MOST LIKELY

MOST LIKELY

SARAH WATSON

P POPPY
LITTLE, BROWN AND COMPANY
New York Boston

Poppy
Hachette Book Group
1290 Avenue of the Americas, New York, NY 10104
Visit us at LBYR.com

First Edition: March 2020

Poppy is an imprint of Little, Brown and Company.
The Poppy name and logo are trademarks of Hachette Book Group, Inc.

The publisher is not responsible for websites (or their content) that are not owned by the publisher.

Library of Congress Cataloging-in-Publication Data
Names: Watson, Sarah (Television writer), author.
Title: Most likely / Sarah Watson.
Description: First edition. | New York : Poppy/Little, Brown and Company, 2020. | Audience: Ages 12+ | Summary: In 2049, as the president of the United States waits to be sworn in, she reflects on senior year in high school, when she and her three dear friends vied for the attention of the future First Gentleman.
Identifiers: LCCN 2019031221 | ISBN 9780316454834 (hardcover) | ISBN 9780316454759 (ebook) | ISBN 9780316454803
Subjects: CYAC: Best friends—Fiction. | Friendship—Fiction. | High schools—Fiction. | Schools—Fiction. | Presidents—Fiction.
Classification: LCC PZ7.1.W417766 Mos 2020 | DDC [Fic]—dc23
LC record available at https://lccn.loc.gov/2019031221

ISBNs: 978-0-316-45483-4 (hardcover), 978-0-316-45475-9 (ebook)

Printed in the United States of America

LSC-H

10 9 8 7 6 5 4 3 2 1

To Mom and Dad,
for believing I could be anything.
Even the president.
But for being totally cool when I said
I wanted to be a writer.

PROLOGUE

Washington, DC
January 20, 2049

THE MORNING sky is a deep shade of blue, and for a moment, I wish I'd gone with the crimson coat. The contrast of red wool against blue sky would have been powerful. But it's too late to change now. This is what I'm wearing. Cream-colored coat over a crisp white suit jacket and matching pants that the designer made personally for me. We'd originally talked about doing a skirt, but the January air is cold and I'm glad for the last-minute change.

"Diffenderfer."

My husband and I both turn at the sound of our last name, but the Diffenderfer they're looking for is me, of course. The professional young woman whose job it is to tell me where I need to be and when says, "We're five minutes to go time."

Five minutes. The moment is so close and yet it still doesn't feel completely real. My friends will tell you that they always knew. That out of all of us, I was always the most likely to end up here. Respectfully, and with love, I think they're full of crap. The truth is, if someone had told me back in high school that this is where my life would lead, I never would have believed it. In some ways, I still can't believe it's about to happen. And I *really* can't believe it's about to happen to someone with the last name Diffenderfer.

Diffenderfer. Ugh. I wonder for the millionth time why I took his name. It was a choice, of course. But I was heavily advised to choose it. Even in this day and age, people felt that it would make me seem more relatable. More approachable. More... "traditional" is the word that one brave soul used before I kicked him out of my office. The reason it pissed me off so much is because I knew he was right. As much as I hate to admit it, it's important to put on a bit of an appearance. So as much as I hate my husband's last name, I made the *traditional* choice and took the damn thing.

I look over at the man who gave me the gift of being a Diffenderfer and smile. He winks back. "Big day," he says.

"Is it?" I tease, and take his hand. I'm surprised to find it shaking slightly. He's nervous, and this fills me with such a sudden sense of tenderness that I'm momentarily overwhelmed. I give his hand a squeeze. He squeezes back. Twice. To tell me that he loves me. "Don't be nervous," I whisper.

"Aren't I supposed to be saying that to you?"

"But I'm not nervous."

"Of course you're not."

I lean in and kiss him. My makeup artist, Margot, will have to refresh my lip gloss, but I don't care. I may not love his name, but I do love this man. I have ever since high school. I've told the story of senior year and that first kiss close to a thousand times now. People apparently like that my love story is uncomplicated. *Uncomplicated.* It always makes us laugh. It's only uncomplicated because they don't know about the complicated parts—which are actually my *favorite* parts. Those definitely wouldn't have helped my image, though. So we've kept it our little secret. Thinking about this makes me smile. I like that, in spite of everything that's happened, there are still a few things that belong only to us.

The young woman with the headset walks up to tell me that it's time. My husband gives me a look. "You ready?"

"Yes," I whisper back, even though the answer is no. How can I ever truly be ready for something like this? I take comfort remembering that the most important moments of my life have been the ones that terrified me. Like that first kiss. Not the story we've told a thousand times. The real one. The one that was messy and excruciating and painful and exhilarating. The one that broke my heart and healed it all at the same time.

I take a deep breath and give my husband's hand one

more squeeze. I suppose it doesn't really matter that I share my last name with him. Because the title they're about to put in front of it will belong only to me.

I, and I alone, will be president of the United States of America.

CHAPTER **ONE**

LOGAN DIFFENDERFER kept a strong pace as he rounded the track. His sweat-soaked shirt clung to his body, and his brown hair bounced as if to the beat of some tragically hip but perfectly rhythmic song.

It was completely annoying.

The space underneath the bleachers was usually the best place at William McKinley High School to have a private conversation. CJ couldn't believe she'd forgotten about cross-country practice when she suggested that she and her three best friends meet there after school. "Maybe we should go somewhere else," she said. Up until this year, CJ had been on the team too. She'd never been a particularly strong runner, and she reminded herself that quitting made sense. She needed the time in her schedule to study for her SATs. (Another thing she wasn't particularly strong at.) Still, it was weird and maybe even a little sad to watch her old team practice without her. "We could try the library. Or that spot behind the cafeteria dumpsters."

Martha looked at the time on her phone. "I have to be in the car in five minutes. Not walking toward it. *In it.*" CJ didn't hold it against her for being in a hurry. Martha was the only one with an after-school job. She was also the only one without a car, so she looked desperately to Ava, who had agreed to give her a ride. "Please tell CJ it's safe to talk here."

Ava shrugged. "It's totally fine. Literally nobody can hear us."

This prompted Jordan to look up from her phone. "That is literally not even remotely how you use the word 'literally.'" She closed out of Snapchat and opened Instagram. Earlier that day she'd posted a photo of herself in her new '50s-style midi dress with the "J" for Jordan embroidered on the pocket in a shade of purple that perfectly matched the stripes of color running through her hair. CJ was more of a "jeans and T-shirt" kind of girl and didn't totally get Jordan's look, but she'd clicked on the little heart next to the post and left a comment. Because that's what you do when one of your best friends is trying to boost her social media following. "Ava has a point, though. Literally. Nobody."

Martha looked at the time. "Four minutes. I have four minutes."

Jordan put her phone away. "So, tonight, who's going to drive and who's going to bring...wait. What do we even need to bring?"

They all traded looks and shrugs. None of them had ever done anything like this before.

"Something sharp, I guess," CJ finally said.

"I'll handle that," said Ava. "But how sharp are we talking?"

As they debated just how sharp of a sharp object Ava should bring, a loud whoop came from the track behind them. They all turned to see that Logan Diffenderfer had just crossed the finish line. As he slowed to a walk, catching his breath in big heaping gulps, he pumped his fist triumphantly into the air and let out another whoop. CJ felt a pang of jealousy. She missed that feeling of crossing the finish line in a flurry of relief and excitement. She watched as her old cross-country coach handed Logan a bottle of water and gave him a pat on the back.

CJ felt another pang. Everything always came so easily to Logan. Not that he didn't work hard. Back when she was on the team, they were the only two who consistently logged extra miles and didn't roll their eyes when their coach shouted inspiring things at them in the middle of practice. For Logan, this extra work resulted in first-place medals and broken records. For CJ, it barely put her in the middle of the pack.

Sometimes CJ couldn't understand how Jordan had ever dated him. (Sure, it was only for about five minutes during freshman year, but still.) He was too perfect. It made him boring. Right then, Logan peeled off his shirt and used it to dab the sweat off his chest. Well, that certainly wasn't boring. It *was* intimidating, though. With his shirt off, his tan skin and carved shoulders, which he'd earned teaching summer swim lessons at the rec center pool, were on full display. CJ folded her arms over the pooch of her stomach self-consciously. She'd spent all summer swimming too, and all it had given her was a face full of freckles.

"Maybe I *am* into dudes."

This was Martha talking. Instead of drinking the bottle of water he'd been given, Logan touched it to the back of his neck. Ohio summers had a way of lingering, and the air was heavy with humidity. Sweat and water dripped down his shoulders.

"You can be into dudes," Ava said. "But please not that one." Logan started running the bottle of water up and down the line of his neck. Up and down. Up and down.

"Oh, come on," Ava huffed. "He's doing that on purpose. He wants people to stare."

"It's working," Martha said.

CJ laughed. Martha's sexuality had been a question ever since they all watched the second-to-last Harry Potter movie. After it was over, CJ announced that she wished she could be Hermione Granger, and Martha announced that she wished she could make out with Hermione Granger. Whether her feelings were specifically directed toward Gryffindor's most notorious female or toward females in general was yet to be determined. Martha was waiting to actually kiss a girl before she officially declared her sexuality.

"Come on, ladies," Jordan said. "Martha's gotta get to work. So what's the deal?"

"I'll drive," CJ said. "Ava's got the sharp thing covered—"

"Right. But seriously. Like how sharp?"

"Your choice," Martha said. "I'm working until eight. Pick me up then?"

This would make them late. They'd be some of the last to arrive. But it's not like they could ask Martha to blow off work. She was already a total stress ball about how she was going to pay for college next year.

So they agreed on eight PM, and then they discussed and settled on an appropriate level of sharpness, and that was that. They'd been talking and dreaming about this night for so long that it almost seemed surreal that it was finally happening.

As they walked away from the bleachers, CJ looked back for a second. She'd meant to catch her old cross-country coach's eye. She wanted to give her a nod, a wordless way to let her know that even though she'd quit, she was still thankful for three years of coaching. CJ accidentally caught Logan's eye instead. He quickly glanced away, but not before she realized that he'd been staring at one of them. What was impossible to tell, what she did not know, was which one of the four of them it was.

CHAPTER **TWO**

AVA, CJ, Jordan, and Martha (they always listed themselves in alphabetical order out of fairness) were a loyal and inseparable foursome. But their remarkable friendship had a fairly unremarkable origin story. There was no great moment of triumph, no great moment of tragedy. No magic pants. They simply met in a park one day when they were five. It was late summer and the line for the slide was long and they started talking while waiting for their turn. They were still a few weeks away from starting kindergarten, and each girl was nervous about it for her own reasons. There was a profound relief when they realized that all four of them had been placed in the same teacher's class. One of them declared that it was fate, and all of them nodded even though two of them didn't know what that word meant. By the end of that first day, they decided that they should all be best friends. It was as easy and natural as that.

Twelve years later, they still liked to say that it was fate that brought them to that particular park on that particular day. Though it's hard to credit divine providence when every kid in the area practically lived in Memorial Park that summer. It's not just that it had the best slide and the tallest set of monkey bars, but there was a certain curiosity and fascination with the names that were carved into the soft wood of the old jungle gym. At the time, Ava, CJ, Jordan, and Martha didn't know why the names were there. They could barely even read. But that didn't stop them from tracing their fingers over the letters and trying to sound out the words as the afternoon sun burned overhead and the sweet smells of summer seemed to stretch on forever.

That day felt like a million years ago and it felt like yesterday. That's what Jordan was thinking as they drove to Memorial Park that night. They were running late, which was annoying even though it was basically her fault. She'd changed outfits about a million times before going back to the one she'd tried on first.

CJ pulled her car to the curb even though they were still around the corner and several blocks away from the park. "What are you doing?" Martha asked from the back seat.

"In case the cops show up," CJ said. She turned off the ignition. "I don't want my car placed at the scene of the crime."

"Clarke Josephine Jacobson," Jordan said. "You're being ridiculous."

CJ wasn't listening. Or if she was listening, she was doing an excellent job of ignoring Jordan. She climbed out of the car and the others followed. Then she put her keys into her backpack and pulled a black sweatshirt out of it. She zipped the hoodie all the way up despite the fact that the night was warm and muggy. Jordan watched with curiosity as CJ pulled the sweatshirt hood around her face and tugged the strings so tightly that only her green eyes remained visible in the darkness. As she tied the strings into a crisp little bow, the others traded a look.

Long ago, the four girls had promised never to talk trash about any member of the group behind her back. They took their promises seriously, so when CJ looked over at them and uttered a muffled "What?" from behind the cotton/polyester blend of her hoodie, they didn't make fun of her behind her back. They made fun of her to her face.

"You cannot be serious," said Martha.

Ava looked her up and down, and tilted her head to the side. "Aren't you a little hot in that?"

"I think she looks adorable," said Jordan. She turned to CJ. "Smile."

"Huh?" Right as CJ turned, Jordan snapped a picture.

"So cute," she said, looking at the photo.

"Ha ha. You guys are hilarious. I don't want to get caught."

It's not like what they were about to do was a felony or anything—they'd looked it up just to make sure—but it's not like it was completely legal either. (It was a misdemeanor.) Jordan tried out different filter options on the picture.

"Don't you dare post that," CJ said in a slight panic.

"Why not? Look how cute you are." Jordan held her phone out.

CJ took the phone and her eyes widened in horror. "I am not even remotely cute."

The picture wasn't exactly flattering. CJ's face was all squished up by the hoodie, which made her freckled button nose—arguably her best feature—look a little *too* buttony. Wisps of blonde hair clung sadly to the sides of her face, and she looked tall. She *was* tall—the tallest girl in the class—but if she'd known the picture was coming, she probably would have done that weird thing she always did where she jutted her hip out to the side and shifted her shoulders down in a way that she claimed made her look normal heighted. Jordan watched as CJ deleted the photo.

"Hey!" said Jordan.

"I am not getting arrested because you posted this on social media. That one picture could destroy my whole future."

Jordan took her phone back. "Don't you think you're being a little dramatic?"

"I might want to go into politics. What if this is the thing that keeps me from getting elected president? Wouldn't you feel terrible?"

"Don't worry," Jordan said. "They'll still let you be president of the Justin Bieber fan club."

"Ha ha," said CJ.

"Relax, CJ," said Ava. "We're minors. Nothing you do as a minor counts." Ava's mom was a lawyer.

"Then let's commit all the crimes while we still can," Martha said.

"Agreed," said Jordan. "Come on. I have the least amount of time left." She enthusiastically linked arms with Martha and they broke into a skip.

"Assholes," CJ said as she caught up to them.

Jordan stopped skipping when she noticed the broken window on the corner house. The area had changed so much since they were kids, shifting from "quaint" into "kinda scary" practically overnight. Martha lived only a few blocks away, and even though she pretended like it didn't bother her, Jordan knew that she was sensitive when the other kids at school referred to the area as a shithole. Jordan didn't have to imagine how much that must hurt, because whenever people saw them together, it wasn't Martha who they assumed lived here. Being half black meant that people looked at Jordan and decided that she was the one who belonged in the neighborhood with the broken windows and the high crime.

Jordan's phone made the *ding* sound that meant she had a new text. It was from Logan Diffenderfer. It wasn't totally unusual for him to text her. She was the editor of the school paper and he was the photographer. So they had a lot of professional business to sort out. His messages would usually start with "Hey, boss," and say things like "Sent you the photos so check your e-mail." Her replies were equally professional: "Got it, thanks," "Final layout approved," or "If you send me another dick pic, you're fired." (They were never *actually* obscene pictures. They were pictures of guys named Dick, and Jordan always pretended like she didn't think they were funny.) The message today was a little different.

Looking for you. You here yet?

She didn't know why he was looking for her, and she didn't like that the fact that he was made her heart beat just a little faster. It made it harder to pretend her feelings for him were gone. Jordan looked over at Ava and wondered if she'd seen the text. She hoped not. She didn't want to have to try to explain it. Not that she would ever lie to her friend. Well, that wasn't completely true. She'd lied once. When they were freshmen, she had told Ava that the reason she dumped Logan Diffenderfer was because she didn't care about him anymore. That wasn't true. She cared about him then, and she still cared about him now. The truth was, the reason Jordan dumped Logan was because of Ava. Because of what Ava had overheard him say. And how it had hurt her.

Next to her, Ava unzipped her cross-body bag and dug around for something. Jordan found herself watching Ava carefully the way she often did. Ava seemed good. She seemed happy. But with Ava, appearances could sometimes be deceiving. Only her closest friends knew about the pain that was locked away down there. Jordan smiled at her and Ava smiled back. Then she found the thing she'd been digging around for and pulled it out of her bag. It was a large chef's knife.

Jordan jumped back. "Holy crap, Ava! What the hell?"

The blade glinted under the streetlight. "What?" Ava asked nonchalantly. "You said to bring something sharp. This is sharp."

CJ took the knife. "This is a Wüsthof, Ava. This is your mom's chef's knife."

"So?"

"So we can't use this. Your mom will kill you."

"I'll put it back after we're done."

CJ turned the knife over in her hands. "You're going to put it back destroyed."

"She'll never notice."

"How could she not notice?"

"Uh, because she doesn't cook. Like ever. I mean, have you met my mother?"

It was supposed to be a joke, but the truth was that even after twelve years of friendship, the other girls didn't know Ava's mom very well. She was always working. Jordan knew that when people heard that Ava was raised by a single mother, they always made assumptions. They'd look at the moody Latinx girl who hated speaking up in class and sometimes stayed home from school for cryptic reasons, and they would create a narrative of poverty. The reality was very different. Ava's mom was a senior partner at one of the biggest law firms in the city.

"I cannot allow us to ruin a Wüsthof." It's not like CJ liked cooking, but she did like cooking shows. "And look at this thing. We're liable to take a finger off."

Ava took the knife back a bit defensively. "Then what are we supposed to do? You put me in charge of the knife. I brought a knife."

Martha opened up her own backpack and produced something that she showed to CJ. It was a steak knife, old and dull with time and use. The tip of the blade was more of a nub than a point. "What about this?"

"That," CJ said, "we can destroy."

———

The knife felt strange in Martha's hand. Her mother had given it to her earlier that afternoon after showing up unexpectedly at the movie theater where Martha worked.

Both of Martha's parents were Cleveland lifers—class of 2003 at the same high school Martha now attended—and she'd always known that her parents had committed the same misdemeanor that Martha and her friends were about to. It wasn't exactly a crime you could hide. She'd seen the evidence. Martha and her mom never really talked about it, though. Not that they really talked about anything. Martha lived with her dad, and her relationship with her mom ranged from difficult to nonexistent. They saw each other so infrequently that Martha barely even had a relationship with her half brothers. They were twins, and even though they weren't identical, Martha still sometimes confused them. That part of her family didn't feel like family. That's why it had been such a surprise when her mom showed up with the knife. Her voice had caught when she handed it to Martha and told her that it was the very same one she had used when she was a senior.

The girls turned the corner and Martha saw the size of the crowd. It looked like every senior in their class was there. Martha liked to self-identify as cynical and had been pretty vocal about thinking this tradition was kinda dumb. But as she turned the knife over in her hand, it didn't feel "kinda dumb." It must have been a pretty big deal for her mom to keep this knife for almost two decades. Maybe tonight was going to matter a lot more than she thought.

"Here we go," Jordan said.

"Time to add our names to history," said Ava.

For more than fifty years, seniors at William McKinley

High School had gathered at Memorial Park on the first Friday of the school year to carve their names into the old wooden jungle gym. Tonight Ava Morgan, CJ Jacobson, Jordan Schafer, and Martha Custis would add their names to the list along with the rest of the class of 2020.

Unfortunately, things for these seniors were about to get complicated. As they got closer to the jungle gym, the girls realized for the first time that the crowd wasn't actually gathered *in* the park. They were congregated along the edge of it. Memorial Park, which was usually open to everyone, was now completely sealed off, surrounded by a chain-link fence and topped with loops of barbed wire. At first, they thought it was just an annoying effort by the local cops to keep them from participating in a tradition that was technically vandalism. Then they saw the sign: an official proclamation from the city that told them they would never get the chance to join the generations before them in carving their names into the jungle gym. Their legacy would not continue on—at least not in this particular form—because the park was scheduled for demolition.

Everyone was shouting over everyone, but it was Grayson Palmer whose voice kept rising to the top. "They can't keep us out. Does someone have some bolt cutters or, like, a crowbar or something? Because I say we break in!"

The crowd erupted in cheers. Ava looked to her friends and was happy to see that Jordan was already doing her journalist thing. She had her phone out and was typing the name of the park into her search engine to get more information. Logan walked up to her. "Finally," he said to Jordan as a greeting. "I've been texting you. I think we've got a front-page story here."

"Already on it," Jordan said. "Are you taking pictures?"

He nodded.

"I can boost people over the top," Grayson shouted. "Girl with the shortest skirt goes first."

More cheers and more laughter. Grayson was the group's de facto leader now. He was tall and he was loud and that was enough to put him in charge. Ava wanted to tell everyone that there was no point in breaking in if the city was just going to tear the park down. But her voice was the kind that you could never hear in a crowd.

Jordan looked up from her phone. "I'm on the city website. It's taking forever to load."

Ava, CJ, and Martha huddled around Jordan and peered at the electronic glow of her screen, waiting impatiently. Logan leaned in too, and Ava had to step awkwardly to the side to make room for him. His presence felt like an invasion. Just being near him always made her feel insecure. Small and inferior. Insignificant and stupid. Intellectually, she knew that she was none of those things. Okay, small, yes. Only physically, though. And she definitely wasn't stupid. Years ago, Logan had said that she was. Not to her face. It was behind her back, which actually made it worse. It meant he really believed what he was saying. Even now, it was hard for her to not feel dumb whenever he was around. Ava did the thing that Dr. Clifford told her to do when flashes of insecurity bubbled up. She recited a mantra to herself. *I am smart. I am smart.* Then she added a second part that definitely wasn't part of her doctor's advice. *Logan Diffenderfer is an idiot.*

Something popped up on Jordan's screen, and Logan scooted in even closer to try to read it. This time Ava held her ground. "Sorry," Logan said and backed up.

Jordan used her fingers to widen the text on her screen. "Bingo," she said. "I found the information about the proposed development."

"I like the word 'proposed,'" said CJ. "That means it's not a done deal yet."

"I don't like the word 'development,'" said Ava.

"Me neither," Logan agreed. Ava looked at him, and she must have been making a weird face because he said, "What? I'm agreeing with you." She looked away, and he turned back to Jordan. "What are they developing?"

Jordan followed another link. As her phone loaded, a deep thumping beat boomed from a nearby phone. Someone was playing a song about fighting the power, and a few people started dancing. Cammie Greenstein announced that her parents weren't home and that her older sister could buy beer. For a second, it looked like the crowd might scatter. But Grayson shook his head. "No. Nobody's leaving. We came here to do this. We're doing this." He drifted over to the fence and seemed genuinely upset as he wrapped his fingers around the links of fence and stared at the jungle gym. It was so close and yet so far away. "Anyone drive a truck here tonight? I say we just ram the whole gate down."

Jordan groaned. Not at Grayson. She was reacting to something on her phone. "Well," she said, "I have good news and I have bad news. What do you want first?"

"Bad," said CJ.

Jordan held up her phone. "It's a giant-ass office building."

On the screen was an architectural rendering of a ten-story tower. Martha took the phone out of Jordan's hands so she could look at it closer. "Assholes," she said. "They want to put this in the middle of my neighborhood?" She handed the phone back to Jordan. "What's the good news?"

"There's a city meeting in three weeks to discuss it. It's open to the public. Anyone with concerns is welcome to voice them."

"Good," Logan said. "Because I think there are quite a few people here who would like to voice some." He turned to the crowd and put his hands up to his mouth like a megaphone. "Hey! Everybody! Listen up! Cut the music." The fight-the-power song stopped on his command. "This isn't over. We've got a plan."

Everyone listened. They hung on his every word. Just like they'd done with Grayson. Ava wondered what it would be like to have a voice like that. Loud and commanding. She wondered how she'd use it if she did.

When Martha got home that night, she found her dad in the living room reading on the couch. Until recently, he'd been on the night shift, but he finally had enough seniority at the warehouse where he worked as a loader to get a more normal schedule. It still wasn't enough hours to qualify for health insurance, but it was a huge improvement.

"Hey, Patsy," he said, looking up from his book. Martha knew that she should have outgrown the cutesy term of endearment long ago, but she liked that her dad still called her that. Patsy was the childhood nickname of the woman she was named after. Her great-great-great-great-great-great-great-grandmother, Martha Washington. "Aren't you back kind of early?"

She plopped down on the couch next to him. "Aren't you up kind of late?"

Since his shift change, he was usually in bed by ten. Martha glanced at the time. It was pretty obvious he'd been waiting up for her. Maybe her mom wasn't the only one who was sentimental about the tradition. Her dad closed his book and set it to the side. "How was the big night?"

"It was a total bust, actually. The whole park was closed off. They want to tear it down."

"Why would they do that?"

Martha picked up the book he was reading. It was a biography of Abraham Lincoln, and when she cracked it open, it had that fresh library-book smell. "Some developer wants to put in an office building. Right in the middle of our neighborhood."

"This seems like a weird area for an office building," her dad said.

"I know. It's such a bummer." Martha set the book down. "There was still space by your name on the jungle gym. I checked a couple of weeks ago. I was thinking it would have been cool for my friends and me to put our names next to yours."

Her dad smiled, and Martha remembered the first time she'd learned about the names. She was just a little kid when her parents had taken her to the park and told her the story of the night they carved their names in together. Her dad had held her up so she could trace her fingers around the letters. "Oh well," he said with nonchalance. "Price of progress, I suppose."

"It's not over yet," Martha said hopefully. "There's a meeting in a few weeks for the developer to present the project.

After she's done presenting, anyone who wants to can voice concerns."

"*She?* They let ladies be developers now?"

Martha punched her dad playfully in the arm. He loved to tease his only daughter about being a feminist. She didn't care. She knew he was proud of her. For an old-school guy, he was pretty new-school about a lot of things. When she'd finally gotten up the courage to tell him, *Hey, Dad, I think I might like girls*, he'd been quiet for a long time. When he did eventually speak, it was to say, "Well, at least you and I finally have something in common."

Martha had laughed. Mostly out of relief. But what he'd said was true. She and her dad were nothing alike. He was a voracious reader. She was a math nerd. He was a former athlete. She once faked Morgellons disease to get out of PE. He liked country music. She liked anything but. And yet, she loved him so much that sometimes it scared her. How was it possible to love one parent so much more than the other one? There was something so obviously screwed up about it that she knew something must be wrong with her.

"Hey, Dad," she said, trying to sound casual. "I was thinking that maybe you'd want to go with me. To the meeting. We're all going to say something and so are a bunch of the other seniors. I think it would mean a lot to hear from someone whose name is already there. You're kind of a part of history."

His look was tough to read. "I don't know, Patsy. You're the good speaker."

Martha knew it was more complicated than that, though. These were memories that Martha wasn't sure her dad wanted to hang on to. She nodded and tried not to look disappointed. Sometimes she wished her dad was the kind of guy who would swoop in and save the day for her. Other times she liked that she was the kind of girl who didn't need him to. She looked over at him, and he smiled at her briefly. Then he picked up his book and went back to reading.

CHAPTER **THREE**

AVA FELT tense during the weeks leading up to the city meeting. Not that this was anything particularly new or different. She basically existed in a constant state of feeling slightly anxious about something, so it was hard to tell how much of this was related to the fact that her friends were forcing her to speak at the meeting and how much of it was just her brain chemistry. She blamed at least some of it on the college counselor who had visited everyone's homeroom and scared the crap out of them with information about deadlines and essay topics and their last possible chance to retake the SATs. She mostly blamed her friends, though. They were the ones making her talk in front of a group of people.

When they arrived at the auditorium on that Thursday night, the room was already packed. Because of "unusually high interest" in the meeting, everyone who wanted to speak was required to sign up before it started. The girls were directed to a long line that snaked the length of the room. CJ crossed her arms in an irritated sort of way and counted the number of people in line ahead of them. The meeting was limited to two hours, and that meant that not everyone who signed up would be able to talk.

"It's going to be tight," CJ said.

Thank god, Ava thought.

She could feel Jordan glance over at her. "Hey," Jordan said. "You okay? You look…"

The sentence did not need to be finished. Ava looked exactly how she felt. Like she was going to pass out. Or hurl. Or maybe both. Probably both. She shoved her toes against the edges of her shoes and held them there for a count of five. This was something her therapist had told her to try in moments of stress. Sometimes it actually helped. Today was not one of those times.

Martha gave Ava's arm a squeeze. "It's okay. You don't have to talk if you don't want to."

"Yes, she does," CJ said abruptly. Long ago, CJ had decided that it was her job to be the "tough love" best friend. She saw it as an admirable quality. Ava was still on the fence. CJ was always pushing her to do things that were out of her comfort zone. Just last week she'd forced her to submit one of her paintings to a local gallery. Ava knew there wasn't a chance in hell that the Coventry Art Gallery would pick the painting of a high school amateur over all the professionals and more experienced artists who would be submitting, but sometimes it was easier just to do what CJ said rather than argue.

"I'm sorry, Aves," CJ said. "I know you hate this. But you're going to thank me later."

Ava seriously doubted that. But it was impossible to slow CJ down once she got excited about something. If there was a problem, she wanted to solve it. The girls were only twelve when CJ dragged them to their first protest. Ava contributed the artwork for their signs. That was the extent to which she was comfortable sticking it to the man.

"Look at her," Martha said, pointing to Ava. "She's like...an unnatural color."

"She's not an unnatural color." Ava could feel CJ's eyes on her, evaluating and processing. "Okay, maybe she's slightly paler than her regular color. But only *slightly*."

"I'd say it's dramatic," said Jordan.

Ava clenched her eyes shut while her friends argued about her. She wished she could just astral project right the hell out of there. When she opened her eyes, she was disappointed to discover that not only had her soul not left the room but that Logan Diffenderfer was walking up to them. *Great.* That's all she needed right now. Even worse, he had his camera around his neck.

"Hey," he said to Jordan. "I've been getting some great shots for the paper."

"Good," she said. "I'm thinking front-page spread for sure. Let me see what you've got."

He held up his camera and clicked through a few images. Ava had to admit that he was good. She'd never say it to his face, but secretly she loved his work. Jordan complained that his shots were often too artsy for the paper, but Ava loved them. His photos weren't just beautiful. They told a story.

He clicked forward and paused on a picture. *Oh god.* It was a picture of her. She really did look pale. Logan lowered his camera, and it seemed like he was about to say something to her. Ava was thankful that Martha jumped in before he could.

"Hey, Diffenderfer," she said. "You weren't in AP Physics today. Mr. Young said you're dropping it."

Logan glanced down at his camera. "Yeah."

"Why?" Martha asked.

Logan hesitated and a commotion stirred up in the line ahead of them. He looked pretty relieved about the distraction. Ava recognized the look. It's how she felt every time something happened that took the focus off of her.

They all turned and saw that a couple of their classmates were arguing with the woman supervising the sign-in sheet. It was getting loud. "We have rights," someone said. It was

Kaia Huber. She was one of the best writers in school other than Jordan.

Jordan turned to Logan. "Get your camera ready. Come on."

The line dissolved as the commotion got bigger. Jordan was already pulling her notebook and a pen out of her bag. She quickly jotted down quotes. CJ followed right behind her. Ava would have preferred to stay out of it, but Martha grabbed her arm. "Come on. Let's see what's up."

They reached the table where a mob of their classmates surrounded the woman with the sign-in sheet. "I'm sorry," she said. She was older and had the distinct look of someone who watched a lot of public television. "But only constituents can speak at these meetings."

Ava didn't know what a constituent was. She thought about discreetly googling it, but Logan Diffenderfer asked the question for her. "What's a constituent?"

"It's a voter in this district," answered Kaia with annoyance. "None of us are registered. So they won't let us speak."

"Well, we would register," CJ said to the PBS woman. "But we can't. We're not eighteen."

"I'm sorry," she said, not sounding that sorry at all. "These are the rules."

"But we're the ones most directly impacted by the park closure. We should get to talk about it," Martha said.

The woman looked frustrated and tired and completely unmoved. "You're welcome to sit and listen."

"But we don't want to sit and listen," Logan said. "We want to stand and be heard."

There were cheers from their classmates, and Ava had to admit it was a pretty good line. She saw Jordan jot it down in her notebook. The public television woman put up her hands as if she were staring down an unruly mob. "If you insist on making a scene, I'm going to have to ask you all to leave. This is not appropriate behavior."

Martha scoffed and rolled her eyes. "Not appropriate? Are you kidding me? We're just asking for two minutes."

It was starting to dawn on Ava that she was getting her wish. She wouldn't have to get up in front of the crowd while her voice quavered and her cheeks turned bright red. The relief didn't feel as wonderful as she'd thought it would.

"Hey," CJ said, pointing to someone at the door. "Isn't that the councilman?"

Ava, Jordan, and Martha followed her gaze to an older man in a tailored suit. He walked with a level stride of self-importance and was trailed by a younger man, who was also wearing a suit, though not nearly as expensive-looking.

"That's definitely him," Martha said. "I recognize his picture from the district website."

Councilman Kenneth Lonner looked like the kind of guy whose voting record favored large developments. Which it did. They'd learned that from the district website too.

"Well," Jordan said, straightening the skirt of her dress and tugging at the top to make sure everything that should be covered was covered, "everyone back up. If they're not going to let us speak, then I guess it's up to the press to solve this." She turned quickly to Logan. "Get as many shots as you can." Then she broke into a fast walk. "Councilman! A minute of your time, please."

Ava watched with awe as Jordan walked right up to him and got in his face. "I'm with the McKinley *Blaze* and wanted to ask you about your decision to ignore the input of students at tonight's meeting."

The councilman looked up from the file that he'd been thumbing through as he walked. He closed it and handed it to the young man next to him. The young man was very young. Probably close to their age. An intern or something.

"I'm sorry," the councilman said. "Which paper did you say you work for?"

"The McKinley High School *Blaze*. I'm the editor. Jordan Schafer."

She put out her hand, and the councilman took it and flashed a charming grin. "I love it when kids get involved in our civic process, Jordan. I really do. But I'm afraid I'm a bit overscheduled tonight. If you call my office, we'd love to give you a tour. My associate here can set it up for you. Best of luck to you, Jordan."

He reached into his pocket and handed her something that she awkwardly took. Then he continued toward the front of the room, where a seat was waiting for him. Ava, CJ, and Martha scrambled to get to their friend. Logan hung back and took a couple of pictures.

"What *was* that?" CJ asked. "What did he give you?"

Jordan looked stunned. She finally opened her hand. It was a campaign sticker. "I asked for a hard-hitting interview," she said. "And he gave me a sticker."

Jordan went to bed angry that night, and she woke up angry the next morning. After they'd learned that they weren't allowed to speak, a lot of their classmates had left. Not Ava, CJ, Jordan, and Martha, though. They'd sat right in the front row and tried to look intimidating. Jordan was pretty proud of her epic scowl, but it's not like a rude facial expression was going to solve anything. The meeting had not gone well for them. The developer was convincing, and even though several people spoke out in favor of the park, their remarks were rambling and all over the place. They hadn't practiced and prepared like the girls had. The night ended with Councilman Lonner saying he would support the development. It still needed to be approved by the city, but with the councilman's support it was considered a done deal. If they were going to save the park, they needed a real plan and they needed it now.

Jordan opened her laptop so she could search for "successful protest ideas." Maybe a letter-writing campaign coupled with a demonstration. They could have sign-making parties and then descend on City Hall en masse. She wondered if one of her classmates would suggest that they chain themselves to the park fence. Ordinarily, Jordan didn't agree with extremist measures. But that was before the councilman had called her a kid and handed her a sticker.

She saw that she had an e-mail from Logan and opened it. He'd sent her the pictures from the city meeting. She clicked through them and stopped when she got to one of her. Logan had managed to capture the exact moment when the councilman handed her the sticker. Her head was cocked slightly to the side and frozen in an expression of bewilderment.

She'd felt so good going into that night too. She'd been wearing her vintage-style swing dress in a bright-red apple print that her little brother said made her look like a wicked queen. He didn't mean it as a compliment, but she took it that way. The dress usually made her feel powerful. Now, looking at it in the pictures, it seemed like a childish thing to wear to an important event. Jordan was used to people not taking her seriously when they first met her. Not just because of her clothes. People loved to say that they didn't see color, but she could read the lowered expectations in their faces. That usually shifted as soon as she opened her mouth. They would tell her that she was "well-spoken" and express awe at how smart she was. She hated that she had to be smarter, better, and more eloquent than her white classmates, and yet she loved that she was.

Councilman Lonner had misjudged her. He'd looked at her and dismissed her as just a kid. Which, okay, technically and legally speaking, she was. What he didn't know was that she was a kid with a stack of newspaper awards. She was the reason that the school had been forced to switch cafeteria food vendors after she'd published an article taking the vendor to task for their unethical business practices. She'd won national recognition for her story about mismanaged funds within the music program. She wanted the councilman to know all that. She wanted him to look at her and acknowledge that he'd been wrong.

An idea came to her. She knew how to get her wish. It was simple and yet completely effective. She fired off a quick text to her friends even though she knew they wouldn't be up yet. She was too excited to wait. Now that she had a plan, she felt giddy about it. Councilman Kenneth Lonner had messed with the wrong kid.

The sound of an air horn rocked Martha out of a deep and blissful slumber. She bolted upright and searched for the source of the noise. Her phone usually made a soothing bell sound when she got a text, but someone had changed it. CJ, most likely. They'd been in a cell phone prank battle since summer.

The air horn sounded again, and Martha opened the texts while simultaneously plotting her revenge. Both messages were from Jordan.

I KNOW HOW TO SAVE THE PARK!

That councilman messed with the wrong kid.

After the text was a black fist emoji.

Martha didn't respond. She padded into the bathroom and cringed when she saw her reflection in the mirror. She hadn't bothered to wash her face last night, and her eyes were dark with smudged eyeliner. As she scrubbed her face clean, she thought about everything the developer had said at the meeting. And how convincing she'd been. She'd talked about how the new office building would create about three hundred jobs once it was built. How that would give the local restaurants a boost and bring in a lot of tax revenue. She said it would revitalize the neighborhood. She had facts and figures to back it up.

Face clean, Martha turned her attention to her hair. She never quite knew what to do with it. Her natural hair color was a mousy brown, but over the summer, Jordan had helped her dye it a shade of black called Urban Death. Her mom had cried when she'd seen it, which made Martha like it even more. She pulled it up into a messy bun. *Three hundred jobs.* Martha couldn't stop thinking about that number. Maybe her dad could get one of those office jobs. And even if he didn't, somebody's dad would. Or somebody's mom. Or somebody.

Martha hated that her dad had to work a crappy loading job. It hadn't always been that way. Martha still remembered what it was like when he was a production supervisor at the Ford engine plant. The people who worked for him called him sir. He even had his own business cards. His name and title embossed onto a shiny white card. He'd given one to Martha to keep in her backpack in case she ever needed to call him at work. She took the card eagerly even though she knew the number by heart—*still* knew the number by heart. Then the plant closed in 2012 and Martha's parents got divorced not long after that and she moved into this tiny two-bedroom apartment with the gray carpeting in the neighborhood that made Ava's mom purse her lips together every time she drove into it. Revitalizing it didn't sound like such a bad thing.

The air horn sounded again and Martha jumped. This time it was CJ.

I'm in.

CJ punctuated her statement with a fist emoji in her signature shade of beige.

Ava's response came not long after that.

As long as I don't have to talk in public.

She added a brown fist emoji.

Martha stared at the fists and wondered which was worse: letting her friends down or letting her neighborhood down. She only had to think about it for a second. She typed her response and hit send.

It was an extremely pale white fist emoji.

CHAPTER **FOUR**

CJ WAITED for her friends in the quad. Jordan had told everyone to meet there twenty minutes before the first bell, and as usual, CJ was the only one who was there on time. She was eager to hear Jordan's big idea and hoped it wasn't anything too extreme. There was no way in hell she was chaining herself to the park fence or doing anything else that might jeopardize her chances of getting into Stanford.

She checked Find My Friends to see where everyone was and saw that she had a new e-mail. It was from the school college counselor. *SAT Sign-Up Deadline Approaching/ FINAL CHANCE.* CJ opened the message, expecting to find a general reminder to the entire class. The e-mail was addressed only to her.

Hi, CJ. I look forward to sitting down with you to discuss your college plans. In the meantime, I wanted to make sure you were aware that the deadline to register for the fall SAT test is quickly approaching. This is the last chance for your scores to count for this application year. Given your current score and your academic goals, I highly encourage you to sign up to retake the test.

Best,
Ms. Fischer

CJ's cheeks burned. Did Ms. Fischer seriously think CJ wasn't already aware that her SAT scores blew? She was aware. She was *painfully* aware. The first time she'd taken the test, she'd been shocked by her results. 1150. She assumed it must have been some kind of mistake, and if it wasn't a mistake, then it was certainly an anomaly. Just a bad test day. Everyone had them. So she rallied and regrouped and studied harder and took the test again. 1150 again. When she saw her score this time, she was furious. Not at the SATs and not even at herself. She was angry at everyone who had ever told her that she was special, that she was smart, that she was gifted, that her hard work would pay off. Her parents, her teachers, her friends. They were clearly all wrong. CJ Jacobson wasn't special. She was average.

She knew that this was her last chance to take the test. The date was circled in red on her calendar and seared permanently into her brain. She would need to score at least in the high 1400s to have a shot at Stanford. She was doing everything she could to get that score. Over the summer, she'd used almost all of her babysitting and birthday money to take an SAT study course. She'd quit cross-country so she could study harder.

"Hey, babe." CJ turned and found a bubbly Jordan bouncing her way over.

"You're late," CJ said.

"And you're grumpy. What's up?"

"Nothing. I thought we were meeting twenty minutes before class."

"When have I ever been punctual? Where are Ava and Martha?"

"When have *they* ever been punctual?"

Ava and Martha arrived a few minutes later with a trail of apologies. That only left a few minutes for Jordan to reveal her big plan. "I want to interview the councilman," she said.

Ava, CJ, and Martha traded looks. Unimpressed ones. Although CJ *was* relieved that Jordan didn't expect her to chain herself to anything.

"Um, you already tried that," Martha said.

"I tried it as the editor of a high school newspaper. Not as an adult journalist."

"Adult journalist?" Ava said. "Like porn?"

Jordan shot her a look. "I mean a journalist who is an adult."

CJ had no idea where this was going. "But you're not a journalist who is an adult."

"He doesn't have to know that," Jordan said. "If I call and request a phone interview, he won't have any idea how old I am. Once I get my interview, I'll run it in the *Blaze*. He'll be stunned when he sees how good it is. He'll never underestimate a kid again."

"And this saves the park how?" Ava asked.

"One step at a time," Jordan said.

The bell rang and CJ tensed. She and Martha both had AP Physics. They had their first quiz of the semester and CJ was nervous. Math and science had never come easily to her, and she'd been lost and overwhelmed since the first day. Martha belonged in that classroom. CJ didn't. She was a fraud.

"Wait," Jordan said. "I need one of you to help me create a fake online imprint." CJ and Ava both pointed at Martha. She was good at coding. "Sure," said Martha.

"Nothing too extreme. It's just in case he tries to look me up. Give me a different last name. James. It's my mom's maiden name. She always wanted her legacy to live on.

I'm thinking a LinkedIn profile and some links to clips of mine. But attributed to adult newspapers." Ava was right. It sounded like porn when you said it that way. "Oh, and I'll need some help researching the councilman. Past voting record. Donor lists. Everything."

Ava and Martha both pointed at CJ. Which was fair. She was the best at research. If she could find the time. CJ thought about her already monstrously long to-do list. She had the SAT and APs to study for. College essays to write. She had an interview after school with a volunteer program. The food bank where she used to give her time had shut down over the summer because of budget cuts, and she was itching to do something worthwhile. And, okay, she also wanted it because she was worried about how the gap in her volunteer hours would look to colleges. Now, on top of everything else in her life, Jordan wanted her to do a full background check on a politician. CJ honestly didn't know how she was going to balance it all.

———

Ava was usually the first person in her art classroom every morning. Mrs. Simon opened the door one hour before class started, and since Ava still hadn't worked up the courage to tell her mom that she wanted to apply to art school, she figured it was safer to work on her application portfolio outside of the house.

As the second bell rang, Ava said a quick hello to Isla and Tobin, the class's other star artists, before hurrying to her spot in the front row. On the first day of school, Mrs. Simon had told everyone to choose where they'd like to sit. Art was the only class where Ava didn't mind being in the front row. It was the only time she felt okay when people stared. The classroom was divided into pairs of easels, and Ava was the only one without a partner next to her. She didn't take it personally. It wasn't because they didn't like her. It was because they were intimidated by her.

Mrs. Simon paced the room and gave a few instructions before telling the class to pick up their hand mirrors and get to work. Their first project this year was a self-portrait, and Ava found the assignment a little uncomfortable. She didn't know if all adopted kids did this, but Ava would often stare in the mirror for long periods of time and study her own face. She'd never seen a picture of her birth mother, so she could only imagine that her mother had the same expressive eyes and long lashes, the same small nose and cowlicked hair. Ava's own face was the only clue she had about what her biological mother looked like.

Ava always wanted her paintings to be about something, so she decided to make this one an expression of the complicated relationship she had with the woman who had given birth to her yet remained a mystery. She decided to paint an image of a female figure looming deep in the background and watching her. Since she had no idea what her birth mother looked like, she would keep the image hazy— a blurred mystery woman.

As Ava painted, she wondered about a lot more than just the shape of her birth mother's face. The questions floated through her with each stroke of her paintbrush. Was she artistic too? Was it hard for her to make her voice loud enough to be heard in a crowd? Did she sometimes get sad for no reason?

Ava was immersed in her work when the classroom door flew open and broke her concentration. A flustered Logan Diffenderfer walked in. "Hey. Sorry. Sorry. I didn't know where the art classroom was. Am I in the right place?"

Mrs. Simon looked up. "Yes. Can I help you with something?"

Logan held up a note. "Yeah. I'm supposed to be in this class now. I guess it was the only first-period class with room."

Mrs. Simon walked over and took his note. After a second, she nodded. "Welcome to Advanced Art, Mr. Diffenderfer. There's an empty spot up front."

She directed him to the only open easel in the classroom. The one right next to Ava.

"Turn right in fifty meters."

The electronic voice of CJ's GPS belonged to a British woman.

CJ was annoyed by the accent, but she would be late if she stopped to mess around with her phone settings. The British woman was a gift from Martha. CJ had been up late the night before studying for their physics quiz, and she'd been so tired that she fell asleep during fifth period. Hard enough that she didn't even notice when Martha used her thumb to unlock her phone. While CJ continued napping, Martha changed all of CJ's settings. She'd meant for it to be funny, and on any other day, CJ probably would have laughed—she certainly deserved it after that whole air horn thing—but she'd cried instead. Martha was so stunned that she immediately apologized and changed everything back. But she'd apparently forgotten about the British woman.

"Keep left at the car park," said the regal voice.

The e-mail from the college counselor had broken her. She was already worried that she wasn't good enough for Stanford even before Ms. Fischer's message arrived in her in-box.

Stanford had been her top choice for as long as she could remember. It was a campus dappled in golden light and lined with palm trees, where nobody laughed when you said you wanted to change the world. They encouraged big ideas, loud ones, disruptive ones. The kind that CJ kept locked deep inside her because she was too scared to say them out loud. She wanted to do something with her life that would matter. Something bigger and more important than painting protest signs and recycling her milk carton. She just didn't know how. Stanford would give her the tools. It would also give her the credibility to use them. She would never feel like a fraud again.

"In one hundred meters, you will arrive at your destination."

The destination was the office for Sensational Recreational, an after-school program that taught sports to kids with physical disabilities.

"In fifty meters, you will arrive at your destination," said the British voice.

CJ was ten minutes early. She should put that on her Stanford application. *Always punctual.* She reminded herself that the volunteer coordinator had e-mailed her almost immediately after she'd sent her résumé. He'd been impressed by her cover letter. Because that's the kind of girl she was. The kind who was on time and wrote exceptional cover letters. So what if her SATs were a little lackluster? Even Hermione Granger stumbled from time to time.

"You have arrived at your destination," the British voice said, and CJ realized that it actually sounded like a grown-up Hermione. It gave CJ confidence. She pulled into the parking lot and paused before getting out of her car. She was going to get this volunteer job and impress Stanford with how beautifully well-rounded she was. But first she needed to Hermione Granger the shit out of this interview. She took a breath, exhaled, and adjusted her posture a bit. This was a thing she did when she was talking to anyone important. Shoulders back, head high, confident smile, and...

She walked across the parking lot and opened the rec center door. A blast of music greeted her.

Duh. Duh, duh, duh.

It was the music from *Rocky* and it was so loud that CJ actually cringed. Was she in the right place? A sign tacked to the back wall told her that she was.

A guy about her age sat behind the front desk doing some paperwork. He clearly hadn't heard CJ arrive over the music. His shaggy brown hair fell over his face as he worked. CJ said hello in her most professional voice.

When he looked up, CJ found that she was staring into a pair of brown eyes that were more mature than the shaggy brown hair suggested.

"Hi," he said over the music. "Alexa, turn it down." The music continued blasting. "Alexa. Shut up!" This time the music stopped. "Sorry. I'm working on an inspirational playlist. Is the *Rocky* theme too obvious?"

Totally too obvious. Instead of telling him that, CJ put out her hand and said, "Sorry to interrupt. I'm CJ

Jacobson." He stared at her outstretched hand as if confused. He was definitely cute, but he was also definitely giving her generation a bad name. She had been taught that when someone puts out a hand, you stand and shake it.

"Can I help you with something?" he asked.

Still holding herself in her professional posture, CJ consulted the details of the e-mail that she'd been sent in response to her application. "I have a four o'clock interview with...Wyatt." She checked the e-mail again. "I'm sorry. No last name was provided."

"I'm Wyatt No Last Name Provided," said the guy who was giving her generation a bad name.

"You're him?"

"I am he."

There had to be more than one Wyatt.

"Wyatt the volunteer coordinator?"

"Wyatt No Last Name Provided. Wyatt the Volunteer Coordinator. I answer to either. But I'm confused. I have a meeting with..." He turned to *his* e-mail as if challenging hers. "Clarke Jacobson."

"I am she."

"Huh," he said, looking her up and down. She knew from experience what this up-down look meant. He wasn't checking her out. He was registering the fact that she wasn't a dude. "I thought you were..."

"A guy. Yeah. I get that a lot. I'm not."

"Evidently."

She felt flustered. It was his smile. It was incredibly disarming. Not in *that* way. It's just that this interview was not going well and she needed it to go well.

"My legal name is Clarke. But everybody calls me CJ."

CJ was the fourth child, and with three older sisters, she was her father's last chance for a boy he could name after himself. When CJ came out all feisty and tough, he decided to give her his name anyway.

Wyatt pulled out her résumé from a stack of other résumés. It made her heart sink a little. She didn't like thinking about the competition.

"Your résumé is impressive, Clarke," he said. Either forgetting or not caring that she went by CJ.

"Thank you."

"But I was really looking to hire a guy."

"Pardon?" she said. Because obviously she'd heard him wrong.

"I was hoping to hire a guy."

It's not like she was naïve. She knew the world hadn't changed so much that misogyny didn't still exist, but she certainly thought it had changed enough that nobody would be dumb enough to come right out and admit it. CJ was ready to call the ACLU right then and there but not before giving him a piece of her mind.

"Well, Wyatt. I'm sorry to be the one to break it to you,

but not only are your hiring practices completely illegal, they are also totally small-minded, since I assure you that I can do anything a man can."

Wyatt didn't seem at all flustered by CJ's passionate speech. His smile had shifted a little bit, but it was still there on his face. It made him look...She wasn't exactly sure how it made him look.

"You can?" he said. "You can do anything a man can?"

"Oh, I can."

"You can go into the boys' locker room and help them change?"

Smug. That was the look on his face. He was smug.

"Oh. Uh...oh. Well...I guess not that."

His smugness shifted to amusement. "I'm not sexist. But the locker room thing is a concern. We have more boys than girls in the program. It's probably still technically illegal for me not to hire you because of your gender, but it's an unpaid position, so..."

It was a fair point. While suing a nonprofit organization that empowered kids in wheelchairs would certainly be something that colleges would notice, she guessed that it wasn't quite the kind of experience that Stanford was looking for. So she politely and somewhat sheepishly thanked Wyatt No Last Name Provided for his time and turned to leave.

"Nice meeting you, Clarke," he said when she reached the exit. "Sorry that we weren't meant to be."

She put her hand on the door but paused before opening it. "Hey. Why *do* you have more boys than girls? In the program?"

He shrugged. "Don't know. This is the first month. Well, of the expanded program. It used to only run once a month on a weekend. So we had kids coming from all over the state. But I talked my bosses into letting me try out a weekday version. I just feel like the kids deserve more than once a month, you know?"

CJ nodded.

"But that means it's only been the local kids. And so far it's mostly boys. We do have one girl, though."

CJ couldn't help but laugh. "Sorry, it's just…that's your 'more boys than girls' breakdown? You've got *one* girl?"

"It's a start. Hey. I'm just happy kids are showing up."

"Boy kids."

"And one girl."

CJ shot him a look.

"Yeah, okay," he said. "I know I can do better. And honestly," he added, "I don't think the one girl is having a very good time."

"Why do you think that?"

"Because every time she comes, she tells me how much she hates it."

CJ nodded. It would seem she wasn't having a good time, then. CJ had been on coed teams before, but they had always had a pretty close gender balance. She'd never been the only girl. She wondered what that would feel like.

"A female leader could help," CJ told him. "It would probably be less weird and more fun for her if she wasn't the only girl in the room."

Wyatt looked up. She could tell that he was considering what she'd just said.

"I'm just saying, if you're really committed to expanding this program, it would help to have a female role model."

"And you would be that female?"

She'd found herself an opening. That was all she needed. Now she just had to close this. Shoulders back, head high, Hermione Granger, and...

"Look, I work hard, I'm enthusiastic. I'm a people person."

Wyatt seemed to be considering. "Go on."

"I've played sports all my life, so I know what it takes to be a good coach."

She was thinking of her best coach now. Ms. Chandran. She had been CJ's cross-country coach. CJ wasn't the best girl on the team, not by a mile. Sometimes literally. She felt clumsy and huge next to the other girls who looked like sleek greyhounds in their tiny track shorts. CJ possessed the kind of body that people politely called "stocky." It wasn't built for distance, and she opted to stick to the shorter runs. She would never forget the day that Ms. Chandran unceremoniously told her that she was going to compete in the long course. CJ shook her head. Her legs couldn't go that far. Ms. Chandran assured her that they would. CJ assured her that they wouldn't. This went on for several rounds until Ms. Chandran finally rested her hands on CJ's shoulders, looked her in her terrified green eyes, and said, *Your legs aren't what's holding you back, CJ.*

CJ ran the race. She ran it with every bit of Ms. Chandran's coaching advice pumping in her ears. *Dig deep, CJ. Dig!* She ignored the ache in her lungs and the burn in her legs, and kept digging until she exploded over the finish line, collapsing in a heap of exhaustion and emotion and absolute awe at what she'd just done. She'd come in second to last, and yet she'd never been prouder of herself. She didn't feel intimidated by the greyhound girls after that.

"And I know"—CJ's voice caught a little and she played it off with a cough—"I know what it means to *have* a good coach. Your one girl needs that. She deserves that."

Wyatt looked CJ up and down again. She could tell he was impressed. "Okay, Clarke. You're hired. I mean, not hired. No money will exchange hands, but..."

She smiled. "You will not regret this."

"I doubt I will. But you might."

He was smiling now. In a way that made her wonder what she'd just gotten herself into.

"Come on," he said. "I've got some paperwork for you in the back. Follow me."

Feeling triumphant, CJ stepped forward. Wyatt did not. Step, that is. He rolled his chair back from the desk. With a sweatshirt slung over the back of his chair, CJ hadn't noticed that the reason Wyatt hadn't stood when she'd extended her hand wasn't because he was rude. It was because he couldn't stand. Wyatt was in a wheelchair.

"Something wrong?" he asked.

"Nope," CJ said.

She gave him a smile and followed him into the back.

The movie theater where Martha worked was a dusty old singleplex. The best thing about working there was also the worst thing: It was boring. They only showed artsy movies that weren't exactly popular with the unsophisticated masses of their Cleveland suburb, and there were some days where not a single customer showed up. Martha hoped today would be one of those days. She'd dragged Ava to work with her because she wanted to pick her brain about Jordan's plan with the park. Martha had concerns. So far, though, Ava was only interested in talking about Logan Diffenderfer.

"He's violating my safe space."

Martha slid her key into the lock and pulled the door

open. "I'm pretty sure he didn't sign up for art just to ruin your life."

Ava followed her inside. "And yet that's what happened. Why did he drop physics, anyway?"

Martha shrugged. She'd been wondering that herself.

"Art is the one place—the *only* place—where I don't always feel completely self-conscious."

"First of all, that's ridiculous," Martha said. "You should feel like a badass at all times. Second of all, show him how good you are at art and make him feel insecure. That seems like a fun way to spend first period every day." Ava didn't respond, and Martha seized on the four seconds of silence to change the subject. "So...I've been thinking about what Jordan wants to do. And also about what the developer said at the meeting."

But that was as far as she got because that was the exact moment she noticed someone standing in the middle of the lobby. "Hi," said the intruder.

Martha jumped. The door had been locked. Which meant that for this girl to be standing here... "Is this a robbery?"

The girl laughed. She looked to be about Martha's age. "OMG. Hilarious. Uncle Benny told me you were funny."

Ava leaned over. "Who's Uncle Benny?"

Martha had absolutely no idea. "I'm sorry," she said to the girl. "Who are you?"

"I'm Victoria." She had an accent, though it was difficult to pinpoint where it was from. England maybe. "My uncle is your boss. Anyway, nice to meet you."

Victoria gave a little wave. Her nails were painted a light shade of pink, and her impossibly tiny wrist was wrapped in a Tiffany charm bracelet that Martha guessed was real. That still didn't explain why in the hell Uncle Benny's vaguely British niece was standing in the lobby. "This is Ava. I'm Martha."

Ava gave a slightly awkward nod. She was always awkward with new people.

"I know. Uncle Benny, Boss Ben, whatever we want to call him, told me. He said you're named after Martha Washington. That you're related to her. Great-great-grandmother or something."

It was a few more years back than that. But Martha nodded. "Yeah."

"That's so funny that you're related to George Washington."

Martha didn't know why it would be funny. Not that it really mattered since she actually *wasn't* related to George Washington. Only to Martha. George never had biological children. Most people didn't seem to know or care that the father of the country wasn't actually a father.

"I'm named after Queen Victoria. But not really. I mean, she's not a relation. My mum just liked the name. But how funny is it that I'm named after English royalty and you're named after American, well, not royalty, but you get what I'm saying. So, do we have uniforms?"

Martha looked at Ava, who merely shrugged. "Huh?" Martha said.

"Uniforms? Like anything that identifies us as theater employees?"

And that was how the great-great-great-great-great-great-great-granddaughter of Martha Washington learned that she had a new coworker.

"Um, no. No uniforms."

"Too bad. I thought it would be fun to have a uniform. Oh well. I'm ready to start training whenever you are."

Ava took that as her cue to leave. "It seems like you might be busy today after all. Talk later?"

Martha nodded. "Definitely. I'll call you tonight."

"Nice meeting you, Eva," said the girl who was named after Queen Victoria but wasn't actually related to Queen Victoria.

"You too," Ava said politely, not bothering to correct her. She gave Martha a hug and whispered into her ear. "Don't worry about the park. We'll figure out how to save it. Also, that girl is weird. Text me if it gets creepy."

Then Ava was gone and Martha was alone with the strange new girl.

CHAPTER **FIVE**

THE NEXT morning Ava pulled herself out of bed, poured a big bowl of Cocoa Puffs, and flopped down on the couch. The house was quiet since her mom was already out for her Saturday morning run. Not too long ago, her mom had tried to get Ava to go running with her. After several attempts, she'd finally accepted that it was never going to happen. Ava looked at her phone and saw their group thread already showed texts back and forth between CJ and Jordan about the councilman. Ava took a bite of cereal. It felt a little weird that she was the only one without a specific role in this plan. Not that she really wanted to create a fake LinkedIn profile or research the councilman. It's just that she thought it would be nice if sometimes people pointed at her when they needed a job done. Ava was about to put her phone down when she saw the e-mail.

"Holy shit!" Ava shouted at the exact same time her mom opened the front door.

Her mom yanked both earbuds out of her ears. "What? What? What's wrong?"

Ava read through the e-mail again just to make sure she hadn't misunderstood. "Oh my god. Oh my god."

"Ava, what is it?" Her mom's earbuds dangled around her neck, and Ava could hear the faint sounds of Vivaldi's *Fifth* coming out of them. Seriously. Vivaldi. The woman's power jam was a classical concerto. "Ava, you're scaring me."

"Sorry, Mom. It's not bad. It's good. It's so good. The Coventry Art Gallery. My painting was selected."

Ava beamed. That made her mom beam back although she was still confused. "Wait. What are you talking about? Selected for what?"

It's not like her mom had forgotten that Ava had submitted a painting to a major art gallery or wasn't a present parent or anything. It's just that Ava had never bothered to tell her since she thought she'd never get selected. She was so mad at CJ for pushing her to submit in the first place. She'd been ready to call CJ and yell at her for constantly believing in her and making her do things she had no business doing. But they'd picked her. The e-mail said that there'd been more than two hundred submissions and they had picked hers.

"That's incredible," her mom said when Ava finally

caught her breath enough to read the entire e-mail out loud. "What a fun thing to be a part of."

Fun? It was actually quite a bit more than fun. "The Coventry Art Gallery is a real showroom." It wasn't some bullshit teen competition either. "Submissions were open to everyone. I beat out professional artists."

"That's amazing. You should be so proud of yourself," her mom said. "And"—her voice was bubbling with enthusiasm now—"this will look *great* on your college applications."

This would have been a perfect time for Ava to tell her mom that she wanted to apply to art school. There would probably never *be* a more perfect time. She tried to psych herself up. *Come on, Ava. You can do it. You can do it.* She opened her mouth. "Yeah. Totally," she said.

Her mom eyed the cereal bowl that was resting precariously on the couch. Her mom didn't like Cocoa Puffs and she particularly didn't like Cocoa Puffs on her nice linen sectional, but she'd long ago given up nagging her only daughter about what she put into her body and what she put on top of the furniture. So she just kept eyeing the Cocoa Puffs like she could psychically keep them from spilling. Ava picked up the bowl and her mom finally relaxed.

"I'm telling you, Aves, the smaller liberal arts universities aren't going to care about your one bad semester. This gallery thing will show them you're a well-rounded applicant."

"Sure, Mom." Ava didn't want to talk about the one bad

semester. She didn't like thinking back to that time. "I'm gonna text the girls."

"Okay," her mom said. "I'll leave you alone, then." She walked toward her bedroom and paused just before going inside. "Oh. While I'm thinking of it...Did you remember to take your pill this morning?" Her voice was breezy, as if the thought had only just occurred to her. It had not just occurred to her. Her mom had a reminder on her phone that went off every morning at seven thirty on the weekdays and ten on the weekends. Not that she needed it. Her mom never forgot.

Ava never forgot either. "Yup. I remembered."

"Ava." Ava looked up. "I'm really proud of you."

Ava didn't know how to take compliments. She was relieved when her phone chimed. "That's probably one of the girls. I should..."

Her mom nodded and left her to it. As soon as her mom closed her bedroom door, Ava checked her message. The text was from a number she didn't recognize.

Congratulations on the Coventry Art Gallery!

It must be from the gallery people. The curator or the director maybe.

Another message popped up.

I'm seriously in awe. Like majorly.

That didn't sound like an art professional.

I read the announcement on the gallery's Instagram

and about shit myself when I saw your name. So seriously.
Congrats.

This was definitely not somebody from the gallery. Ava typed out a response.

Who is this?

She watched the blue dots form as her mystery fan revealed himself.

Oh. Sorry. Should have started with that. I got your number from the class directory. It's Logan.

Ava never responded.

Which made it completely awkward on Monday when she saw him in class. She got there early, and Logan was already at his easel, staring in bewilderment at his hot mess of a self-portrait. It turned out that his talent with a camera did not translate onto the canvas.

Mrs. Simon lit up when Ava entered. "Ava! Get your professional artist butt over here."

"I guess you saw the gallery announcement?" Ava was very aware of Logan on the other side of the room. "Pretty cool, right?"

"It's amazing. And further proof that you have got to apply to art school. It doesn't have to be RISD. The Art Institute would be lucky to get you if you want to stay in Ohio."

Ava shot a look in Logan's direction. "I'll keep thinking about it," Ava promised quietly.

The bell rang and Ava went to her easel.

"Hey," Logan said.

"Hey," she said, eyes forward.

"You never texted me back."

"I, uh, got busy."

"You seemed to get conveniently busy once you knew it was me texting."

"Nope. Just busy."

"All weekend?"

"Yep."

"You must be pretty excited. About the art show."

Ava kept her eyes forward. How was he so bad at picking up on social cues?

"I guess," she said curtly.

"Why are you being weird?"

"I'm not being weird."

Ava was totally being weird. She couldn't help it. When it came to Logan Diffenderfer, she didn't know any other way to be.

"God, Ava."

"What?"

"I'm seriously so confused. I thought sending a congratulatory text was generally a nice thing. I don't understand why you're being such a—"

She turned to look at him, daring him to finish that sentence. He did not. "Never mind. So...you're applying to art school?"

Shit. Ava crammed her toes into her shoes harder than she ever had in her life.

"Undecided. It's...complicated."

"Why's it complicated?"

Ava shot her hand in the air. She would ask to switch easels. She would say she preferred a spot in the back row. "Mrs. Simon?"

Mrs. Simon saw her hand but motioned for her to put it down. "One second, Ava. I want to get everyone started on something new." She paced the rows as she addressed the class. "I've been really happy with the progress on your self-portraits even though some of you still need to keep working." She paused behind Logan, then continued walking again. "But overall, I'm seeing excellent work. Now it's time to switch gears. What you're going to discover is that it's one thing to paint a face that you already know intimately. It's quite another to have to figure out the features of somebody who isn't as familiar to you. I think you'll find it an interesting challenge. So put away your mirrors and turn to the person next to you."

This could not be happening. This seriously could not be happening. Ava turned to her right and found Logan Diffenderfer staring at her. "Well," he said, "this should be real fun."

———————

"What the hell is Ava's problem?"

Jordan closed her locker door to find Logan Diffender-fer on the other side of it.

"Seriously, why is she always such a—" Jordan's eyes widened and then narrowed in a way that made Logan's mouth snap shut.

"Such a what, Logan?"

"I'm always nice to her and she always treats me like... like I killed her puppy."

"She doesn't have a puppy."

"You know what I mean." Jordan pulled her backpack over her shoulder and started walking. He followed. "Come on. Why is she like that?"

Jordan wished she could just tell him what Ava had over-heard. He wouldn't take delight in knowing that he'd hurt her. He'd feel awful. This is the part she wished Ava could understand. He was a guy who said a bad thing. He wasn't a bad guy. But as much as she wanted to tell him, Jordan couldn't violate Ava's trust. "I have no idea why she doesn't like you," Jordan said.

Logan sighed. "You're lying."

Jordan's phone buzzed with an incoming call. She glanced at the number. "Oh my god!"

"What. Who is—"

"Quiet!" She cleared her throat. Then cleared it again. Then she took a deep breath and answered. "This is Jordan James," she said as calmly and professionally as possible.

"Jordan James?" Logan repeated. "Who are you talking—"

Jordan put her hand over Logan's mouth. He looked surprised. Far too surprised to try to move it.

"Good afternoon, Ms. James," said a male voice.

It was the councilman. *Oh my god.* Her heart was pounding. She'd only submitted the press request this morning. She hadn't expected to hear back so quickly.

"Jordan is fine."

"Hi, Jordan. My name is Scott Mercer."

Jordan deflated slightly but recovered. "Oh. Hello... Mr. Mercer."

"Scott's fine. I'm the legislative deputy to Councilman Kenneth Lonner. The councilman is buried in committee meetings about the billboard ban, so I'm afraid he won't have time to speak with you about the park."

"Oh, okay." Jordan cringed. Not only at the way her voice sounded, young and kid-like, but at the words. A real journalist wouldn't take no for an answer. A real journalist would press. "Well, what I mean is, if that's the case, I'll have to run the article without a comment from him. And given the nature of what I'm running, I would expect that he'd like a chance to respond."

Logan tilted his head curiously to the side. Jordan's hand moved along with his face.

"I see," said Scott Mercer. There was some movement

on Scott Mercer's side of the call. Some typing. "Uh…can I put you on hold for just a second?"

"That would be fine."

Jordan heard the line click. She took her hand away from Logan's mouth and did a little excited dance right there in the hall. "Oh my god. Ohmygod, ohmygod, ohmygod."

Logan wiped his mouth with the back of his sleeve. "What the hell is—?"

Jordan slammed her hand back onto Logan's mouth as the line clicked on.

"Jordan? Are you still there?" said Scott Mercer.

"I'm here."

"Here's what I can do. As the councilman's legislative deputy, I'm well versed on the development issue and have been authorized to speak for him."

"Oh," Jordan said. "That would be an, uh, amenable solution for me."

"Does Thursday at eleven AM work for you?"

"Absolutely," she said quickly, before remembering that she would be in school at eleven AM. "Oh wait. Sorry. I just consulted my calendar, and I have a prior, um, engagement." He didn't need to know that her prior engagement was AP English.

"What about three PM?"

Jordan considered. It was perfect. The newspaper office would be empty and quiet after school. She could do the call from there.

"Three PM will work fine."

"Fantastic. Is this number a cell phone?"

"Yes. So you'll call me here? Or should I call you or..."

"I'll text you the address of the field office. We can meet there."

An in-person meeting? That would never work. The whole idea was that she didn't want him to see how young she was. "Actually, um—"

Brrrrrring!

"What is that?" asked Scott. "It sounds like a school bell."

It *was* a school bell. It was ringing right over Jordan's head. "Thursday will be great see you then thanks bye!"

She hung up as fast as she possibly could. Logan removed her hand from his mouth. "What just happened?" he asked.

Her heart was pounding. It would be fine. She could make it work. She could make herself look older. She could cut her last class of the day. That would give her more than enough time to drive across town. It was US History and she could always get the notes from Ava. Actually, CJ took better notes. This would all be totally and completely fine.

"Um, Jordan," Logan said. "Did you just imply to that person on the phone that you had damaging information about the development?"

Oh, right. She'd done that too.

"Shit," Jordan said.

That afternoon, CJ studied for her SATs at the desk she'd inherited when her oldest sister left for Brown. Jordan had begged all of her friends to go shopping with her that day. She needed to buy an outfit that would make her look old enough to interview someone called a legislative deputy. Ordinarily, CJ would have let herself be dragged around the mall, but the SATs were only a few weeks away. She had to say no. Ava was busy too, and that left poor Martha to take one for the team.

CJ flipped through her giant stack of vocabulary flash cards and stared at one of the words. "Arboreal." She felt like an idiot for not remembering what it meant. She flipped the card over and read the definition: *Of or relating to trees.* CJ tried a trick she'd learned in her prep class and visualized the meaning of the word. She imagined the old maple tree in Memorial Park, the one they'd picnic under in the summer and that turned brilliant shades of orange and red in the fall. CJ wondered if they would have to cut it down to make room for the office building. Probably.

Now that she was thinking about the park, something nagged at her. The developer had cited the park's declining popularity as a reason to close it. She claimed that attendance had dropped off significantly in the last ten months. CJ had taken the developer at her word, but now that she thought about it, it didn't seem true. She drove by on the way to

Martha's all the time, and the park was always filled with kids. She went online to see if she could verify the attendance numbers and stumbled onto something very interesting. The park hours were different now. It used to be open until ten PM. That had changed recently. Ten months ago, to be exact. Now the park closed at sunset. In the winter, that could be as early as four PM. There was more information and CJ kept reading.

"Holy shit," she said out loud.

As quickly as she could, she dialed Jordan's number. When Jordan didn't pick up, she called Martha.

"Hey," Martha said.

"Put Jordan on."

"Well, hello to you too."

"I found something huge."

"I'm still going to need you to say hello. Because manners. Also, Jordan has now tried on ten thousand skirts and I'm bored out of my mind and you owe me so hard."

"I think the councilman has been actively trying to kill the park."

"What? Hang on." CJ heard a fumbling noise and then Martha's voice, now distant and hollow. "You're on speaker. Jordan's right here. Should I conference in Ava?"

"Yeah. Get her."

Ava was at her mom's office working with her fancy French tutor. Or maybe it was her fancy calculus tutor. Her mom hired a lot of fancy tutors. CJ waited for the call to connect. She felt impatient and excited all at once.

"We're all here," Martha said.

Ava started to say hello, but CJ cut her off. "I think the councilman is helping the developer kill the park. Is he allowed to do that?"

"What?" said three voices in unison.

CJ's call waiting clicked. She checked the number. It was Wyatt, her new boss at Sensational Recreational. She wasn't sure why he was calling. She wasn't starting until next week.

"I have to take this other call," CJ said.

"Wait, no. Don't go," said Jordan.

"I have to. I'm sending you a link. The reason park attendance is down is because someone shortened the hours. You'll never guess who."

"Who—" shouted three voices before CJ clicked over and cut them off.

"Hello?" CJ said. She tried to sound calm even though she was absolutely buzzing. It wasn't just *someone* who had shortened the park hours. It was the councilman. Why would he do that unless he wanted the park gone?

"Clarke. I hope I'm not catching you at a bad time." He was speaking loudly, practically yelling over something happening behind him. It sounded like screaming.

"What is that?"

"Not important. I know you're not supposed to start until next week, but is there any way I could persuade you to come down sooner?"

"Uh...I mean...how soon?"

CJ heard a crash and then more screaming. She said, "Oh my god! What is that?" at the exact same moment that he said, "How fast can you get here?" Then they both said, "What?" at the same time. Then there was a long pause.

"You first," Wyatt said.

"What is that sound?"

"That, Clarke, is the sound of children at play. Now how fast can you get here?"

CJ pulled into the parking lot of the rec center fifteen minutes later. As soon as she got out of the car, she heard the screaming. It was coming from the gym. CJ quickly locked her doors and half walked, half ran across the parking lot. When she opened the double doors, she was surprised to see that Wyatt had been telling her the truth. This *was* the sound of children at play. A dozen or so boys in wheelchairs were spread across the basketball court playing a game that she would later learn was flag rugby. It was completely confusing, totally violent, and the boys absolutely loved it.

CJ saw Wyatt, wearing a striped referee shirt and following along with the action of the court. Occasionally, he blew the whistle that hung around his neck, and the boys would either cheer or shout depending on the call. Wyatt noticed her and waved her over.

"Clarke," he said as she approached. "What took you so long?"

Was he serious? She didn't think he was serious. But maybe. "Uh...I drove straight here. But I'm ready to get to work. Where do you need me?"

Wyatt's attention shifted to something on the court, and he blew his whistle so loudly that CJ jumped. "Sorry," he said. Then he shouted something at one of the kids, who argued with him before finally accepting the penalty. Wyatt turned back to CJ and said, "I feel really bad, but it turns out I dragged you down here for nothing. There was a crisis, but it's over."

"What happened?"

"Dakota. My one girl. She was miserable. Like *really* miserable. And I thought that maybe you could come down here and do your female thing. You know, that thing you pitched me in your interview. Make her see that this is actually fun. I mean, doesn't this look like fun?"

CJ watched two boys collide into each other and then shriek with laughter. It did look like fun, actually.

Wyatt blew his whistle. "Dudes. Dudes. This is *flag* rugby. No contact!" He turned back to CJ. "Dakota ghosted right before you got here."

"Oh my god." CJ was worried now. "Should I look for her? Do you have any idea where she went?"

"Yeah. She went home. With her mom."

CJ relaxed. "Oh. You said 'ghosted.'"

"Yes. She ghosted."

"If she told you where she was going, that's not ghosting. Ghosting is when you just disappear with no explanation. Like you would do to someone you're dating."

"Well, I would never do something like that in a dating situation. That's horrible. So I use the term differently. But I respect your cool teen slang."

"You know I'm only two years younger than you, right?"

"But they're big years."

CJ tossed him a look.

"Anyway, sorry to drag you away from whatever you were doing. I hope it wasn't anything important."

"All good," said CJ, trying to keep it light even though she was dying to get back home. She had about a thousand texts from her friends. Most of them were in all caps. She was pretty sure they were on the cusp of uncovering something huge. "So I'll see you Monday?"

"Wait. As long as you're here, stick around for a few. I want to introduce you to the dudes." Wyatt blew his whistle. "Dudes! Time out! Huddle up. Come meet Clarke."

CJ followed him onto the court. "You know I go by CJ, right?"

Martha couldn't believe what CJ had found. Of course she also couldn't believe that she was the only friend available for Jordan to drag around the mall that afternoon. She usually worked on Mondays, but that was before Victoria came along and the entire schedule got turned upside down to accommodate her boss's niece. Martha decided that if she was going to be stuck at the mall, she was at least going to make the most of it. So while Jordan paid for a pencil skirt and a boring white blouse that made her look older, Martha popped over to the food court. She wanted to pick up some Chinese to take home to her dad for dinner. He was a hopeless cook and would probably die of malnutrition if Martha ever moved out.

As she walked across the mall, Martha tried to process what CJ had found. She didn't really think it was that big of a deal at first. Then Jordan pulled up a picture of some serial-killer whiteboard she had in her room. She was using it to keep track of everything she knew about the councilman. It was completely thorough. And vaguely creepy. She'd listed the names of all the councilman's political donors and the dates of their contributions. The developer happened to have written him a pretty big check just two weeks before he limited the park hours. It did seem weird. Although, at the moment, Martha was more irate about something else she had noticed on the serial-killer board. Jordan had also noted his stance on an upcoming vote about a minimum-wage increase. He was opposed. She hadn't been following the issue that closely, but she was vaguely aware that they were considering a city-wide initiative to raise the minimum wage by fifty cents. It made Martha livid that he would oppose that. An extra fifty cents an hour would be life changing for some people. It would certainly make a difference to her. Especially if this Victoria girl kept taking her hours.

"You look like someone who's about to graduate," said a male voice from just up ahead.

Martha looked around to see who was talking to her. She shriveled up a little on the inside when she saw who it was.

"So, am I right?" he asked. "Are you about to graduate?"

Staff Sergeant Broderick stood in front of the Army Recruitment Center, the one that was a staple of pretty much every mall in a blue-collar town. His name wasn't on his uniform, but she knew it because he'd handed her his business card before. Several times, actually. He always tried to talk to her and yet somehow never remembered her face. After the second time it happened, Martha did some googling. She learned that he was expected to sign up a certain number of people each month, which explained his aggressiveness. She also learned that thirty-five was the oldest recruitment age.

"No," Martha said. "I graduated a while ago. I'm thirty-six. Sorry."

"Ha ha," he said lightly. "Good one. So what's the plan after graduation? You want to come in and talk about it?"

Martha did not want to come in and talk about it. Inside the recruitment office, a uniformed woman sat at one of the desks. Martha accidentally caught her eye as she was looking for an escape. The woman was older, forties probably, with a no-nonsense look that Martha liked. Martha also liked that she kept glancing up at the conversation and seemed to be rolling her eyes at Staff Sergeant Broderick.

"How much do you know about the army?" Broderick asked in a dude bro tone.

"Well," Martha said, "I know that they haven't hit their recruitment goal for women in several years." She'd read this online too. "So I know you're desperate for people like me."

The woman at the back desk looked up again.

"That's exactly right," said Broderick. "Which is why we're offering forty grand in bonuses on top of student-loan repayment."

Martha's jaw must have been on the floor, because he took this as his opening.

"Come on in and we can talk about it."

Martha shook her head and backed away.

CHAPTER **SIX**

ON THURSDAY morning, Jordan stood in front of the bathroom mirror and tried to figure out the best way to hide the purple stripes in her hair. Her new outfit was packed carefully in her backpack for later, but she was still worried that the purple stripes in her hair would give away her real age. She'd been trying to follow a YouTube video about how to pull it into a sleek but effortless topknot. As she stood back and frowned at the results—which were neither sleek nor effortless—her little brother walked by the bathroom.

"What the hell is wrong with your hair?" Lucas was in eighth grade and all attitude.

"Nothing is wrong. Get out."

"You look terrible."

"Mom!" Jordan shouted. Her mother appeared in the doorway looking mismatched in a business suit and a pair of old clogs that she referred to as her comfies. She always waited until the last second to put on her heels. "Make Lucas leave me alone."

"Lucas, leave," said her mom.

He rolled his eyes and walked away while muttering something about women. Jordan pointed to her head and turned to her mom. "Help."

"What's the end goal here, because..." Her mom eyed the knot curiously. "What are you even trying to do?"

"I don't know. I just want to hide...these." She grabbed desperately at the purple stripes. "I need to look professional." Jordan had already told her mom about her interview with the legislative deputy. She always told her mom everything.

"You don't have to try to be something you're not. He's expecting a high school student. Not Barbara Walters."

Okay, maybe she didn't tell her *everything*. She'd conveniently left out the part where she told him she was older. "Please, Mom. I also have my meeting with the college counselor today. I'm afraid she won't take me seriously."

This part was absolutely true. Jordan had woken up feeling nervous. She knew her first-choice schools might be unrealistic, and she wasn't sure what she'd do if the college counselor told her that. "I want her to look at me and see somebody who looks...I don't know...collegiate."

"Oh, honey. You already look way more collegiate than

half the burnouts I went to school with. But okay. I get it. Sit."

Jordan sat dutifully on the edge of the tub, her back to her mom. She shook out her hair, and her mom combed through it with her fingers. Jordan loved this feeling more than almost anything in the world. It calmed her down and kept her from worrying about the interview. There was nothing else she could do to prepare. She'd practiced and practiced all week, forcing her friends to play the role of the legislative deputy. Her plan was to toss him a couple of softballs first. She would let him get nice and comfortable. Then she'd hit him with everything she knew and see how much he flinched.

Her mom worked quickly, pulling Jordan's hair upward with a thin comb. She was great at this. As a kid her mom had spent about ten thousand hours practicing on all of her friends. She'd grown up in a mostly black community and almost all of her childhood friends had hair like hers. Jordan sometimes wondered what that would be like. There would be a shorthand and a shared experience. She wouldn't feel people staring at her when she walked down her own street. Her neighborhood wasn't as white as Ava's—which was alarmingly white—but she did stand out.

"Don't let the college counselor talk you out of aiming high," her mom said as she combed through Jordan's hair. "I don't care if she thinks Columbia and Northwestern are too much of a stretch. There's absolutely no harm in applying."

Jordan didn't want to think about it. She just wanted to relax and enjoy this feeling of sitting on the tub with her mom. "Can we talk about something else? I'm already too nervous."

"What do you want to talk about?"

Jordan shrugged. "I don't know. Anything."

"Okay. I've got something." Jordan could hear the smile in her mom's voice. "How's Logan Diffenderfer?"

Jordan tried to turn her head so she could shoot her mom a look. "He's fine, Mom."

Her mom loved Logan. He was polite and charming, and knew how to talk to adults. He also wasn't afraid to let Jordan shine. Her mother had once noticed him beam when Jordan received news about a newspaper award she'd won. She was convinced that Jordan and Logan were going to get married someday. Which was ridiculous for about a million reasons. Not the least of which was, who even married someone they met in high school anymore?

"Ava still hates him, Mom. But thanks for checking."

Jordan could never date someone one of her best friends despised.

"All right," her mom said. "But someday she won't. I'm just saying, he's a very nice boy."

"Noted."

Her mom finished with her hair and said, "Voilà." Jordan turned around to look at herself in the mirror. Her stripes were almost entirely hidden underneath other pieces of her hair. It was still possible to notice them but only if you were really looking, and Jordan doubted that a guy with the title of legislative deputy would be really looking.

Martha took the bus to work that afternoon. She was supposed to get a ride from Ava, but Ava had sent some cryptic message that she had to bail because Logan Diffenderfer was ruining her life.

Martha got off at her stop and walked the three blocks to the theater. She was surprised to find the door already unlocked. Inside, Victoria greeted her chipperly in her vaguely British accent. "Good afternoon."

"Did I misread the schedule?" Martha asked, her voice dripping with passive-aggressive annoyance. "I thought I was working today."

Only one employee was usually scheduled to work on weekday afternoons. Martha couldn't afford to keep losing out on hours.

"Yes. I mean, yes, you're working. No would be the answer I should have given. Since you asked if you'd misread the schedule."

"Huh?" Martha said.

"I'm here to see the movie." Victoria shifted her weight. She was wearing pink jeans, which Martha didn't know was a thing people did. "I can pay. Should I pay? Uncle Benny didn't tell me if we got free tickets or not."

"We don't. But I'll let it slide."

Martha walked over to the concession area and began setting up. Victoria followed her. "So, how's it going?" Victoria asked.

Martha hated small talk. "The weather is lovely," she said flatly, hoping that Victoria would take the hint.

Victoria did not. "Interesting. I find it lovely too. So many people complain about the humidity, but I'll take it over the dreary cold any day."

Realizing that they were going to have a conversation whether she liked it or not, Martha decided to at least get some information. "Hey. Can I ask something? Where is your accent from? It's..." She was going to say "weird" but settled on "tough to pinpoint."

"Well, my mum is American. But I call her 'Mum' because I was born in London. Dad's British. But we moved to Paris when I was five. I went to an English-speaking school, but my teachers were mostly Canadians. After Paris, it was London again. Then here."

"How do you do all that and end up in Cleveland?"

"Nasty divorce," Victoria said. Then she quickly corrected herself. "Not me. My parents."

"Yeah. I figured." She didn't tell Victoria that her parents had divorced nastily too.

Victoria grabbed a box of assorted candy bars from the storage cabinet and started filling the display rack.

"You don't have to do that," Martha said. "Besides, the movie is about to start, and I don't think anyone will show up for a three-hour documentary about urban farming."

Victoria made a face. "Is that what we're showing? I didn't even know."

"Then why are you here?" Martha realized that her question came across as a little blunt. "I mean, look, free country. You can hang out wherever you want. But why here?"

Victoria shrugged. "I needed to escape my house."

"Oh, sorry. Everything okay?"

Victoria stacked the candy carefully. One bar on top of the next with the labels facing the same way. "It's fine. It's not like I'm running from anything dramatic. Just boredom, really. We only moved here about a month ago. Nobody at my new school talks to me."

"Where do you go?"

"Hawthorne Academy," Victoria said. "Do you know it?"

"Yeah." It's where Ava's mom had tried to send her after everything that happened freshman year. The school was as famous for their rigorous academics as they were for their students' large bank accounts. Rumor had it that everyone there drove a BMW and had an Adderall dealer on speed dial.

"It's not exactly an easy place to be the new girl. And I'm like an expert at being the new girl. Here. I'll do that."

Victoria took two big stacks of napkins from Martha and got to work filling napkin holders.

"It's fine. You're not even getting paid right now."

At least Martha hoped she wasn't. She was still nervous about this cutting into her hours.

"I don't mind."

Victoria smiled, and Martha realized for the first time how pretty her new coworker was. She was definitely weird. But a quirky weird.

"So tell me, what's cool to do in Cleveland? I'm still figuring out my way around."

"Nothing's cool to do in Cleveland."

Martha's phone buzzed. It was probably Jordan. She'd promised to text as soon as her interview was over. Martha was dying to know how it went. She grabbed for her phone so fast that it flew out of her hand. Victoria bent over to pick it up at the same time that Martha did, and it was frankly a miracle that they didn't bonk heads. Their fingers did touch for a second, though.

"Sorry," Martha said. "I've been waiting for an important text."

She checked it and found a message from Jordan.

He's running massively behind. I'm still waiting in the lobby. Now I have to pee, and I'm terrified that if I go to the bathroom, he might come out to get me and then he'll think I left. WHAT DO I DO?

"Everything okay?" Victoria asked.

"Yeah," Martha said, laughing. "Sometimes I think my friend has it all together, and other times, not so much." Martha typed out her response.

Pee, you idiot.

"So," said Martha, "which parent did you get? In the divorce?"

She correctly assumed that any child of divorce would know what the question meant.

"My mum. Dad's still in London."

"I got my dad. My parents are divorced too."

"Sorry."

"It's fine. It gets easier. I don't know how far into it you are. But it becomes normal. Weirdly normal."

"I hope so. Things with them were never great. It was inevitable. Dad was always working, so not having him around doesn't even seem that different. Cleveland's been the biggest adjustment. It's been lonely. I think that's why Uncle Benny offered me the job. He told me how cool you were. I think this is like a setup."

Martha swallowed. Hard. "Oh?"

"Since I need friends."

"Oh," Martha said again. Then her phone buzzed. "Hold that thought." Martha read the text. "Uh-oh."

"What's wrong?"

Jordan had sent the message in all caps.

MAJOR DUCKING PROBLEM.

Victoria peered over her shoulder. "What's a ducking problem? Is that like an American thing?"

Martha was absolutely sure that Jordan had not meant to type "ducking."

Ava and Logan were staring deep into each other's eyes when she heard her phone buzz. "I should get that," she started to say.

Logan shook his head. He somehow did it without breaking eye contact. Which was frankly a little unnerving. "We're not supposed to look away."

"It's probably Jordan," she said, still keeping her eyes on his. "She might be done interviewing that city guy."

"Do you want to start this over? Because I sure as hell don't." They went on with the staring. After a minute, Ava's eyes started to drift. "Nope," Logan said. "Right here." He made his fingers into a V and pointed them at his eyes.

Ava hated this. She didn't blame Mrs. Simon for making them both stay after school. She knew her portrait of Logan was subpar. She'd rushed through it, just wanting it to be done.

"This is weird," Ava said.

"I know."

Ava had expected Mrs. Simon to give them both extra

instruction on how to properly shade a nose or paint the lines of a neck. She did not expect her to ask them to stare into each other's eyes for an uninterrupted fifteen minutes.

Logan scratched an itch on his arm. "How long do you think it's been?"

Ava had set a timer on her phone, but she couldn't look at it without breaking eye contact. "No idea."

"Oh, wait," Logan said. "If you move your head slightly to the left, I think I can see the clock behind you."

Ava tilted her head without moving her eyes, and Logan groaned. "What? What's wrong?"

"Three minutes," he said. "It's been three minutes."

Ava wanted to crawl out of her skin. Another minute or so passed. The silence was almost as awful as the staring. Logan must have felt it too because he said, "Let's ask each other questions or something."

"Okay. What's your favorite color?"

"Gray."

"Gray? *Gray?*"

"Yes. Gray. You have a problem with gray?"

"It's not a color."

Logan somehow managed to roll his eyes without looking away. "Fine. Will you accept blue?"

"Sure. Now ask me something."

"Why do you hate me so much?"

She didn't say anything.

"Come on," he said. "That's my question. You have to answer."

"Fine. Because you're annoying."

It wasn't a lie. It just wasn't the whole truth.

"Whatever. Your turn."

"Favorite food?" she asked.

"My dad's baked ziti. Patented Diffenderfer family recipe. Your questions are terrible. Ask me something real."

"It's your turn," Ava said.

Logan took a second to think. "Okay. I've got one. Who is the woman in the picture? The one in your painting?" He angled his head slightly toward her self-portrait.

"Well, it's called a self-portrait because—"

"I know it's you. I mean the woman in the background."

Ava hesitated.

"Or we can just ask each other dumb questions all day," Logan said. "Whatever."

"It's my mom. Not my adoptive mom. My birth mom."

"Oh."

"I don't know what she looks like. I assume she has brown hair and brown eyes, and probably looks somewhat like me. But I don't really know. That's why I kept it fuzzy."

"That's...really cool," he said. "Are you going to submit that one to RISD?"

"It's my turn to ask a question."

She thought for a second, and Logan sighed. "My favorite sport is running. My favorite book is *Catcher in the Rye*. My favorite band is Amen Dunes. My favorite—"

"Why did you drop AP Physics?"

Logan shut his mouth.

"Why?" she asked. "I want to know."

His eyes were locked on hers when he answered. "Because I had a panic attack."

She blinked. "Oh," she said. "I didn't—"

"It's fine. I mean, it's not fine that it happened. But it did. My mom was there and she freaked. She wanted me to see a shrink but...no way."

It took all of Ava's strength not to look down at her feet.

"So she said if I wouldn't see a shrink, I had to lighten my schedule. Art was the only first-period elective left with room. I didn't do it to torture you, even though you seem to think so."

"Why didn't you want to see a...shrink?"

Ava hated the word "shrink." It made her feel tiny and broken. Like she wasn't normal.

"You already got your question," Logan said. "It's my turn."

She prepared herself for what was coming next. "Okay."

"What's *your* favorite color?" he asked.

She was mad at him for copping out. It felt like a

letdown. Like all the air had left the room. They asked each other a few more questions after that. Mostly insignificant ones. And then they went back to silently staring. It felt less intense in some ways and more intense in others. As she looked into his eyes, she also noticed his other features. She could see all the things she'd gotten wrong in her painting. His ears did stick out, but not in a way that made him look ridiculous. They made him look boyish. Like he was still figuring out how to grow into himself. She could see that his smile was slightly crooked, and she could tell that it was because there was a hint of something else behind it. Not sadness. But not exactly happiness either. Her portrait had only revealed the first layer of Logan Diffenderfer. She'd missed all the layers underneath.

The alarm on her phone finally went off. They'd survived their fifteen minutes.

"Please don't tell anyone," Logan said. "About the panic attack. I don't want people to think I'm..."

Logan didn't finish the sentence. He didn't need to. Ava knew what he was going to say. *Crazy.*

Ava picked up her phone to silence the alarm. "Uh-oh," she said.

"What?"

She showed him the text from Jordan.

MAJOR DUCKING PROBLEM.

CHAPTER **SEVEN**

JORDAN STOOD in the doorway of the legislative deputy's office and prayed to the universe that he wouldn't recognize her. Which hardly seemed possible. She had recognized him the second he'd looked up from his desk. This truly was a major ducking problem.

He'd been on the phone, which is how she'd been able to quickly text her friends. Now she was waiting for him to finish his call. The receptionist who had escorted Jordan from the lobby was still standing there waiting to introduce them. Maybe Jordan should tell her she needed the bathroom again. She could go and never come back.

Scott Mercer hung up the phone. "Sorry about that," he said.

"This is Jordan James," the receptionist said.

Jordan pushed her shoulders back and raised her head

high. It was something that CJ swore made her feel more confident. Scott Mercer stood and did that politician thing where he buttoned his jacket and extended a hand in one swift move. Jordan didn't know what else to do, so she shook it. When their hands touched, his blue eyes narrowed into a squint. "We've met before, haven't we?"

"I don't think so."

But they had—the night of the community meeting. He was the young man who had been walking with the councilman when she'd asked for an interview.

"You sure? You look so familiar."

"Definitely not," Jordan said.

The receptionist turned to leave, and Jordan seriously thought about running after her. She might have gone through with it too were it not for the stilettos she'd borrowed from her mom's closet without asking. She felt wobbly in them. Like a little girl in her mother's shoes. Which is exactly what she was.

"Well, come on in, Jordan. I'm getting pulled into a meeting with the councilman, so unfortunately I can only give you twenty minutes." He started to sit back down but then stopped. He looked at her like something had just occurred to him. "I know exactly where I recognize you from."

Jordan's shoulders slumped. She knew she owed him an explanation. She may as well tell him the truth. *I just wanted to be taken seriously.*

"I—"

"You were at the young professionals' mixer."

She blinked a couple of times. "Uh..."

"The one at the Hyatt Regency."

All the adrenaline that had been coursing through Jordan's body suddenly stopped at once. It made her feel heavy. "Oh yeah. The young professionals' mixer. That must have been it."

"See? I knew we'd met," Scott said. "Do you need to deal with that?"

Jordan hadn't even realized that her phone was dinging over and over and over.

"Shoot. Sorry. Guess I forgot to silence it."

She glanced at her phone and saw that the texts pouring in were from Martha.

What's the ducking problem?

(My "ducking" is intentional and for comedic purposes.)

But seriously? Are you okay?

Oh my god. ANSWER ME.

Hellllooooo?

"It's my editor. Just give me one second." Jordan quickly typed a bunch of letters so that he'd see her texting.

czopiuvawerawlu

She hit send and silenced her phone. "Okay, that's done, so..." She took a deep breath. She had only twenty minutes. She needed to pull it together. She sat down and crossed her legs because she felt like it made her look more professional. "Is it okay if I record?"

"Of course," Scott said as Jordan fumbled for the record button. "So you're right out of college too?"

Jordan looked up. "Oh, uh…" She tried to remember how old Martha had made her on her LinkedIn profile. Did it even include an age?

"The young professionals' thing. That was the one for recent grads, right?"

Jordan nodded. "Right. Yes. Recent grad." She needed to calm down. She was flustered and scattered.

"I go to so many of those things, it's hard to keep track. I'm working on building up my professional network."

"Yeah," Jordan said. "It's all about who you know, right?" She smiled and took a quick breath to center herself. Then she set her iPhone down on the desk between them and saw that both Martha and CJ were responding to her string of gobbledygook.

MARTHA: *Is this a cry for help?*

CJ: *Seriously? Are you okay?*

MARTHA: *Are you being kidnapped????*

CJ: *If you are being kidnapped, drop us a pin.*

Jordan snatched her phone off the table. She turned it to airplane mode and set it back down. "Okay," she said. "How about I dive right in?"

"Great."

She took a breath and reminded herself of her strategy. Start off on a friendly tone. Get him to establish facts. Picture Hermione Granger if you get nervous. (That was CJ's advice.) Then go for the kill.

"I want to start by getting a sense of the councilman's attitude about parks in his district."

"Of course," he said. "Parks are an incredibly vital part of a community and something he prioritizes."

Jordan made a note. "I see. Then talk me through the ordinance he introduced last year to limit hours in Memorial Park. I'm particularly interested in the timing—"

Scott's desk phone rang, and he put up a finger. "Hold that thought." He answered, "Office of Councilman Kenneth Lonner. Scott Mercer speaking." He nodded as someone spoke. "I understand. And what is the location of this pothole?"

Jordan's eyes squinted. Pothole? He had cut off her question to take a call about a pothole? She watched him write down an address and a couple of other details. When he hung up, he turned to her. "Sorry about that. You were asking about timing?"

She felt like her rhythm was off now. "Actually, let's back up. I noticed that the ordinance only impacted Memorial Park. None of the other six parks in the district had their hours cut."

"That's correct."

"Why was that?"

"Well, I'm not sure how familiar you are with the location of Memorial Park."

Jordan had been riding her bike there since she was five. "I've done my research."

"Then you know it's in an area with a lot of crime. A lot of drug deals were happening after dark. That's why the hours were limited."

This was perfect. This is the answer she expected him to give. It was the answer she *wanted* him to give. Now she could corner him.

"Yes. I do see that. But according to my research, crime was at an all-time high *five* years ago. And it's actually been in a slight decline for the past several years."

"Right. Only slightly, though."

"Yes. That matches what I found. I'm curious"—Jordan kept her voice as even as possible—"about the timing. The councilman introduced the city ordinance two weeks *after* he first met with the developer hoping to build an office building on that property."

She leaned back and waited for him to squirm. His phone rang again. "Sorry," he said. "I have to get that." Jordan felt robbed as he picked up the receiver. "Office of Councilman Kenneth Lonner. Scott Mercer speaking. Oh, hello, Mrs. Montgomery." Scott hit mute on the phone. "This one might be a minute. She calls every single week about a sober-living facility that's being built on her street. She's not happy about it. And not brief."

Jordan couldn't believe this. Was he taking these calls on purpose? To break her rhythm? To eat up all her time? What would a real journalist do? She wouldn't tolerate this, would she? "If I only have twenty minutes—"

Scott put his finger up as if to say, *Hang on.*

"I understand, Mrs. Montgomery. I assure you that I am passing your complaints on to the councilman. I understand your concerns but...Okay...Uh-huh." He muted the phone again. "I really am sorry. But I can't ignore these calls. During city business hours I have to be available for constituent complaints. Part of my job is to log them for the councilman." He unmuted the call. Mrs. Montgomery's voice was loud enough that Jordan could hear it. As she watched Scott get reamed out by an old lady, it occurred to her that maybe his title wasn't as fancy as she'd thought it was. The woman finally exhausted herself, and Scott hung up.

"Sorry," he said. "So you were asking about the restricted park hours?"

"Actually, I was asking about the timing. The developer met with the councilman. *Then* he shortened the park hours. Are you telling me that was a"—his phone rang again—"coincidence?" she said under her breath.

"Office of Councilman Kenneth Lonner," he said as he

picked up. "Oh, hello, Councilman. Yes. Of course. Right away."

He hung up the phone and stood in one solitary motion. "I'm afraid I have to cut this short. I'm getting pulled into a meeting now."

Was he serious? She met his eye. "But you haven't answered any of my questions."

"I really am sorry."

Jordan was too angry to be intimidated by him anymore. "You promised me twenty minutes."

Scott sighed, and at that exact moment, his phone rang again. He laughed at the absurdity of it. Jordan did not. So he stopped laughing too. "One sec," he said to her. "Office of Councilman Lonner. Scott Mercer speaking."

Jordan couldn't believe this. She grabbed her phone from his desk and tossed it in her purse. "Thank you so much for your time," she said flatly, and started to walk out.

"Jordan. Wait."

She turned back.

"Can you hang on for just a second?" he said into the phone. He put the call on hold. "Look, how about this. If you can come back, I'll give you your full twenty minutes. It'll give me time to talk directly to the councilman and get you an answer on what you were asking about. Because I honestly don't know. But I'll get you an answer, and I'll give you your twenty minutes. You have my word."

Another line on Scott's phone rang. He threw up his hands like he couldn't believe it. This time Jordan did laugh. So Scott laughed too. "And, Jordan, maybe we should make it outside of business hours. Do weekends work for you?"

Jordan nodded. "You had me at 'I'll give you your full twenty minutes.'"

"How about Saturday? Elevenish?"

"Let me consult my iCal." Jordan knew she was free, but she made a big show of checking. "I can make that work."

"Great," Scott said. He smiled and his blue eyes sparkled. "It's a date."

" 'It's a date'?" CJ was sprawled across Ava's mom's king-size bed with Ava on one side of her and Martha on the other. The three of them were staring at Jordan's phone like it was an old-timey radio, not an iPhone balancing upright on a purple PopSocket playing back a recording of her interview. "What a creepy thing to say."

Jordan poked her head out from the master bedroom closet. "It didn't come out that way. I think he was just flustered." She smiled triumphantly. "I flustered him."

"Hell, yeah, you did," said Martha before rolling onto her back. She grabbed a pillow and clutched it to her chest. "Did you hear that the Tylers started a YouTube channel about saving the park?"

CJ nodded. The Tylers were Tyler Welles and Tyler Ziegler, and they were best friends. Mostly because they were both named Tyler. "But have you seen it?" CJ asked. They were asking people to share their fondest park memories. In theory, it was a great idea. In execution, it was a disaster. "I'm not sure that a video of Grayson fondly remembering the time he got stoned underneath the slide is really going to help our cause."

Jordan hovered in front of the closet. "I feel weird about this." She turned to Ava. "Are you sure your mom won't mind?"

"She won't even notice anything's gone. The stuff for Goodwill is in the back. It should be in a grocery bag."

If Jordan was going to pull off a second interview, she needed a new professional outfit. Ava had graciously offered up the suits from her mom's reject pile. As Jordan rooted around in the closet, Martha pulled up one of the Tylers' videos. Sasha, a drama-club girl with bright-green eyes and a vacuous personality, delivered an overly dramatic monologue about how evil the city was for "oppressing our right to self-expression." It was not convincing, and it made CJ feel tense. Like everything was up to them. She sat up and rubbed at her temples.

Sasha's video finished, and Martha clicked on the next one. CJ was too distracted to watch. Something that had happened earlier that day was nagging at her. She grabbed the pillow from Martha and held it to her chest.

"Hey," said Martha. "There are like ten other pillows on this bed. Take one of those."

CJ didn't give the pillow back. She hugged it tighter. "I had my meeting with the college counselor today."

Jordan emerged from the closet. "Is this it?" She held up a grocery bag. "What's wrong with CJ?"

CJ loosened her death grip on the pillow. "You had your meeting with Ms. Fischer today too, right?"

"Yeah," Jordan said.

"Was it..." CJ didn't know how to finish the sentence.

"It was...fine," Jordan said tentatively in a way that made CJ think it was better than fine. "Why? How was yours?"

"Not fine. When I said that Stanford was my dream, she pursed her lips. Like, literally. She said that it was admirable to shoot for the stars but that we should talk about some realistic options too."

"That's just how she is." Martha snatched the pillow back. "She told me to give myself more options too."

"Me three," said Jordan. "Sorry, CJ. You're not special."

Ava didn't add anything to the conversation. She was the only one who hadn't had her meeting yet.

Jordan dumped the contents of the grocery bag onto the floor. Designer clothes scattered everywhere.

CJ grabbed another pillow from the head of the bed. This one had fringe at the edges, and she ran her fingers through it. "She told me that BU would be a good option."

"Really? Me too." Jordan sounded excited. "Maybe we *will* end up at college together. How fun would that be?" Jordan sifted through the pile of clothes and pulled out a little black suit dress. "This is cute." She held it up to herself. "She said it's a perfect safety school."

Ms. Fischer had not called it a safety school when she brought it up to CJ. They spent the rest of the meeting focusing on CJ's SAT score. Ms. Fischer came at her with a stern warning about making the time to study even if it meant sacrificing her social life for a few weeks. CJ hated how meek her voice had sounded when she asked if there were other things to focus on to make up for her SAT score.

Ms. Fischer had acknowledged that CJ's GPA was outstanding and that her long list of extracurriculars would mean something. *Maybe if you nail the essay. And I mean, really nail it. You don't want to have to rely on that, though.* Then she gave CJ practical tips about SAT study guides and free computer programs. CJ was too embarrassed to say that she'd done all those things already.

Jordan unbuttoned her pants and kicked them off. She stood there in her Wonder Woman undies eyeing the dress. CJ wished she could be that relaxed in her underwear. Even around her friends, she was always doing the thing where she crossed her arms in front of her stomach to hide it. She stood up. "I have to go."

Jordan was just stepping into the dress. "Wait. No. You can't."

"I have to."

"What about the park?" Jordan asked.

"I'm sorry," CJ said. She couldn't focus on the park right now. She would focus after the SATs were over. She needed to get home; she needed her SAT flash cards in her hands to feel like she was doing something. "I'm sorry," she repeated. Then she left.

CHAPTER **EIGHT**

MARTHA ONCE saw a documentary about veal production. She learned that the calves were housed in restrictive
pens because the lack of movement made their meat more
tender. That's how she felt whenever she worked in the tiny
movie theater ticket booth. Like a constricted, doomed calf.

It was Saturday morning, and she was perched on the
stool in the little booth, painting her nails with Wite-Out
and thinking about next year. College applications had
everyone in knots. Martha included. Though her knots
weren't so much about getting in as they were about how
she would pay for it when she did. Everyone told her to
apply for financial aid like it was no big deal. Like they
didn't understand that the money had to be paid back. Her
top choice, MIT, was more than fifty grand a year. Once
you added room and board, Martha calculated that she'd

be graduating $280,000 in debt. At least. It made her feel sick. If she went to Cleveland State, she could probably get enough scholarship money to cover tuition. She could live at home and save even more money that way. She could keep working at the movie theater. Thinking about it made her feel more relaxed. It also made her feel like veal.

"I'm bored." The voice came from behind her. "I'm so borrrrrred."

Martha turned to find Victoria in the doorway. She was dressed in a pair of tiny tattered cutoffs (the kind that were tattered by Abercrombie & Fitch, not by life) and a scoopy little top that showed her delicate collarbones.

"Weird," said Martha, carefully painting her pinkie nail. "I'm having the time of my life."

"Is that a joke? American humor is sometimes hard for me to get."

Martha put the cap back on the Wite-Out and shook her hands to dry them. "Definitely a joke."

There wasn't a lot of space in the ticket booth and only one stool, so Victoria leaned against the counter. She was so close to Martha that their knees were practically touching. "What do you do to pass the time?" Victoria asked.

Martha blew on her nails in an obvious and exaggerated way.

"Oh. That's a boredom thing," Victoria said. "I assumed it was a style choice." Martha laughed, and Victoria turned around so she could look out the window. "It's so strange, all these people walking by and living their lives while we're stuck in here."

Martha considered telling her about the veal documentary. "Saturdays are always slow. Maybe you can talk to your uncle about his choice to show obscure foreign films that no sane person would ever pay money to sit through. I'll bet you one George Washington that we don't get a single customer today."

Victoria's eyes lit up. "I will take that bet," she said quickly. She leaned forward, which caused her butt to press up against Martha's knees. "Hello, good sir," she said into the microphone. "Are you here for the obscure foreign film?"

Victoria had been blocking the window—she was *still* blocking the window—so she had seen what Martha had not. A real live customer walking up to the ticket booth.

"You have to press the button or they can't hear you, weirdo." Martha playfully shoved Victoria out of the way to reveal a customer looking very confused on the other side of the glass. Martha sighed when she saw who it was. She pressed the button that activated the microphone. "What do you want, Diffenderfer?"

Logan blinked a couple of times. "Oh. Hey, Martha. I'll take a ticket for the matinee."

"And I'll take that dollar," Victoria said to her with a smirk.

Martha muted the microphone. "You haven't won yet, Queen Victoria. It may seem like you have the advantage now, but this is going to end just like the Revolutionary War did." Martha grabbed the microphone and spoke into it. "You sure, Diffenderfer? The movie is obscure. And it's Polish."

"Actually, it's French," he said. "The director is Polish." He shoved his hands in his pockets, then immediately took them out again like he was embarrassed that he knew this. "So could I get a ticket? Just one. It's just me. I'm by myself." Or maybe he was embarrassed about being alone.

Victoria gave Martha a triumphant smirk and pressed the microphone button. "That'll be seven dollars, please." He gave her the money, and she gave him the ticket. "I'll meet you at the front to take your ticket. Enjoy the show."

After he walked off, Martha did a slow clap. "Well played, Queen Victoria."

Victoria curtsied. "If England had had a queen instead of a king at the time of the American Revolution, the war would have ended a little bit differently." Then she smiled and put out her hand for payment. "That'll be one dollar. One George Washington, please."

Martha reached for her wallet. "Fine," she said. "But you forgot something." She took a coin out of her wallet and pressed it into Victoria's hand. "George Washington is also on the quarter."

Victoria laughed, and Martha noticed that it was a good laugh. She also noticed how warm and smooth Victoria's hand felt when she put the quarter in it.

"Come on," Victoria said. "Let's sit in the back and watch the movie."

"You want to sit through a Polish film about sadness?"

"It's French. And that guy is *cute*."

Jordan felt strong and prepared as she pulled into the parking lot of the district field office. Scott had warned her that the receptionist didn't work on Saturdays and that she should text him when she got there. He came outside to let her in, and she saw that he was weekend casual in a pair of jeans and a preppy button-down. She felt ridiculously overdressed in Ava's mom's suit dress. "I have a thing later," she blurted. "A luncheon. At a fancy place. Hi."

"Hi," he said. "Nice to see you again." He put his hand out and she shook it. "Come on back."

As she followed him down the hall, she noticed that most of the offices were dark today. They stopped in front of a large glass-walled conference room. "I thought this would be more comfortable than my tiny office."

"Great," she said, shifting and tugging at the edge of her dress.

"Are you okay?"

"Uh-huh."

The dress was stupidly tight, and she could barely breathe. She sat carefully in the chair that was offered, tucked one stilettoed foot behind the other, and tilted her knees slightly to the right. It was the "duchess lean," popular with British royalty, who did it to keep from flashing their royal undies, and repurposed now by Jordan who did it to keep from exploding out of her dress. "Let's get started," she said, sucking in as hard as she could.

"I really do apologize about before. Coffee?"

The only time Jordan ever drank coffee was when she ordered a blended mocha with extra whipped cream, and she guessed that wasn't what was being offered. "No, thank you."

She watched impatiently as Scott poured himself a cup from a pot on the back table. She was desperate to start the interview. Mostly because she was desperate to go home and unzip this dress so she could breathe again.

"So," he said, "how's your Saturday?"

Jordan shifted. "I'd love to get started." It came out curt and she tried to recover. "Since I have that luncheon later."

"Sure," he said. He seemed nervous. She hoped he was. It would mean that they had really uncovered something worthwhile. A nefarious plot to support a developer. Maybe her article would win an award. It might even get so much attention that the admissions people at Northwestern would see it. She leaned over to dig her phone out of her bag—it was already in airplane mode this time—and set it between them.

"Okay," Jordan said. "The question I was asking was about timing. Councilman Lonner introduced an ordinance that limited the hours at Memorial Park just two weeks after the developer first submitted her proposal. How does he explain that?"

"I spoke with the councilman about it," he said. "The reason he introduced that ordinance was because of neighbor complaints." Jordan waited for Scott to go on. "You know how part of my job is to log constituent complaints? The people who live along the park, one household in particular, became very vocal about their frustration with the drug dealing that was going on there. They felt that it was becoming unsafe. The councilman met with them and agreed that their concerns were valid, so he introduced the initiative to limit park hours."

"And that happened right after the developer met with him? Seems a little coincidental." Jordan leaned forward, waiting for him to crumble.

He didn't.

"No. The constituent meeting was before, actually. It always takes a few weeks to draft an ordinance. I guess that does seem pretty coincidental, though." He shrugged. "Yeah, I could see how that looks weird. But no. It really was a coincidence. Are you sure you don't want coffee? Or some water?"

Jordan shook her head. She jotted down some notes to give herself a second to regain her composure. She had one more question, and she wanted to make sure it came out with strength. "How does the councilman justify the developer's donation to his campaign?"

She knew the exact amount. It was written on her whiteboard. The developer had given the maximum legal limit.

Scott sipped his coffee. He seemed genuinely confused. "Justify it?"

"The developer contributed the maximum possible donation. Now the councilman is supporting her project."

"Ah," he said. "I see where this is going. The councilman takes donations from a lot of people. With a lot of opposing viewpoints. I can assure you that they in no way sway his decision-making."

Jordan watched him carefully. She noted that he didn't show any signs that he was lying. There was no change in his voice or body language, and he maintained eye contact. His calmness bothered her. She'd hoped to nail him with this question. She would have to press harder. She wasn't willing to entertain the other possible option: that he was telling the truth.

––––––––––––

CJ barely left her house that weekend. Her friends sent her constant updates, so she knew that Jordan's interview hadn't gone the way they'd all hoped it would. CJ felt guilty for not being with them as she sat at her desk and studied her cards and took SAT practice test after SAT practice test. On Sunday night, her dad cracked her bedroom door open and peeked in. "Mom wants to know if you're coming to dinner or if we should just slide a tray under the door prison-style."

CJ turned without smiling. "I think I'm done for the night. I was just taking a break."

"Sitting in front of your computer isn't a break. Come on. Let's shoot some hoops."

CJ grabbed her shoes and met him in the driveway. They both stretched for a minute without saying much, and then he tossed her the ball.

CJ dribbled a couple of times. Her dad faked her out and easily stole the ball. She was rusty. He dribbled and she got low, ready to move. Her three older sisters were girly girls. They liked clothes and boys and makeup. CJ liked those things too, but she also liked wrestling and getting dirty and beating her dad at one-on-one basketball. He'd taught her to be strong at defense, and they'd played enough games together that she knew all his tells. He tried for a fast break to the right, and she was right there to block him. She got the ball and drove to the basket. She shot wide and missed completely.

"Come on, CJ," he yelled. "Take your time. Focus."

Her dad never gave her any slack. He pushed and pushed until she improved. Or cried. Many of their games ended with her in tears and wondering if she'd ever be good enough to make him proud. CJ got the rebound and took another shot. This time it went in with a *swoosh*. Nothing but net. She loved that sound. It was the sound of winning.

They played hard for the next twenty minutes, until her mom came out to tell them that dinner was getting cold. Her parents were traditional in a lot of ways. He worked. She cooked. He made the financial decisions. She let him. CJ tried not to get too judgmental about it, though. It worked for them. Her mom was a good mom. She was a *great* mom. And yet CJ always felt like there was a distance between them. She suspected that part of the reason was because her mom was so much older. Ava's was too, but she didn't feel old in the same way. As CJ's mom once put it, *We're just a very different breed of woman.* CJ's mom had never worked, although she resented it when people described her that way. *Raising children* is *my career.* She'd married CJ's dad right out of college and then she'd had three daughters in a row. CJ was not one of them. Her parents were just becoming empty nesters and her mom was starting to think about finding a career for herself when CJ came along as an unexpected curveball. CJ sometimes wondered if her parents had ever considered other options. She'd never even heard her mom say the word "abortion," though, so she couldn't imagine a world where she actually thought about getting one.

CJ's two oldest sisters had daughters of their own, and the last time her third sister had visited, she mentioned during dinner that she and her husband were "trying." As far as CJ knew, this was the closest that any of the Jacobson sisters had ever come to having a conversation about sex with their mother. All three of her sisters still lived in various parts of the Midwest. Sometimes CJ felt like the weird one for wanting to get out. The world just seemed so much bigger to her.

The next day was CJ's first official afternoon volunteering with Sensational Recreational. She drove there straight after school and pasted on her most cheerful smile as she pulled open the double doors of the gym. Wyatt waved her over when he saw her. A couple of the boys had already arrived and were on the court messing around. CJ carried her gym clothes in her old cross-country duffel bag. The one with the letters of her last name and her number, 33, sun-bleached and cracked along the side. "Hi, Wyatt," she said as she walked up. "I'm ready and excited to be reporting for duty."

"Clarke. I'm ready and excited to have you."

She saw his eyes move to her bag. "I brought a change of clothes. Gym stuff."

"You're a runner?"

"Yeah. No. I was. Not anymore."

"We have that in common, then," Wyatt said.

CJ wasn't sure if it was a joke or not. Was she supposed to laugh? She wasn't sure, so she looked away uncomfortably instead. "Is Dakota here yet?"

"About that," he said. "We should chat." He rolled his wheelchair and she walked alongside him. "Dakota's mom called on Friday to tell me she was quitting."

"Oh no."

"I managed to talk her out of it."

"Oh good."

"I promised her I had something special for Dakota today."

"That's great. What is it?"

Wyatt looked at her and it clicked.

"Oh. Me. Yes. Yes! *Me*."

"Clarke..." He said it in a soft way. "She's having a rough time. Don't expect too much out of her. And don't expect too much out of yourself."

CJ felt a wave of nerves and did her best to shake them off. "Not at all. It's going to be great."

"I'd originally planned to start the kids on basketball today. But Dakota's mom mentioned that tennis was her favorite sport Bee-Dub." When CJ looked confused, Wyatt elaborated. "Bee-Dub. Before wheelchair."

"Is that an expression?"

"No. I've literally never said it in my life. But I like it. I might use it again. Anyway, I figure we'll give tennis a shot today."

The gym doors clicked open and Wyatt angled his head. "She's here."

CJ turned and saw Dakota for the first time. Her hair was bright red, and you could see the freckles that dotted her nose even from across the court. Her mom also had red hair but in a deeper and more intense shade. She was a Sansa Stark to her daughter's Anne of Green Gables.

Mother and daughter both saw CJ and started to come over. One came willingly, the other had to be pushed.

"Clarke?" said Dakota's mom.

"CJ, actually. And you must be Mrs. Gorman. Hi."

"You can call me Margaret." She seemed nervous.

"I'm so excited to work with Dakota today," said CJ.

"Well, she'll see to it that that feeling doesn't last." Dakota gave her mom the kind of withering look that belonged on the face of a teenager, not an eleven-year-old. Her mom sighed. "Sweetheart, please try to have a good attitude today. Wyatt switched to tennis just for you. And CJ is here to make sure you have a good time."

"Good time?" CJ said. "Oh, we're not going to have a good time. We're going to have a GREAT time."

Dakota rolled her eyes and looked at her mom. "Is she serious? She cannot be serious."

Margaret gave CJ an apologetic shrug before turning back to her daughter. "I'll pick you up right at five." She gave Dakota a big kiss and then mouthed two words to CJ, *Good luck.*

As soon as Margaret left, CJ knelt down so she was eye level with Dakota. "So, you ready to have some fun? Let's go pick out the best racket. I saw a really cool purple one in the pile. You like purple?"

Dakota pulled on the two levers that unlocked her wheelchair brakes. She rolled to the sideline and parked herself there. CJ looked at Wyatt. "It's not you," he said. "Don't take it personally."

CJ smiled her best camp-counselor smile. "Not at all. She just needs a pep talk. I give great pep talks."

While the boys huddled around Wyatt and selected their rackets, CJ sidled up to Dakota. "Can I tell you a secret?" CJ asked. When Dakota didn't say anything, she kept going. "I used to get really nervous about playing sports. I thought that the only reason to play was to win. But the best time I ever had was when I lost a race. We're just here to have fun today. Doesn't that look like fun?"

She motioned to the court. Wyatt was being goofy and hilarious as he showed the kids how to hold their rackets. Everyone was laughing.

"It doesn't seem fun to me," Dakota mumbled.

"You won't know until you try. How about you give it just five minutes. I'll even set a timer so we don't go a second over."

Dakota twisted her fingers together and looked up at CJ. She didn't seem angry or sullen anymore. Just sad. "Please don't make me play. Please."

Her voice was edged with tears, and CJ felt completely out of her depth. She responded in the only way that seemed right. "Okay," she said.

CHAPTER NINE

"DO YOU think that Danglehoffner guy is coming again today?"

"Huh?" Martha said. She was leaning on the concession-stand counter, staring at her phone while Victoria absent-mindedly cleaned around her.

"Danglehuffer. Darfenderfner. No. That's not right. What's that guy's name? The cute movie buff?"

"Dinglehopper," said Martha. Then she went back to her phone. She was reading the latest issue of the McKinley *Blaze* online.

"Dinglehopper? Like the fork the Little Mermaid uses as a hairbrush?"

"Yep," said Martha. Jordan had decided to hold off on publishing the park article, and there wasn't anything ter-ribly exciting in the issue.

"Diffenderfer."

Martha looked up.

"It's Diffenderfer, right? Logan Diffenderfer. That's his name?"

After Martha had handed Victoria the quarter, they'd ended up sitting in the back of the theater and watching the weird French film. Only the movie wasn't weird at all. It was beautiful. Sad and lonely and yet somehow deeply hopeful. At one point, Martha was so overcome with emotion that she'd had to rush out of the theater. She barely made it to the bathroom before a huge brimming sob erupted from her chest. Martha wasn't a fan of crying, and she certainly wasn't a fan of crying in front of other people. When she finally composed herself enough to return to the theater, the movie was over, and Logan and Victoria were talking. Closely.

"No," Martha said flatly. "It's definitely Dinglehopper."

There was a knock on the front door and Martha hopped up. "Crap," she said. "One of us should have been in the ticket booth. That's probably a pissed-off customer."

"Maybe it's Diffenderfer," Victoria said, with an eagerness that Martha didn't like.

Martha walked to the front door and opened it. "Dad," she said with surprise.

Her dad had never stopped by Martha's work before. Someone was dead. That was the only explanation. Someone had died horribly. She quickly ushered him in. "What are you doing here?"

"Why aren't you in the ticket booth?"

"Is someone dead?"

"Why would someone be dead?"

Her father took off his baseball cap as he walked through the door.

"You can keep your hat on, Dad. Nobody cares."

"I care. It's rude to wear a hat indoors."

The conventions of society that he chose to cling to were so annoyingly arbitrary. "So what's up?" Martha asked.

"I finished filling out those financial aid forms."

"Oh," Martha said. "Thanks." She didn't want to go into debt, but she didn't want to be veal either. She'd just sent the forms to her dad and her mom last night. Since her parents were divorced, she needed one from each of them.

"It says they need to be scanned," he said. "I thought maybe you'd have one of those scanner thingies here."

She shook her head. "No. But I have an app on my phone. I can take care of it."

Her dad pulled an envelope out of his back pocket. He hesitated before handing it over. "I don't want you to freak out when you see the numbers. They wanted to know about my debt too. When you add it all up in one column, it looks like a big deal. But it's not. It's just how adults live. I know how you get about money and…it's nothing for you to worry about."

Martha took the envelope from him. "Thanks."

"Patsy. Look at me."

She did.

"I wish I had more to give you."

She hated this. She wished her dad knew how to use a scanner thingy or how to fill out a form online like every other parent in the world. She wished he could figure out how to do this by himself so she didn't have to see the shame on his face right now.

"No, Dad. It's fine. Honestly, the less income you have the better off I am. I'll be eligible for a lot more financial aid. So seriously. The worse this is, the better for me."

She was suddenly very aware of Victoria at the concession-stand counter. The sleeves of her dad's shirt were rolled up, showing off the tattoo on his forearm of an eagle soaring over the American flag that he'd gotten on the anniversary of September 11. The ink was faded and blurred at the edges. People always misjudged her dad when they first met him, and she wondered if Victoria was doing it now. What they didn't know was that underneath the rough-around-the-edges exterior was a savagely prolific reader who had had an important job once. They didn't know that in high school everyone thought he was somebody special. Martha had seen his yearbook. He was a football star in the fall and a baseball legend in the spring. Senior year he was voted Most Popular, Best Couple (with Martha's mom), and Most Likely to Be Drafted by the Cleveland Browns. They didn't know that he'd done the admirable thing and turned down a football scholarship at Notre Dame to stay in Cleveland with her mom when she got pregnant.

He took his baseball cap out from under his arm. "See you at home, Patsy."

"See ya, Dad. Thanks for this." She held up the envelope.

After he was gone, Martha heard footsteps behind her. "Patsy?" There was a slight bit of teasing in Victoria's voice.

Martha shrugged. "What? Your parents never called you anything weird?"

Victoria looked stung and Martha backed off. "Sorry," she said.

"You okay?" asked Victoria.

Martha nodded. "I'm fine. Patsy was Martha Washington's childhood nickname. My dad's always called me that. He thinks I'm like her. Like I'm going to grow up and be..." *Remarkable.* That was the word he always used. "Whatever. It's just a dumb nickname."

Victoria smiled. "I don't think it's dumb. I think it's really sweet, actually."

Martha shrugged. Not because she hated the nickname. Quite the opposite. She loved it. It's just that standing there, clutching that envelope, she didn't feel remarkable. She felt scared. "I'll man the ticket booth," Martha said.

"We shouldn't be so lazy about not being in there." She took her envelope and walked away.

Jordan stared at her whiteboard, the one that her friends said made her look like a serial killer. She was convinced that if she just stared at it for long enough, everything would come into focus.

Her brother wandered in and plopped down on her purple beanbag chair. "Dad said we're doing knickknacks for dinner again."

Knickknacks meant that her parents were sick of cooking and everyone was on their own to eat whatever leftovers they could find in the fridge. "Okay," she said.

"What are you doing?"

Jordan didn't respond. She'd written down the date of the meeting with the neighbors and the date that the councilman introduced the ordinance. They were so close together, it was almost unbelievable that it could be a coincidence.

"What...arrrree...youuuu...doooinng?" her brother said again, this time imitating Dory from *Finding Nemo* when she was communicating with the whale.

"I'm trying to save your future. You want to carve your name into Memorial Park, right?"

"Sure." He moved to her desk and picked through her stack of college brochures. "George Washington University?"

"It's in DC." The college counselor had told her it would be a good backup, along with BU, if she couldn't get into Northwestern.

"I don't want you to go to DC."

"Relax. I don't either." It was not an area that interested her. At all.

"Why would neighbors complain about a park?" He stepped in front of the whiteboard, blocking her view.

"Lucas, get out. I'm trying to focus."

"I thought you were doing this for me."

"I am. The neighbors complained because people go into the park to deal drugs and do bad stuff."

"That's not the park's fault." Lucas picked up one of her whiteboard pens and drew a smiley face on the board. Then he put the cap back on the pen. "Dibs on the leftover spaghetti." He walked out.

After he was gone, Jordan stepped closer to her whiteboard. It *wasn't* the park's fault. It also wasn't fair to the kids who lived in the neighborhood. Martha's neighborhood. They would be expected to play inside from now on. The only reason the councilman didn't look like a villain was because he got to say he was doing it for the vocal neighbors. Jordan looked at the two dates she'd written down and then scanned her notes. Scott had given her a date and told her that's when the meeting with the antipark neighbors had taken place. She didn't even think to ask for verification.

Now she was mad at herself. It was his eyes. Those bright-blue eyes that seemed incapable of lying. Jordan reached for her phone. She shut her bedroom door as she dialed. The phone rang only twice before she heard his voice. "Office of Councilman Kenneth Lonner. Scott Mercer speaking."

"Scott. Hi. It's Jordan. Jordan Scha—uh—I mean, James. Jordan James."

"Jordan." He seemed surprised to hear from her. "What can I do for you?"

"I'm still working on my article, and I realized that it would be helpful if I could read the complaints made by the constituents. The ones who spoke up about drug dealing in the park."

There was a long silence.

"Hm," he said. "I'm not sure that I have anything I can show you. The meeting between the councilman and the residents was private, so I don't believe notes were kept."

Interesting. Jordan didn't know if that was unusual. She worried it would show her inexperience if she asked.

"Then how about a name and a phone number for any of the people who made the complaints?" she said. "I can get quotes directly from them."

"I'm not allowed to give out our constituents' personal information."

That seemed legitimate. Though also incredibly convenient. As Jordan sat there, her Spidey sense on fire, she decided that she had to push. "You understand that I could file a records request under the Freedom of Information Act, right?"

Jordan had absolutely no idea what the Freedom of Information Act actually covered. She was taking a gamble that he didn't either.

She thought she heard Scott sigh. It turned out that he was just clearing his voice so he could lower it. Almost to a whisper. "Look," he said. "I can't give you anything on the record. But I'll show you something if you can keep it between us."

"Sure."

"Can you meet me tomorrow?"

"Absolutely. Should I meet you at the office?"

"Definitely not. How about the place where that young professionals' mixer was? The Hyatt Regency. We can meet in the lobby bar."

"Uh…"

"Meet me there at seven."

He hung up. The first thing Jordan did was to call the Hyatt Regency and ask if the lobby bar was limited to patrons twenty-one and up. She was relieved to learn that it was also a restaurant. "Kids welcome." That's what the man on the phone actually said. *Kids welcome.* As soon as that was done, she uncapped her red pen and wrote something down.

Councilman lying?

CHAPTER TEN

AVA DIDN'T mean to look at Logan's canvas. He'd asked her not to look at the painting of her until he was done and she'd agreed. She'd walked into the art room after school because she'd finally had a revelation about how to paint her mother in the background of her self-portrait. After-school art hours were optional, and it was usually just Ava and Isla and Tobin in the room. She'd been surprised when she opened the door and saw Logan, paintbrush in hand. He'd been surprised too. His easel was angled in a way that she could see it. She looked away at first, wanting to keep her promise. Then she couldn't help herself. She glanced back. It was only a quick look.

"You made me white!"

Logan spun around. "You looked? You said you wouldn't look."

"No. Okay, yes. I looked. I couldn't help it. Logan. I'm Latinx. My skin does not look like that. Even white people aren't that white."

Logan stepped back and looked at his painting. Ava could tell he was embarrassed. "I know. It's awful. I can't do this. Mrs. Simon is going to fail me, isn't she?"

"Well..."

"Shit. I can't have anything below a B on my report card this semester. How is art harder than AP Physics? Shit, shit, shit."

Logan was spinning out far more than the situation required, and now Ava felt bad about her reaction. She was going to feel really terrible if he had another panic attack. "Okay, calm down. Mrs. Simon grades on effort, not talent. The fact that you're here after school...and that you're taking this seriously..."

"I'll try to find the right skin color," he said.

While Logan went to the back of the room to get more paint, Ava found her self-portrait. She set it up on the easel and thought about how she was going to do this. Her plan was to paint her own face onto her mother's. Then, using the palm of her hand, she'd drag it through the wet paint to make a blurred shadow effect. Logan came back with the paint and paused behind her.

"You make it look so easy."

"It's not," she said. "I work harder than people realize.

And even then, it doesn't always come together. This one's been really tough. I thought it would be interesting not seeing her face, but it's just weird."

"Do you ever think about looking for her? Your mom?"

Ava grabbed the edges of her sleeves and pulled them over her wrists. "Um, it's complicated. I don't really want to...It's not something I want to talk about." *With you.*

"Sorry," he said. "I'll try to get your skin color right. I really am trying."

He returned to his painting and she returned to hers. She could feel him staring at her from time to time. He'd peek around his easel and squint at her, studying her, trying to get the image right.

Of course Ava thought about looking for her birth mother. Sometimes she thought about it every waking second of every day. She had so many questions. That's why the fuzzy image wasn't sitting right with her. Because a fuzzy image would never be enough. She desperately wanted to meet the woman who had given her away, and she wanted to ask her why.

Suddenly Ava felt goose bumps spring up all over her arms. She looked up and saw that Logan was staring. She knew it was just because of the assignment, but he didn't look away when she met his eye.

"I'm going to get this right," he said.

Ava nodded. Then she dug for her phone and sent out a desperate text.

———————

CJ was already in the parking lot of the rec center when she got the text from Ava.

Logan is staring at me. It's horrible. It's the assignment. But still. It's horrible. Can anyone come hang out in the art room? PLEASE. Like be a Diffenderfer buffer?

Martha and Jordan both texted back right away that they couldn't do it. CJ sighed. She would do anything for Ava. And if she was being honest, she was relieved to have a reason to skip out on volunteering. She felt like such a failure with Dakota. Everything she said was wrong. Like she was just making things worse. She sent a quick text to Wyatt.

So sorry, but I can't make it today. I'm sick.

Wyatt texted back immediately.

Sick of Dakota?

CJ started to type something back about a horrible fever, but she deleted it. Maybe she could tell him she had cramps. He'd never question that. She deleted that too. Before she could come up with a third lie, her phone chimed with a new text from him.

The blue dots betray you, Clarke. I can see you trying to come up with a lie.

I'm not lying.

Okay. I'm lying.

But it's not because of the reason you think.

As soon as she hit send on the last message, her phone rang. It was him. "Hello?" she said.

"Clarke. You don't sound sick."

"I already admitted I'm not."

"Then talk to me. Why aren't you gracing us with your presence today? If it's because you think you failed as a volunteer, please don't be so hard on yourself. You're honestly not as bad as you think you are."

"Well, thank you for that."

"She's a tough kid going through a tough time."

"I know."

"Then what's going on?"

CJ sighed. "The thing is," she said, "I've got another tough kid going through a tough time."

"Are you lying to me again?"

"Not exactly." Ava was seventeen. Technically that made her a kid, so technically it wasn't a lie. "Look, here's the deal. One of my best friends got partnered up for this portrait assignment with her mortal enemy."

"Ah. High school drama. Tell me more."

"Well, it's kind of a long story. Freshman year he said this thing and—"

"You need to learn to recognize sarcasm. I absolutely do not care. Now get your butt down here."

"I know it sounds dumb, but it actually is a big deal. She's..." CJ stopped herself from saying *fragile*. Ava definitely wasn't fragile. If anything, she was the strongest person CJ knew. "She's special."

"Again, Clarke. I don't care. I'll see you in fifteen minutes."

CJ hung up and walked into the gym thirty seconds later. "I was in the parking lot," she said when Wyatt raised a curious eyebrow.

"Clarke," he said. "Don't put so much pressure on yourself. You're not here to change Dakota's life. If we can eventually get her to play some tennis, awesome. But we can't pull her out of this thing she's in until she's ready to come out. She's gotta just be in it, you know?"

Dakota didn't even say hello when she arrived. She went straight to the sideline, as was her habit. CJ waved. Dakota didn't wave back. She thought about what Wyatt had said. That Dakota just needed to "be in it." So she let Dakota be and helped run drills with the willing participants. After about twenty minutes, Dakota looked so sullen that CJ couldn't take it anymore. She turned to Wyatt. "Do you mind if I..."

"Go," he said.

CJ went over to the sideline and sat down next to her.

"Hey, Dakota."

"Hey."

"Where's your mom today? I didn't see her drop you off."

"Angus's dad drove me." Angus was a boy with death-metal stickers all over the back of his chair. "My mom is having coffee with another mom. The mom of my—this girl I used to be friends with."

"You're not friends anymore?"

Dakota shook her head. "She's mean. I hate her. We got in a fight, and now our moms have to have coffee and talk about us."

"What was the fight about?"

Dakota looked away. CJ could tell she'd hit a nerve. "I sometimes fight with my friends," CJ said. "It feels awful, but deep down, even when we're fighting, I know we still love each other."

"It's not the same. She'll never be my friend again. I don't have any friends."

"I bet that's not true. I *know* that's not true. Because I'm your friend."

Dakota gave CJ a pained look. "That's even worse than having no friends. You're just some creepy adult who gets paid to hang out with me."

"I'm not getting paid," CJ said. "I'm not even an adult. Dakota, I'm just trying to figure out everything too. The truth is, I'm kind of a mess. More than people realize sometimes. I get overwhelmed. I get scared. So I might understand better than you think. You can talk to me about anything. That's what friends do for each other."

Tears immediately sprang to Dakota's eyes. Then there was a flash of anger. "YOU ARE NOT MY FRIEND!"

Heads turned and the action on the court shifted into silence. CJ could feel everyone staring. "Dakota..."

Wyatt caught CJ's eye. She gave him a look as if to say that everything was under control. Even though she was fairly certain that it wasn't. CJ leaned over to Dakota. She touched her arm lightly and whispered, "Why don't we go outside? We can talk while we take a walk."

The words that were supposed to keep Dakota from going over the ledge pushed her straight off it. "Don't you get it? I can't take a walk! Just leave me alone! LEAVE ME ALONE!"

The pain in Dakota's voice was almost primal. It stunned CJ into silence. She sat there frozen while Dakota unlocked the wheels of her chair and fled for the exit. It was only when Dakota exploded out of the gym doors that CJ registered what was happening. Dakota was racing into the parking lot.

Wyatt was already on the move.

"Dakota!" he shouted as he went after her. "Dakota!"

CJ could feel all the boys staring at her. This was her fault. This was her fault and she needed to fix it. "Carter," she said to the oldest boy on the court. "Have everyone practice their serves. I'll be..." She didn't even finish the sentence.

Outside, CJ saw that Dakota still had a lead on Wyatt. There were so many cars in the parking lot. So many drivers not paying attention. A minivan came around the corner. CJ saw it before Dakota did. The van slammed on the brakes and honked the horn. The driver opened his mouth to yell. As soon as he saw that it was a child in a wheelchair, he waved instead. "Sorry."

The near collision must have jarred Dakota, because she stopped. Wyatt caught up to her and Dakota spun around. She was breathing hard, and CJ got close enough that she could see tears in her eyes. "I...I...I'm sorry," Dakota said.

CJ decided to hang back and let Wyatt talk to her. She was so scared of saying the wrong thing again.

Wyatt looked at Dakota with deep sympathy. "What are you sorry for?"

"For screaming like that."

"It sounds to me like you needed it."

She nodded.

"You want to scream some more?"

She shook her head. "Everyone will stare."

"Who gives a shit?"

She looked at him, confused but intrigued that he'd just sworn in front of her.

"Yeah. I said 'shit.' You are having a shitty day and you

are allowed to scream about it. I think you need to scream about it. So scream."

CJ shifted her weight. She felt so useless.

"Try it," he said. "Yell whatever you want. Yell whatever is inside of you that needs to come out."

Dakota was still trying to catch her breath. "This wasn't supposed to happen."

"What wasn't? But tell me louder."

"I was supposed to have surgery and everything was going to be fine. My mom said I'd be fine. She promised. But I'm not fine and my friend is scared of me and it's not fair. IT'S NOT FAIR!"

"No," Wyatt said. "It's not. LOUDER."

"IT'S NOT FAIR! IT'S NOT FAIR!"

There were at least a half dozen people walking through the parking lot. Not one of them said anything. A couple of them even looked over and smiled politely. The wheelchairs made everyone so weird and awkward. CJ looked down at her feet. She was weird and awkward too.

Now that the floodgates were open, Dakota screamed. Wyatt raised his voice and screamed with her. It gave Dakota the permission she needed to be even louder. She screamed her truth with everything she had. She screamed until tears streamed down her face. She screamed until the shouting was mingled with laughter. Wyatt pumped his fists into the air and howled like a wolf. Dakota screamed until there were no words left, and then she howled like a wolf too. Their voices blended and carried, and the sound ebbed and flowed between anger and joy, sadness and relief.

It was one of the most beautiful things CJ had ever seen in her life. And the most useless she'd ever felt.

CJ didn't talk to Wyatt about what happened that afternoon. She wouldn't even make eye contact with him. She helped him pick up cones, and she put the tennis rackets back in the office. Then she said good night. Wyatt tried to say something to her, but she told him she had to be somewhere. She raced to her car, and when she got there, she gripped the steering wheel tightly. She'd failed again. This time it wasn't just the SATs or coming in last in a race. She'd failed another person.

CJ turned the key in the ignition and pulled out of the parking lot. She wondered if she'd ever come back. She decided it would be better for Dakota if she didn't.

That night, Martha opened the envelope from her dad. In one column, he'd written his gross income, his debt in another. Martha looked at the numbers and felt like her knees were going to give out. She knew it wasn't her dad's fault that he was in such terrible financial shape. Not that long after his layoff, he'd been in a motorcycle accident. It wasn't even that bad, he was only banged up, but this was back when he didn't have health insurance. The ambulance ride alone had cost two thousand dollars. She'd overheard him complain about it to one of his friends. *Wish I'd never even gotten in the goddamn thing.*

Martha flopped back on her bed. She stared up at the ceiling, where she could still see the yellowed outlines where an entire galaxy of glow stars had once loomed. Her dad had bought them for her and helped her put them up on their first night in the new apartment. Martha was in her astronomy phase back then. For a few years, her dream was to fly to the stars. Now her dream was so much smaller. She just wanted to be able to pay for college.

Martha decided to call CJ. It's not that Ava and Jordan wouldn't try to understand, it's just that CJ actually would. Not totally. Her family wasn't nearly as bad off, but money was still tight. Her parents clipped coupons and complained about the economy and at least that was something. CJ's parents had had to fill out these horrible forms too. When CJ didn't pick up, she called Jordan. Then Ava. Then she tossed her phone across the room and clenched her eyes shut. She wanted to hide. From all of it. The debt and the anxiety and the stars she'd once thought she could fly to.

Martha's phone rang, and she walked across the room to get it from where it had landed. She hoped it was CJ. It wasn't.

"Hello?" she said tentatively.

"Hi," said Victoria. "Am I catching you at a bad time?"

"No. What's up?"

Victoria was probably calling to take more of her hours away. "Uncle Benny" had mentioned that he was going to rearrange the schedule again.

"I was just calling to talk," Victoria said. "I wanted to see how you're doing, I guess. You seemed...I don't know. You seemed like you were having a bad day."

"I don't think you'd understand," Martha said.

"Try me."

"It's financial stuff. That doesn't really seem like a problem for you. No offense."

"It's okay. None taken. I probably wouldn't understand. But I can still listen."

Martha walked back to her bed. She climbed in it and curled up. Then she told Victoria everything while she stared at her stars.

Jordan had learned her lesson with the too-tight suit dress, so when she walked through the revolving door of the Hyatt Regency that night, she was dressed stylishly but comfortably in a pair of her own bright-red cigarette pants. She usually paired them with a funky printed tee and a pair of sneakers, but today she'd made the look more subdued with a simple black tank top and some heels. She felt more like herself—the adult version of herself—and that gave her confidence as she searched for Scott at the bar.

He was seated at a small table with a single candle flickering on it. There was a manila folder in front of him. Jordan's heart leaped slightly when she saw it. She didn't know what was in that folder, she just knew that it was going to change everything.

Scott stood when she approached and shook her hand. He was so unfailingly well-mannered. She could never imagine one of the boys in her high school behaving like this. "Nice to see you," he said as they both sat.

"Is that for me?" she asked, eyes moving to the folder.

He slid it across the table. "That's for you. You can't reference any of it in your article. I could get in a lot of trouble for showing you this."

"Totally off the record," she said. "I promise."

She opened the folder and saw that it contained a stack of about thirty pages. There were handwritten notes on torn-out sheets from a yellow legal pad and printouts of e-mails. She started to read. As soon as she realized what it was, she looked up at Scott. "These are the constituent complaints," she said, somewhat stunned.

He nodded. "I could tell you thought I was lying and I get it. But it's the truth. The majority of the neighbors hate the park. The handwritten notes were taken by my predecessor. From phone calls. The e-mails pretty much speak for themselves."

She barely heard him. She was reading one of the e-mails. The neighbor who lived directly across the street from the park hated it. Passionately. The hardest part for Jordan was that his complaints sounded legitimate. Late-night drug deals. Needles near the play equipment. He didn't feel safe letting his daughter play there anymore. Jordan closed the file. "Thank you for this."

This was Martha's neighborhood. It was so hard for her to see that it had gotten that bad.

"I know it's not what you wanted to see," he said.

Jordan tried to pretend like she didn't know what he was talking about. "I'm a journalist. I'm just here to report the truth. And this is the truth, so..."

He raised a dubious eyebrow. She leaned back. There was no point in lying anymore. "Fine," she said. "I hoped my article would save the park. Sue me."

Scott smiled. "Well, since we're speaking off the record, I guess I'll admit something too. You had me worried for a minute." She looked up. "In our first interview. When you brought up the thing about the timing of the park ordinance."

"Really?"

He nodded. "I've done a couple of interviews about the park now, and no other journalist has made that connection. You know how to dig. You're also very good at being intimidating." He added that last part with a smile, and Jordan sat up a little straighter.

"Really?"

"God, yes."

She let the compliment wash over her. It almost made up for the disappointment she felt now that her article was a total bust. Almost. "I really wanted this piece to work," she said. "I know journalists aren't supposed to let their own opinions influence them, but I can't help it. I don't see how closing the park is a good thing. Don't you think the kids in that neighborhood deserve to have somewhere to play?"

Scott shrugged, though not in a dismissive way. Like he was thinking. "I do think the office building is the right call here. That area needs the economic boost. But between us, it does make me nervous when we start closing parks."

"Why can't you put it somewhere else? Couldn't you do that?"

Scott laughed.

"What?" Jordan asked.

"One, it's not that easy. It's a major project with money and red tape. And two, *me*? I'm flattered you think I have that kind of power. I know I seem like a big deal, but I'm not. I'm basically a glorified assistant. I'm nobody."

"You're not nobody." He met her eye, and she felt her cheeks turn warm. She looked away. "I just mean, you have the ear of the councilman." Jordan couldn't imagine what she'd do if she had that kind of access. "You could talk to him." She finally got the courage to look back up. Scott had a faraway look on his face. Like he was imagining something. "What is it?" Jordan asked.

"I was just thinking about what you said. Why couldn't it go somewhere else?"

His words gave her hope. A tiny little sliver of it. She let him keep thinking. She let him process it.

"I don't know," he finally said. "Maybe."

Maybe was enough. She would take it. "Well," she said, "I guess I should probably go."

Scott nodded. "Yeah, me too." But neither of them stood. "Unless...did you maybe want to stay for a drink?"

Jordan looked up. His question surprised her, but not in a bad way. She realized that she did want to keep talking. Staying for one drink wasn't a problem. Was it? She could order a Coke. It was good to keep a professional rapport.

"Sure," she said.

CHAPTER **ELEVEN**

THAT SATURDAY, CJ took her SATs for the third time. As soon as they were over, she texted Wyatt and asked him if they could meet up. She was still in a fog from her test, but this was just as important. She got to Starbucks a few minutes early and looked around for a place to sit. She was annoyed to see that both of the handicap-accessible tables were being used by people who clearly didn't need them. She thought about saying something, but in the end, she settled for an empty four top at the back of the store. When Wyatt arrived, CJ stood up.

"Clarke," he said. "You don't have to stand."

"Blame my dad. It's how I was raised."

"Well, I hope you won't be offended if I don't do the same."

She smiled awkwardly. Then she said, "Do you want a

coffee?" at the same time that he said, "So, you're quitting, aren't you?"

She looked down at the table. "I think it'll be better for everyone. Especially Dakota. I didn't mean to hurt her."

"You're not the center of the universe, Clarke."

That made her look up. "What?"

"You seem to think you're the source of her problems. Or that you're a failure because you couldn't fix them. Sorry. You're just not that powerful."

She folded her hands and looked down at them. "I want you to be able to bring in someone who isn't terrible at this. Someone who knows how to say the right things. I'm just making everything worse." When she looked back up, Wyatt was staring at her, completely unmoved. "Come on, I'm trying to quit with dignity here."

"Well, you're doing a terrible job of it. I don't accept your resignation."

Someone had carved her name into the table—Laura— and CJ traced her fingers along the lines. She wondered who Laura was and why she'd left her name behind. It made her think about the park. Another thing she couldn't solve.

"Come on, Clarke. I'm not letting you off the hook. Now come outside with me. It's a nice day."

Wyatt pushed himself back from the table and CJ followed him out the door. The sidewalk was too narrow for them to move side by side so they used the bike lane instead.

"That thing that happened in the parking lot," Wyatt said. "With the swearing and the screaming…"

"It was my fault," CJ said. "I totally own that."

"Again, Clarke. You're just not that powerful. Besides, here's what I don't think you get. She needed that. She needed to scream." He looked over at her. "And for what it's worth, I think I did too." CJ saw that his brown eyes were deep and complicated. "You don't know this because you've never asked. And I'm guessing you've never asked because you think it would be impolite, but I haven't been in this chair for all that long."

CJ had noticed the scars on his arms and the one down the back of his neck, so she'd assumed there had been some sort of accident. "I have wondered. And you're right. I did think it was rude."

"I know, Clarke." He said it without judgment. "A lot of people do. Sometimes the politeness just makes it harder, though." He smiled at her. "So, is there anything you'd like to ask me?" His expression was warm. This wasn't a trick.

"What happened to you?" she asked.

"Well, the short answer is extra-long sheets."

"What's the long answer?"

"I had just moved into my dorm room at Ohio State. But the thing you might not realize is that college dorm beds need extra-long sheets. Honest to god. It's the craziest thing you've ever heard. But you need them. I was driving back from Bed Bath & Beyond. A guy in a minivan blew through a red light. I never even saw it coming."

"I'm sorry."

"Why? You weren't driving."

CJ shot him a look. "If I have to ask questions that make me uncomfortable, you have to stop making jokes."

"Fair," he said. "That's very fair. We all have our coping mechanisms."

They heard a bike behind them and moved to the side of the road until it passed.

"One of the things they tell you when you wake up and they drop the news that you're never going to walk again is that everybody thinks that they're going to be the miracle. Everybody thinks they'll be the one to defy the odds."

"Is there a chance? That you'll be able to walk again?"

"Do you believe in Santa?"

CJ looked over. She correctly assumed that this was not a real question.

"The injury is at my T10 vertebra. So barring some sort of Christmas miracle, it's not really that likely. They tell you not to pray for a miracle because the sooner you accept it, the sooner you can start to grieve. And the sooner you grieve, the sooner it gets easier."

"When did you start to grieve?" CJ asked.

Wyatt looked at his watch and pretended like he was

doing math in his head. "When was that thing in the parking lot?"

She glanced over at him. "Are you being serious with me or are you joking again?"

He shrugged his shoulders. "A little of both, to be honest. I've accepted I'm not the miracle. But I don't know how much I've grieved. So I have to say, screaming my feelings out in a parking lot felt pretty fucking good, actually."

He smiled and she smiled back.

Wyatt had taken the bus to get there, so CJ offered to give him a ride home. She asked him if he needed help getting into the car and he said yes. He showed her where to stand and how to hold her arm so he could steady himself against her. She could smell the clean soapy scent of his hair and the sweetness of his fabric softener.

Wyatt lived with his parents in Gates Mills, a nice community about twenty minutes from where CJ lived. She pulled into the long driveway and turned off the car. She took his wheelchair out of the back seat and unfolded it for him. Then they repeated the same process that they'd done before, only in reverse this time. Wyatt leaned against her, and his skin felt smooth and warm. He wheeled himself up the metal ramp that extended the length of the porch steps. A faded Ohio State football flag flapped in the breeze. From his doorway, Wyatt paused and turned back. "Hey, Clarke. How'd your SATs go?"

She was surprised he remembered. She'd brought it up only once and barely in passing.

"It's just a stupid test," she said. "It's not important." He stared at her in a way that told her he knew she was lying. "Okay. Fine. I care. A lot."

"And?"

"And I think I did really well this time."

It was the truth. Everything about the test felt different this time. Her hard work had paid off. She could feel it in her bones.

"Good for you, Clarke," he said. "I'll see you Monday."

As she said good-bye, CJ realized how glad she was that he hadn't let her quit.

Ava frowned and checked the time when she heard the doorbell ring. It was a few minutes after eleven and Jordan was officially late. She knew it wasn't her at the door since Jordan never used the bell, preferring instead to slap her palm against the side window like an octopus in the way that had been an inside joke for so long that nobody could remember how it started. Ava unlocked the door and opened it. Logan Diffenderfer stood on the porch. "Hey," he said.

Ava didn't know why she'd agreed to this. Jordan hadn't even really asked. She'd just told Ava that she was going to write an article about her painting getting accepted into the

Coventry Art Gallery. Ava hated being the center of attention. She hated the idea of being written about. She hated being photographed. Especially when it was Logan Diffenderfer doing the photographing.

"Jordan's not here yet," Ava said.

Logan adjusted the camera bag that was over his shoulder. "That's okay. I didn't even know she was coming. We don't need her or anything."

He didn't need her. But Ava did. The idea of being alone in her house with Logan was too weird, too awkward. She'd made Jordan promise to be there for the photo shoot.

"Could I maybe come in?" Logan said.

Ava opened the door and ushered him inside. He followed her into the living room. "Nice place."

"Thanks."

"So where's your painting? Where are we doing this?"

"The sunporch probably has the best light," Ava said.

"The light doesn't really matter. I can work with anything. I'd rather the photo tell the real story. Where do you usually paint?"

"Um." Ava checked her phone. Nothing from Jordan. "My easel is in my bedroom."

"Cool," he said, and waited for her to show him the way.

She led him down the hall and he followed her inside. Her eye went straight to the bra lying on the floor by the closet. It was her cute pink one. She didn't know if that made this more or less horrifying. "Maybe we should wait for Jordan, though."

Logan set his camera bag on the floor and unzipped the main pouch. "Why?"

"Uh..." As soon as his head was down, Ava snatched the bra off the floor and threw it in her closet. She scanned the room to make sure there wasn't anything else embarrassing. Oh, nothing big. Just her antidepressant medication right there front and center on the dresser. Ava was going to *kill* Jordan. She wrapped her palm around the orange bottle and pressed it to her side. "I have to grab the painting," she said. "It's in the sunporch. Since I thought we'd shoot in there, so..."

"No problem. It'll take me a minute to get set up."

Ava backed out of the room. As soon as she was in the hallway, she shoved the pill bottle into the decorative vase that sat on the entryway table. She hurried to grab her painting, checking her phone again as she did.

Logan was standing at her easel when she came back in. It made her chest physically tighten when she remembered which painting was there. Of all the things in her room that made her feel exposed, this was by far the worst.

"This is incredible," he said.

She nodded and mumbled a thanks. It was a church, simple and plain yet oddly beautiful.

"Where is it?" he asked.

"Mexico City."

She was painting it from an image on a postcard that was clipped to her easel.

"You've been here?" he asked, pointing to the postcard.

"No."

She didn't elaborate.

"Oh-kay," he said.

"I'll move it so we can put my gallery painting here."

It was hard to get a good grip on the canvas while it was still wet, and she accidentally knocked it against the edge of the postcard. It fluttered to the ground and landed message side up. Logan bent to grab it. "Don't!" she shouted so loudly that it startled them both. "Don't read it!"

"I wasn't!"

"Don't look at it."

"Okay!"

Logan looked at the ceiling. Out the window. Anywhere but down.

Ava laid the canvas on an old towel that she kept for this exact purpose. Then she picked up the postcard and put it away in the closet. Logan was still staring at the ceiling. "Can I look now?"

"Yeah."

"I'm not even gonna ask," he said.

Good. Because she wasn't going to tell him. She set her gallery painting on the easel. "Let's just get this over with," she said.

It's not like Jordan meant to forget about Ava. She just lost track of time. Her dad was helping her with her college essays, and even though he could be brusque with writing advice, he was really good at it. She was trying to write an essay about why she wanted to attend Northwestern and was having a surprisingly hard time coming up with a good answer. She knew they had a good journalism program and she'd seen the campus once and she liked it. Her dad didn't think it was a good enough answer to set her apart from the pack.

"Because one of their school colors is purple. And that's my favorite color?" she offered up hopefully.

Her dad told her to put some more thought into it. Jordan didn't get very far into the thinking process before her phone chimed.

I can't stop thinking about what you said.

The number wasn't saved in her phone, but she knew exactly who it was. Scott Mercer. She could see that he was still typing. A second later, another message appeared.

You're right. That neighborhood does deserve a park.

More typing and then a third message.

Can you talk?

Jordan looked over at her dad. "I'll be right back. I have to do something."

He waved her away without even looking up from the computer screen. Jordan texted a response.

Give me thirty seconds.

She went into her bedroom. She wanted to be near her whiteboard. And she wanted privacy. She took a breath and dialed.

"Hey," he said.

"Hey. So you've been thinking about the park?"

"Yeah." He paused. "But this has to be completely off the record. Is that cool?"

She wondered why he was calling her, then. "Okay."

"I wish," he said. "I wish the councilman was handling this differently. I wish he could see that the park has value for the community."

She stared at her whiteboard. "Why doesn't he?"

She heard Scott sigh. "How much time do you have?"

Jordan stretched out. "I've got all the time in the world." Then she remembered where she was supposed to be. "Shit!" Jordan bolted up. She'd forgotten about Ava.

"What? What's wrong?"

Jordan scrambled to find her shoes. "I'm late. Oh my god. I'm so late for something."

She almost fell over as she pulled one of her boots on.

"I hope it's not important."

"It is. It's very important. My friend is going to kill me."

"Oh god. I hope she doesn't. I was enjoying talking to you. Well, go run. And if you're still alive later, maybe give me a call."

Jordan hung up. Her heart was thudding in her chest for about a million different reasons. She quickly dialed Ava and it went straight to voice mail. Jordan left a frantic message. "I am *so* sorry. I'm on my way now. Be there in fifteen minutes. Actually, ten. I'll speed. Because I am so, so, so sorry. Love you. Bye. On my way."

She paused for one second to catch her breath. She needed to steady herself. Scott wanted her to maybe call him later. And she maybe wanted to.

Ava felt awkward and stiff in front of Logan's camera. At least he didn't tell her to pose or say cheese or anything like that. He told her to just act natural. As if that were possible.

"Who are your favorite artists?" he asked while taking a couple of test shots.

"Frida Kahlo, David Hockney, Cabrera, Reyes, Léger, Sorolla."

Logan took a couple more shots. "Better," he said. "You're relaxing."

"Ah. The question was just a ploy."

"Of course," he said. "People are more natural when they're talking about something they like."

"I could list a million more if it helps me get this over with faster."

He laughed and took a shot. His camera made a *click, click* sound with each picture. "You're like me with directors."

"Directors?"

"Movie directors. Stanley Kubrick, Max Ophüls, Orson Welles. Those are probably my top three. Kathryn Bigelow and Kimberly Peirce if we're talking modern day."

"Is that what you're going to study? Film?"

"That's what I would *love* to study. But no. Prelaw."

"Why?"

He shrugged. "So I can be a lawyer?"

"That's what you want to do?"

He shrugged again. "Not really. But my parents are both lawyers. They have their own firm and want me to join it. It's the family name. It's like my destiny, basically. I've been groomed for this since birth."

"Yeah," Ava said. "But if it's not what you want…if it's not your dream…" She paused. "I don't know why I said that. I still haven't told my mom I want to apply to art school."

Click, click. Logan took another shot and checked it. "This one's great. I got you in a really interesting moment."

He raised his camera back up. "So you're going to do it, though? You're going to apply?"

"I really want to. Really, really want to." *Click, click.* "But I don't know. I probably won't even get in, so it won't even matter. RISD is so competitive."

"Ava. You're going to get in. There's no way you're not getting in. You're the best artist in the whole school."

The compliment made her feel weird. "That's not really saying much. I love Mrs. Simon, but it's a public school art program. I'd be going up against art magnet students and kids who have studied with actual artistic masters. It's a different level of competition."

"Is the postcard painting for your portfolio?" Logan asked.

If he was trying to get her to relax, this topic was not going to do it. "No."

Click, click. He checked the photo he'd just taken. His expression changed and he looked up at her. "Did I say something wrong? You seem...tense."

Ava shifted. He was right. "That painting is just for me," she said. "The postcard was from Mom. My birth mom." He lowered his camera. "It's the only thing I have from her."

He didn't say anything, but his expression did. A combination of compassion and *Holy shit.*

"I do think about finding her," Ava said. "It's complicated. I can't do anything until I'm eighteen, though. And maybe I won't even then."

Logan raised his camera, then lowered it again. Raised and lowered. He wasn't uncomfortable exactly. He was thinking about something.

"What?" she asked.

"I don't know if I should say anything. This is so not my business. But I think I know a way you could find her," he said. "Even before you turn eighteen. If you ever wanted to."

Ava looked away. Was he seriously about to mansplain how to find a birth parent to someone who had lived with this question her entire life?

"I'm being serious," Logan said.

"Logan. You don't know anything about my adoption."

"I help out at my parents' firm when they get busy. Just doing filing or whatever. They have this private investigator who works there. We've actually gotten pretty tight. He's a cool guy. He does stuff like this. He usually charges a lot, but I bet I could get him to do me a solid. If you're interested..."

"Nope," Ava said. "I'm not interested." It was a lie. She wanted to find her birth mother almost more than anything in the world. Freshman year, when she'd been at her lowest, she'd been so desperate for that connection that it felt like a giant gaping wound that wouldn't close until she at least got to see her, to touch her, and to ask her why. She'd brought it up with her mom, and they'd talked it over with Dr. Clifford at one of their family sessions. Dr. Clifford and her mom decided that it was not in Ava's best interest. Everyone was always deciding what was best for her. Everyone except for Ava. "Definitely not interested," she said.

She wondered if he would be able to see that she was lying when he took her picture. She stood there and waited until he lifted his camera. Just as he did, she heard a slapping sound from the side of the house. Like an octopus beating a tentacle against a window.

"What the hell is that?" Logan asked.

"That," Ava said with relief, "is Jordan."

CHAPTER **TWELVE**

EVEN THOUGH it was technically fall now, it didn't feel like it. It was mid-October, yet neither Martha nor her dad wore coats as they walked across the long mall parking lot. By now, the air should have been crisp and filled with the scent of wood-burning fireplaces. Martha's dad still called it an Indian summer, because no matter how many times she tried to explain it to him, he didn't get why that was problematic. He held the door open for her and followed her inside. He'd been called in for an interview with a company that built motorcycle parts. If he got the job, it would mean driving two hours each way. It would also mean health insurance, a good paycheck, and retirement benefits. Martha was going to help him pick out a button-down shirt for the interview.

They had to walk past the Army Recruitment Center to get to JCPenney, and Martha peeked inside. The female recruitment officer, Major Malone, was at her desk. Martha was fascinated by her. She didn't fit Martha's image of a soldier. Martha knew it was a weird thing to do, but after the first time she'd seen her, she'd googled her. She hadn't found much, just one picture of her holding her pilot's helmet and standing in front of an Apache helicopter. Martha couldn't imagine what it must feel like to pilot a helicopter. She'd never even been on a plane before.

Whatever. Why was she even thinking about this? It's not like the military was known for their friendly relationship with the lesbian and bi community. At least she knew it used to be like that. She honestly wasn't sure what it was like now. Maybe she should ask. Of course maybe she should figure out if she even fit into one of those categories first. Martha's mind drifted to Victoria. It had been doing that a lot lately.

"What's going on with the park?" her dad asked.

"Huh?" Martha's cheeks felt hot. She blamed the weather before remembering that they were inside, where it was air-conditioned. "Oh. The park."

Ever since they'd realized that there was no massive political conspiracy, they'd basically stopped thinking about it. Around school, their classmates were still talking about the park, but they were talking about other things too. College applications and midterms. The football team and the upcoming rivalry game against Walsh Jesuit. Jordan had found out from the legislative deputy guy that the city was waiting for the results of something called an environmental impact report that could, in theory, kill the whole project.

"Nothing really. There's this environmental thing we're waiting for. It doesn't look like it'll help us, though."

"Oh well," he said. "I suppose that's the price of progress."

He'd said the same thing to Martha's mom after the plant closed. Martha could still remember sitting under the table in the dining room, unnoticed as her parents argued in the kitchen. Her mom was spinning out and demanding that her dad do something. "What do you want me to do?" he'd said. "Production moves overseas and plants close. The world is changing and there's nothing I can do about that. That's the price of progress." She'd never heard her mom yell before that time. After the plant closed, there was nothing but yelling. *That* was the price of progress as far as Martha knew.

They took the escalator to the menswear section and found a rack of button-down shirts that were on sale. Martha picked out a blue one and held it up to her dad. It was a beautiful shirt. She hoped it would be good enough.

Ava was literally the last senior to have her meeting with the college counselor. She'd put it off over and over again, hoping that the counselor would eventually give up. The counselor did. Her mom, however, did not. She came to Ava frustrated and impatient, and stood over her while she sent an e-mail to Ms. Fischer to reschedule the appointment. Ava's mom put it into her own calendar. There would be no missing this one.

The first thing Ava noticed about the college counselor was her flowy turquoise infinity scarf. It was the only pop of color on her otherwise all-black outfit. She wore round tortoiseshell glasses that gave her an air of intellectualism mixed with hipster elitism. Ava was immediately intimidated. She felt the anxiety spread across her entire body, and it made her think about her mother. Not Lynn. She was thinking about the one whose face was a smeared blur in the background of her painting. She wondered if her birth mom's heart raced and her palms got sweaty before big meetings too.

"Ava?" said Ms. Fischer, extending a hand. "Come on in."

Ava limply shook the offered hand. "Hi," she said, in a voice as weak as her handshake.

"Have a seat."

Ms. Fischer angled a chair for Ava and another one for herself. After the counselor sat down, she leaned forward—a gesture that was supposed to be welcoming but that Ava found off-putting—and said, "So, are we waiting for your mom?"

"My mom?" Ava was still thinking about her biological mom, so it took her a minute to realize what Ms. Fischer was asking. "Oh. My mom. No. Are parents supposed to be here? I thought it was just me."

"Generally, yes. But if a parent wants to be involved, I'm not opposed. And your mom has e-mailed a few times."

Ava cringed as something that had happened that morning suddenly made sense. She remembered her mom asking about this meeting. She wanted to make sure Ava hadn't forgotten, and maybe she did say something about planning on being there. Ava had been in a rush and was only half listening, since CJ kept honking at her from the driveway. They were trying to carpool more because of climate change and CJ was always early on her days.

Right then, there was a quick knock on the door. Before Ms. Fischer even finished saying, "Come in," it opened.

"Hi, hi," said Lynn. "Sorry I'm late. I didn't miss anything, did I?"

"Not at all." Ms. Fischer rose and Ava's mom shook her hand firmly. It was the kind of impressive grip that Ava could never manage.

"Sorry for being late. I was coming from downtown and traffic was murder."

Ms. Fischer grabbed a third chair and arranged them into a triangle. Like they were about to have a séance. Maybe they were. Ava wouldn't put it past her mom to employ a medium to get her into college. Ms. Fischer kicked off the meeting by talking a little bit about herself. She went over her credentials as if they couldn't see the diploma framed on the wall behind her. She also had a master's in education from Penn. At the mention of that, Ava's mom practically wet herself.

"I was there for law school."

Then there was a back-and-forth about their Penn glory days, and Ava wondered if they would even notice if she left the room. Before she could test that theory, her mom got a moony look on her face, and said, "It would be such a dream for Ava to go there. I know it might be a bit unrealistic." Ava crammed her toes into her shoes. "Ava is such a special girl. Incredible, really. I know everyone says that about their kid, but it's true. She's worked so hard, and..." Her mom was getting emotional. Ava turned to look at her. Her mom never got emotional. "You have, Ava. And you deserve to go anywhere you dream."

The compliments were so unexpected and felt so wonderful that Ava almost whispered the truth. *My dream is RISD.* The words were there on her tongue, but she couldn't get them out of her mouth.

Ms. Fischer removed her glasses and wiped them clean with her infinity scarf. "I've been looking at Ava's grades, her test scores, and extracurriculars, and here's the thing: Ava is an ideal candidate to shoot high."

Ava's mom turned to her. "I knew it. Didn't I tell you not to limit yourself?" She turned back to Ms. Fischer, waiting expectantly.

"Ava, you've got one tricky semester on your report card, but you did exactly what universities want to see. You pulled yourself up and you kept your grades high. You should be incredibly proud of yourself."

Ava smiled sheepishly. "Thanks."

"What's going to tip you over the net, one way or the other, are the personal essays."

"Of course," said her mom. "One of the other partners at my firm gave me the number of a college-essay advisor. I'm told she's phenomenal."

"That'll be helpful," said Ms. Fischer. Then she turned back to Ava. "I also spoke to your art teacher, Mrs. Simon." Ava felt her mouth go dry. "She told me that you're one of the most talented students she's ever had."

Ava shrugged. "I guess."

Her mom gave her a small nudge and whispered to her, "Ava, take the compliment."

"Thank you," said Ava.

Ms. Fischer smiled. "She was very effusive. She also mentioned that you've been working on a portfolio for the Rhode Island School of Design."

"Uh..." Ava said. "Um."

Her heart thumped deep in her chest, and she could feel her mom staring at her. At that exact moment, an unexpected image popped into Ava's head. It was Logan

Diffenderfer. She thought about him with his camera and his list of favorite directors. He had a dream and he was ignoring it. She didn't want to be like that.

"That's my top choice," Ava said. "I want to go to RISD."

Ava's mom smiled thinly. Ava couldn't even make eye contact with her.

"Oh?" said her mom.

The mood shifted in the room. They talked for another thirty minutes, but Ava couldn't hear much over the blood rushing through her ears. Her mom sat with her legs tightly crossed and her hands rigidly folded. It was unsettling not to know what she was thinking.

As soon as they got to the car, Ava found out. "It's not that I don't support your art," her mom said, hands tight on the steering wheel. "It's just that you are capable of so much more. Do you even understand how incredible you are? It takes guts and strength to do what you did freshman year. You rebounded from something horrible and are now one of the best students in that school. Just think of what you can do with your life. Your choices are limitless."

"I want this, Mom. It's what I love doing."

Her mom pulled into traffic without really looking. A horn honked and a car swerved. "I have the right-of-way, jerk!" she shouted, even though she didn't. "You can still take art as an elective. But be practical. What are you going to do with an art degree?"

Ava released her toes. She didn't even remember when she'd started clenching them. "I would be an artist."

Her mom sighed and threw her hands up for a second until she remembered they should be on the steering wheel. "That's not a realistic career."

There were brake lights ahead, and her mom slowed down as the traffic piled up.

"I know it's hard to understand when you're still in high school and everything is taken care of for you, but as you get a little older, you are going to see the value in being financially secure. You don't ever want to be in a position where you have to rely on anyone else. That's when choices get taken away from you. I worked hard to get you on a good track so you won't ever have to rely on a man. Or woman," she quickly added. At least she was giving Ava some choice in her life.

"I'm not going to rely on a man, Mom. I promise. Why don't you want me to follow my dream?"

Her mom gripped the steering wheel hard. "Oh, Ava. Why do you think they're called dreams? Because they're not realistic. You are too smart—"

"What if I'm not?" Ava said it quietly and calmly.

Her mom whipped her head over. "Of course you're smart. Your GPA—"

"Is only high because you've hired a million tutors. What if I only do well because of all the extra help? What if I'm actually dumb?"

It was Ava's greatest fear. It was the thing she overheard Logan Diffenderfer say when they were freshmen. He'd called her dumb, and every day since, she'd wondered if he was right.

"Ava, come on." Her mom was trying to balance her attention between the road and her daughter. "You are smart."

"I'm not. I know it. The school knows it. I know that they wanted to drop me out of the advanced track freshman year."

Ava could see the panic in her mom's face. She hadn't known that Ava knew.

"I know what you did, Mom. You're the only reason they didn't dump me like they should've. I've known this whole time."

This was back before Ava had a diagnosis, before she had a name for what was going on with her. She just knew that it was getting harder and harder to get out of bed. Some days it was so hard that she couldn't go to school, and most days it was impossible to go to the fancy tutors who made sure that she excelled in her classes. She wasn't the least bit surprised when the letter came to her house saying that she would be dropped down. She didn't care. But her mom cared. Oh my god, did she care. It was like if Ava wasn't in advanced English and history, then what was the point of living? So her mom went to the principal and shifted into scary lawyer mode and demanded that they keep her daughter in the advanced track even though she didn't deserve it.

"I'm not like you," Ava said. "I don't have your genes. So let's just be honest for once. I'm dumb, Mom. I'm dumb."

"Ava—"

"You know it. Deep down we both know it."

"Ava. Stop saying that."

"I'm dumb!"

"Ava..."

Her mom looked at her. With her eyes off the road, Ava saw what her mom did not. The car in front of them had stopped.

"Mom!"

Her mom screamed as she slammed on the brakes. Ava put her hands up and braced for impact. They stopped inches before they made contact. The sensor system in their Mercedes beeped rapidly, telling them just how close they'd come. The shock was too much, and her mom did something that Ava had never seen her do before. She cried.

"Mom?"

The tears tumbled out hard and jarring. Even when the cars behind her honked and someone yelled at her from their car window, she kept crying.

"Mom?"

"I'm doing my best, Ava. All I've ever done is my best, and I'm still failing you."

CHAPTER **THIRTEEN**

CJ COULDN'T sleep. She felt vaguely unsettled. Like she'd forgotten to turn the iron off or something. CJ had never actually ironed anything in her life. It was just that kind of feeling. She didn't know what it could be, though. School was fine. Everything with the park was basically on hold. Her friends were good.

CJ grabbed her phone to numb out with Instagram. She wanted to lose herself in the little pictures that always helped put her to sleep. As she scrolled, her eyes started to get heavy. She was half asleep when she saw the video. Her eyes snapped wide open and she sat up. The caption read: *The results are in. #SATday #1490 #Yasssss.* A junior girl who CJ knew from cross-country was dancing and celebrating to Kool & the Gang while pointing to the enviable SAT score she'd just looked up online.

That's what CJ had forgotten. Her SAT results. They'd posted today. CJ darted out of bed. How could she possibly have forgotten? She didn't even bother to put it in her calendar because she'd figured there was no way she could ever forget. And yet she had.

She smacked the space bar until her computer woke and then went to the SAT portal. She typed out each letter, number, and numeric symbol of her password carefully. Her score popped up and CJ stared at it. She felt nothing. Literally nothing. She sat there for a minute or two, and then she did something that she hadn't done since quitting cross-country. She put on her running shoes.

CJ crept out the back door, the one that didn't squeak, and quietly slipped outside. She got into her car and turned the ignition. It was almost midnight, so it took her only a few minutes to drive to school. She felt calmer once she was standing on the track. The night air was refreshing and not nearly as cold as it should have been this time of year. CJ knew that it was probably because of global warming and that she should really be angry about it, but in that moment, all she wanted to do was drink it in.

She started out slowly, letting her legs get used to the motion. Soon she fell into the steady rhythm that always felt like a form of hypnosis. She waited for her mind to click off like it usually did. She even mentally called out the footsteps to help it along. *Right, left, right, left.*

She was trying to forget what had just happened. *Right, left, right, left.* The way her fingers had clicked against the keyboard as she entered her log-in information. *Right, left, right, left.* The moment that her results had popped up. *Right, left, right, left.* The realization that her score had not gone up. It had not remained the same. It had gone down. Ten points lower in verbal. Twenty points lower in math. *Right, left, right, left.* Her brain wasn't turning off. Why wasn't it turning off? *Right, left, right, left, right, left, right, left.* It wasn't turning off because CJ couldn't outrun this. She wasn't good enough. *Not good enough. Not good enough.* The words looped in her head.

CJ ran harder. She shifted into a sprint without even realizing it was happening. Her coach would have yelled at her to slow down. She could never sustain this pace for an entire race. But this wasn't a race and her coach wasn't there. So she ran harder and harder. Faster and faster. *Not good enough. Not good enough.* She would run until she collapsed if that's what it took to drown out the words. She could outrun it all if she could only go fast enough.

That's when she heard the voice. "Hello?" it said.

CJ slowed. "Is someone there?" she called out.

This time she heard the words sharp and clear. "CJ? Is that you?" She recognized the voice immediately.

It was Logan Diffenderfer.

Ava couldn't sleep. She was pretty sure she'd taken her Lexapro that morning, but she counted out the number of pills left in her bottle just to be sure. As long as the drug was in her system, she shouldn't feel like this, should she? She paced her room and the cloud of gray paced with her. She wasn't supposed to feel this sad over something as small as a fight with her mom. Except that it was so much more than a fight. It was her entire future. Maybe the way she was feeling was normal. She paced some more. She didn't feel normal.

Ava took the chair from her desk and pulled it over to the closet. She stood on it to reach the shoebox tucked deep into the back on the top shelf. The box held photos and concert tickets and a Denny's napkin from a particularly wonderful night with her friends that Ava wanted to remember forever. It's also where she kept the postcard when she wasn't painting it. The one with the picture of the church in Mexico City. She flipped it over and read the words she'd read a million times before.

Dear Baby Girl,
    I've tried over and over to write this letter, but I don't

know what to say. I always thought this church was so beautiful. I've never seen it in person, only on this postcard that your grandmother kept with her until she died. It's where she used to pray before she came to America. You have her eyes. I wasn't expecting that, and it made all of this so much harder. For the brief moment that you were in my arms, I loved you. I'm so sorry.

It wasn't signed. There was no name. No return address. Just a postmark from California.

CJ didn't need to ask Logan why he was at the track in the middle of the night. It was pretty obvious that he was doing the same thing she was. So when he said, "Feel like doing a few more laps?" she said, "Definitely."

After they'd fallen into a steady rhythm, CJ asked, "So... what problem are you trying to outrun?" She couldn't see his expression in the dark. She only saw his head swivel in her direction. "Diffenderfer," she said. "It's the middle of the night. You're not out here for fun. What's up?"

"Nothing specific," he said. "Just everything. You?"

He was being guarded. That was his choice, but she felt like being honest.

"I got my SAT scores and they're not good enough. There's pretty much no way I'll get into Stanford."

His head turned back toward her. "Sorry," he said. Then he laughed slightly.

"Did you just laugh at my crap SAT scores?"

"No. No. That wasn't about you. Sorry. It's just...I'll sound like an asshole if I say it out loud."

"Say it."

CJ's legs were starting to feel the ache of running after a long period of time off. It felt wonderful.

"When you said you'll never get into Stanford, I had this flash of...oh, what's the word..."

"Schadenfreude," she offered. "It's an SAT word. It's when you delight in another person's misfortune."

"Oh," he said. "Then definitely not that. No. Not at all. Opposite, actually. I felt jealous."

Now it was her head that turned. "Why?"

"Because I don't want to go there. I was just thinking how relieved I'd feel if I didn't get in."

CJ resisted the urge to run him right off the track.

She knew that Logan's SAT scores were good. Every year the principal sent out a newsletter congratulating all the McKinley High School students with the highest SAT scores. His name was on the list. Hers, of course, was not. Because she wasn't good enough. *Not good enough. Not good enough.* She ran faster.

"Whoa, slow down," Logan said. "It's not a race."

Everything was a race.

"I can't help it. I hate you right now, Logan. My whole life, all I've ever done is what I'm supposed to do. I did all the right things. And now, because I did bad on one test, my dream is basically over."

"It's not over. You still have a chance."

CJ didn't want just a chance. She'd worked too hard, she'd sacrificed too much, for just a chance.

God, it felt good to run again. There were a million stars out that night and they made her feel small. In a good way. Like her problems weren't so significant in the grander construct of the universe. She remembered when Martha used to be obsessed with the stars. She'd point them out and claim that she would fly to them one day.

"Hey, Logan?" CJ said.

"Yeah?"

"Have you ever had a transformational experience?"

"You're talking about that Stanford essay topic?"

She nodded. It was one of the application essay prompts

that they had to write about. *Describe a transformational experience and how it has shaped you into the person you are today.*

"I don't even know what that means," Logan said.

"I think it's like stepping outside of yourself. Having an experience that totally alters the way you see your life."

"Then definitely not. You?"

"No," she said. But she wanted to. Not just because of the essay. Not just because it was her only shot at getting into a school that otherwise would have nothing to do with her. She wanted to have an experience so profound and so completely significant that it would shift everything into spectacular, amazing, electric color. "I've been volunteering at this after-school program. There's this guy there."

Logan looked over at her. "A guy, huh?"

CJ could feel her cheeks turn red. "Not like that." At least she didn't think it was like that. "He's just blunt and honest and…" She didn't know how to say it without sounding weird. "He makes me wish I could see the world differently. Actually, you might—"

"CJ. No offense. But I don't want to hear about some dude."

But Wyatt wasn't just some dude. She was about to tell Logan that, when he turned to her and interrupted her train of thought.

"Now," he said. "I have a question for *you*. It's a serious one."

CJ looked over. "Yeah?"

"Feel like racing?"

He didn't wait for an answer. He took off at a sprint. CJ, never one to turn away from a challenge, kicked up the pace. She sprinted faster and faster. Harder and harder. She sprinted with everything she had left in the tank. As she caught up to him, they collided in the dark. It didn't feel entirely awful and neither of them said sorry. They kept running, and their arms bumped into each other again. CJ wanted to win, she was desperate to win, but Logan was faster. He pulled ahead, and she watched his lead on her widen. It made her want to cry. *Not good enough. Not good enough.*

That's when Logan's phone rang.

"Shit," he said, slowing to a walk. CJ caught up to him, then slowed down too. "That'll be one of my parents, I'm sure. Wondering why the hell I'm not in my bed." He pulled his phone out of his pocket and looked completely confused when he saw the caller ID. "It's Ava."

CJ peered at the screen. "*My* Ava?"

Logan answered somewhat tentatively. "Hello?"

CJ leaned in so she was close enough to hear. Ava's words were quiet, but she could still make them out.

"Does your offer still stand? Because I want to find my birth mother."

CHAPTER **FOURTEEN**

JORDAN STOPPED by Dunkin' Doughnuts on her way to school. She'd woken up to two texts that morning, both addressed to her and Martha. The first was from CJ, saying that Ava had made a rash decision to find her birth mom and that CJ was worried. Then, less than an hour later, there was a text from Ava saying that CJ had gotten her SAT scores, they weren't good, and that Ava was worried. Jordan wasn't sure which friend she was supposed to be more concerned about, but either way, it seemed like a good day for doughnuts. She ordered a dozen.

The weather had shifted overnight, and there was frost on the lawns and rooftops. It was too cold to meet up in the quad like they'd originally talked about, so Jordan sent a group text telling everyone to meet in her car. CJ was the first one to climb in. "Hey," she said. "I know I look like crap. Long night. Lots to tell. Ooh. Doughnuts."

Jordan held out the box and CJ took a cinnamon sugar.

"Sorry about your SATs," Jordan said.

CJ sighed, inadvertently blowing some of the sugar off her doughnut. "Ava told you?"

Jordan nodded. "I'm sorry. I'm so sorry."

"Thanks. I can't even process it. I think I'm still in shock."

CJ's phone beeped and she grabbed it out of her backpack.

"If that's Ava or Martha, tell them to hurry," Jordan said. "It sounds like we have a lot to cover."

CJ looked at the text and laughed. "It's not." She held up her phone for Jordan to see.

The text was from CJ's boss at the volunteer program. Jordan squinted at the tiny picture that accompanied his name. "You failed to mention that he's hot. And is he asking you out?"

CJ shook her head. "No." She giggled. Which seemed strange given the fact that ten seconds ago she was in a complete fog about her SATs. "It's just how he talks."

Jordan read the text out loud. "'Clarke. Would you do me the kindness of accompanying me on a reconnaissance mission tomorrow night? Just say yes and I'll provide details as they become pertinent.' That's how he talks?"

CJ shrugged. "Yeah. He's...I don't...goofy. Smart goofy. He's funny." She grabbed her phone back and typed out a reply.

Yes.

Jordan peered over CJ's shoulder. "Why is he in your phone as Wyatt No Last Name Provided?"

CJ laughed. "It's a dumb inside joke." Her phone chimed with his response.

Aces. Pick me up at eight and don't wear anything restrictive.

CJ laughed again.

"Clarke," Jordan said. "What is happening?"

Both back doors opened at the same time, and Martha and Ava climbed in. The mood in the car shifted quickly. CJ silenced her phone and turned it facedown in her lap.

"Okay," Jordan said. "Only ten minutes until the first bell. We have to triage. Who has the bigger crisis? Second girl gets pushed to lunch. CJ seems okay, so I'm thinking we do Ava first."

"Fine by me," CJ said.

Ava yawned. "I'm okay. Just tired. I don't really feel like talking." Jordan offered her the box of doughnuts. She waved it away. "Honestly," Ava said. "CJ texted you before she called me. I'm fine. She made way too big a deal out of it. No offense, CJ."

CJ turned around so she could look at Ava. "Oh, pardon

me for thinking that calling Logan Diffenderfer at one AM seemed a bit concerning."

"Wait," said Jordan. She felt her entire body stiffen. "You called Logan at one AM?"

"Ho-lee shit," said Martha. "We're going to need some more details."

"He offered to help me find my biological mom," Ava said. "It's a long story."

"Which you will tell," said Martha. She turned to Jordan. "Did you know about any of this?"

Jordan shook her head. She didn't like the way this was making her feel. She'd noticed a comfort between Ava and Logan that day at Ava's house when he'd taken her photo. It had seemed weird at the time. And now, to know that Ava and Logan had been talking late at night. She didn't feel jealous exactly, but it wasn't far off. Jordan knew that Logan wasn't hers, and even if he was, which he totally wasn't, she'd spent the last three years wishing that Ava would finally get over this grudge she had against him. So this was a good thing. Totally a good thing.

"Wait, I'm still confused," said Martha. "So after you talked to him, you called CJ?"

"Not exactly," said Ava. She turned to CJ and gave her a look. "I guess CJ left a detail out."

"It's going to sound weirder than it was," CJ said. "I was with him at the time."

"What?!" Jordan and Martha blurted out in unison.

"Dude," said Martha. "We're going to need to skip first period."

"I can't," CJ said. "You can't either. Physics quiz. Anyway, it wasn't a big deal. It was just a bizarre coincidence. We both went out for a run and ended up at the track at the same time."

"In the middle of the night," Martha said, somewhat dubiously. She turned to Jordan. "Are you believing this shit?"

Jordan didn't say anything. A memory sprang up from somewhere deep inside her, and it was so vivid that it was like it just happened. She was remembering the first time Logan held her hand. They were on the sidewalk outside her house. He'd been so nervous that he asked before he did it. It was so sweet and so kind that she thought her heart might burst into a million little pieces.

Ava looked at the time. "The bell's about to ring," she said. "Talk later?"

Jordan nodded. She hadn't thought about the moment with Logan and the hand holding in years. She wondered why it came to her just now.

Martha caught Jordan looking at Logan Diffenderfer several times that day. The first time it happened, the look was brief and could have been meaningless. The second time, Jordan's eyes lingered. Martha didn't judge her for it. She was actually starting to understand the appeal of Logan. He'd been showing up at the movie theater more regularly, and he always had smart and interesting things to say about the films. He was sensitive and didn't seem afraid of showing emotion. Martha was intrigued by that. Other than spiders and being buried alive, showing emotion was probably her biggest fear.

Logan came to the movie theater again that afternoon. They were screening *Before Sunrise*, and when Martha told him that she'd never seen it, he insisted that it would change her life. Victoria was there too, not working, just hanging out. She'd been doing a lot more of that since Logan had become a regular. The three of them sat in a row in the back with Martha in the middle.

Martha didn't love the movie. It was just two people talking, and she wanted something to happen already. Logan and Victoria kept whispering to her and then across her so they could gush about how beautiful the movie was. Martha was too distracted to appreciate it. Her dad's interview with the plant was that afternoon, and he'd promised to call her the second it was over. He wasn't much of texter.

Her phone finally buzzed during some part that was making Victoria cry. Martha stood quickly and didn't say anything as she rushed out to the lobby. "Hey," she said, answering. "How'd it go?"

"How'd what go?" asked Jordan.

Martha hadn't even looked at the caller ID. "Sorry. I thought you were my dad."

"Is he done with his interview yet?"

Martha walked over to one of the tables and sat down. "No. I don't think so." Then she realized she was too restless to sit and paced instead.

"I'm keeping my fingers crossed," said Jordan. "Anyway, I just got a call from Scott."

"Who? Oh, right." The legislative deputy. For some reason, Jordan and *Scott* were now on a first-name basis. "What did *Scott* say?"

"What's with the attitude?" asked Jordan.

Martha stopped pacing. "Nothing. I'm nervous about my dad. What did Scott say?" she repeated with less 'tude.

Jordan sighed. "The EIR came out." The EIR was the environmental impact report. Jordan had started speaking confidently about city matters in shorthand. In a way, it was kind of cool. She sounded like a real reporter. In another way, it was completely annoying. "There's nothing in it that's going to help us."

Martha sighed. "Okay. So what now?"

"I honestly don't know."

There was a long pause while neither of them said anything. Martha's phone beeped and she glanced at it. "Shit. That's my dad. I gotta go."

"Good luck," Jordan said quickly. "Love you."

"Love you too." Martha clicked over to the other line. "Hi," she said.

"Hey." She could tell from her dad's voice that the news wasn't good. "Well," he said, "they told me that they'll let me know officially by next week, but I don't think it's gonna happen. On to the next one," he said, trying to sound chipper.

"What happened, Dad?"

"They didn't love the huge gap in my résumé. Apparently, I'm not up to speed on the way things work now."

"But you could get up to speed," she said. "Easily."

"It's not going to happen, Patsy." The disappointment in his voice broke her heart. "I should let you go. I don't like bothering you at work."

"Dad, it's fine."

He'd already hung up.

"Dammit," Martha shouted. She thought she was saying it to herself, but when she turned around, she saw Victoria standing there.

"Hey," Martha said, trying to sound casual.

"What's wrong?" Victoria asked.

"Nothing."

It obviously wasn't nothing. It was clearly something. A huge something. Victoria stepped forward and, without any warning at all, put both her arms around Martha and enveloped her in a hug. Martha stood stiffly, arms at her side. "Um, what's happening?" asked Martha.

"I don't know what's wrong," Victoria said. "But something is. I'm sorry. You don't have to tell me. I just thought you needed a hug."

Martha was completely annoyed. Because Victoria was right. She did need a hug. It felt good. Martha lifted her arms and hugged Victoria back.

———————

It took CJ longer than she'd thought to drive to Wyatt's house. Even with the unexpected traffic, she was still ten minutes early. She was always punctual, but even more so when she was nervous. Wyatt still hadn't told her what their mission was. She looked at the clock on her dashboard and decided that it was close enough to the time that it wouldn't be weird to knock on the door. It only took about two seconds before a woman in her fifties answered.

"You must be Clarke," she said.

"CJ. Hi. You must be Wyatt's mom."

"Call me Katherine. Come in. Please."

CJ heard Wyatt before she saw him. He was hollering

from down the hall. "No. Do not come in. She doesn't have to come in, Mom."

A second later, he appeared in the living room. CJ felt both more at ease and more nervous when she saw him. "You're early, Clarke."

"There are three things in life that are certain: death, taxes, and me being ten minutes early to everything."

Katherine clapped her hands together. "She's funny. Oh, Wyatt, She's funny."

"Yes, she's hilarious." Wyatt rolled up to CJ, and neither of them was quite sure if they should hug or shake hands, so they did nothing. "Hi," said Wyatt. "Sorry my mom is weird."

"I'm not weird," said Katherine. "Now come in and sit, Clarke. Tell me about yourself."

CJ sat on the couch. As she looked around the room, there were two things that were impossible to miss. First was the picture of Wyatt in a high school track uniform. It was positioned prominently on the mantel in an obvious place of pride. He had just crossed the finish line and had both of his hands raised in victory. His legs were tan and strong, and he looked so exuberantly happy. CJ would have dwelled on that photo were it not for the second thing she noticed. The room was absolutely filled with pottery. It was everywhere. Seriously. Everywhere. All over the bookshelves, perched on the end tables, and of course there was the giant one at the center of the coffee table. CJ was pretty sure that they were supposed to be vases, although it was impossible to ignore the fact that every single piece had a certain phallic quality.

"Oh," CJ said almost involuntarily as her eyes landed on a particularly questionable and particularly erect piece of art. Wyatt leaned over and whispered, "Don't say anything to my mom. She has no idea."

"No idea about what?" asked Katherine.

"I think Clarke was just noticing your pottery."

Katherine lit up. "See anything you like?"

CJ tried not to stare at anything directly. Was this a test? "Oh, well…"

"My mom made everything in this room."

CJ smiled awkwardly. "How lovely. They're very… elegant."

"It's a new hobby. I'm thinking of starting an Etsy store. But if you see anything you like, I would be honored to make it my gift to you."

Wyatt shot CJ another look, and she tried not laugh. "Wow. That's really kind."

"Pick any piece. Any piece you like."

The more CJ tried not to stare, the more she couldn't stop herself from staring. Her eyes landed on one with a bulbous base and a tall—well, "shaft" was the only word that really seemed to work.

"You like that one?" Katherine motioned to the pottery that CJ was looking at and didn't wait for an answer. "I'll get some tissue paper."

"Mother."

"CJ wants it. And I want to give it to her." Katherine waved Wyatt off and got up to search for the tissue. "So, Wyatt tells me you want to go to Stanford next year."

"Oh, I'm not really sure." CJ folded her hands in her lap, but that felt too formal so she unfolded them. "It's on my list, but I have other things on the list too. So..." CJ folded her hands again. "I don't know where I'll end up."

"Maybe you can talk Wyatt into going back to OSU."

"Okay," said Wyatt, cutting her off. "This has been fun. But we're late."

"Well, I can't find the tissue, but you can just be careful with it."

CJ stood and put her hand out. "It was so nice to meet you."

Katherine waved the proffered hand away and pulled CJ into a hug. Something about it was a little too tight and a little too long. But it was hard to think about it too much, because as soon as the hug was over, CJ found herself holding a clay penis.

As CJ and Wyatt left the house, she decided it would be better to wait until they were both in the car and out of his mom's earshot to ask about the pottery. Once they were both buckled in, Wyatt told her to head east on the main road until he was ready to give her more instructions.

As she pulled away from the curb, she asked, "What's the deal with the vases?"

Wyatt sighed. "Why must we talk of such things?"

She put on her blinker and glanced in the rearview mirror. "Because one of them is sitting in my back seat and I think it's staring at me."

"I don't have the heart to tell her. Nobody does. It's actually my fault."

"You're the reason your mom makes ceramic penises?"

"Clarke. I'm shocked. Is that what you see?" CJ could hear the smile in his voice.

"Come on. No jokes. Tell me why it's your fault that your mom makes obscene pottery."

Wyatt sighed. "Before my accident, she'd always talked about wanting to take a pottery class. But she never did. Then this happened." Wyatt motioned to his legs. "When I got out of the hospital, she was so relieved. She just kept talking about how she was going to start living her life in a new way. You know, doing all the things she'd always thought about doing but never did. So she planted tulips and she signed up for a pottery class. It was all very Oprah. This is her way of living her best life."

"I think it's absolutely beautiful."

Wyatt gave her a dubious look.

"Not the pottery. The pottery is hideous. I think the story behind it is beautiful."

"You're cool, Clarke."

CJ looked over at him, and when their eyes met, she felt a small and indescribable something. She quickly looked away. "What about your dad? What does he think?"

"About the pottery? Hates most of it. But he admits she's improving."

"About your accident."

"Ah," he said. "He's also drinking the Oprah Kool-Aid. Turn left up here."

"Are you going to tell me where we're going?"

"It's a surprise. But not a very good one. So don't get too excited."

"Perfect. That's my favorite kind."

CJ turned the car, and Wyatt went back to talking about his parents. "I think in a lot of ways my parents are in avoidance mode. My mom has her pottery, and my dad keeps talking about patching things up with his brother. I guess they had a big falling-out a million years ago. I've never even met the guy, and all of a sudden it's like *family is the most important thing.* Don't get me wrong. I'm glad I've inspired them to embrace life or whatever, but..."

"But what?" CJ asked.

"It feels like my dad is trying to fix things with his brother because he can't fix"—Wyatt pointed to his legs—"this."

CJ had an urge to reach over and take his hand. She wondered how he'd respond if she did.

"We're here," he said.

"You're joking."

"I joke about a lot of things. But miniature golf? That's something I take seriously."

CJ hadn't been to the Great Lakes Mini Golf and Family Fun Center since Martha's ninth birthday. She'd found the activity rather miserable then and wasn't particularly looking forward to it now. "How fun," she said flatly.

"It won't be," he said. "We're really here to do recon. I want to see if the course is wheelchair accessible. I keep thinking that if we can find the right activity, Dakota might actually have a good time."

CJ smiled and felt her heart warm. "Then I'm all in."

The person at the counter set out two clubs and two colored golf balls. One blue and one pink. CJ took the blue one, because screw gender norms, and followed Wyatt to the first hole. "You know," she said, "if it turns out mini golf is the thing that gets Dakota to smile, well, it's worth you ruining my night."

"Clarke. That started out so beautifully. Then became so mean."

She gave him a grin that he returned. As she followed him to the first hole, she saw his smile fade.

"Well, crap on a shingle," he said. "I don't think we're

off to a great start. Looks like the first hole isn't wheelchair accessible."

CJ didn't want to sound ignorant, but she thought everything in America had to be wheelchair accessible. "Aren't there laws about that?"

Wyatt laughed like she'd just said the most adorably quaint thing in the world.

"Okay," CJ said. "I know there are historical places that don't have proper access. But anything as modern as mini golf has to be accessible, right?"

"There *was* a law passed in 2010," said Wyatt, "that all new mini golf facilities have to have at least 50 percent of their holes accessible."

"Only 50 percent?"

"And only since 2010. The Great Lakes Mini Golf and Family Fun Center is older than shit. So who knows what we're going to get."

They approached the second hole, and CJ saw right away that it would be nearly impossible for Wyatt to navigate. The dragon that guarded the putting green was completely cheesy. It was also so wide that Wyatt couldn't get his chair around it. The third hole was no better. There was an impenetrable castle-and-moat situation. It turned out that only one hole in the entire facility was completely accessible. By the time they got to it, Wyatt was so frustrated that CJ didn't even enjoy it when she beat him by three strokes.

"Come on," CJ said, after Wyatt made an exaggeratedly big deal out of adding up their scores. "You know what *is* accessible to everyone? Pizza."

The snack bar was a series of picnic tables with benches permanently welded in place. "Like prison," Wyatt said in a way that was meant to be a joke but didn't come out that way. The only way Wyatt could pull his chair up to the table was to sit awkwardly at the end. CJ sat down at the corner next to him.

"Sorry," Wyatt said.

"For what?"

"That this night has been such a drag."

"It's exactly what I needed."

He shot her a look.

"I'm being serious. This is a nice distraction."

"What am I inadvertently distracting you from?"

"I got my SAT scores yesterday." She picked at a glob of cheese on her cold pizza. "I tanked 'em. Again. I think my dream of going to Stanford is basically over."

"Clarke, can I say something that might sound offensive?"

She shrugged. "Sure."

"You need better dreams."

"It's just so embarrassing. I work so much harder than everyone I know. Why can't I be one of those people who things come easily to?"

"Because those people are usually assholes." She looked

up. "You have so much empathy, Clarke. I think that's why you can't stand seeing Dakota on the sideline." Their eyes met, and she felt that same indescribable something that she'd felt earlier in the car. "You have a big heart. That's better than a big score."

Ordinarily, CJ hated it when people described any part of her as "big." This time, though, it made her want to cry. She wished she could see herself the way Wyatt saw her. She couldn't help it. Scores mattered. Winning mattered.

"Anyway," he said, "I know Stanford is your dream. But dreams change."

CJ felt her leg accidentally brush against his. She quickly pulled it back. "Hey, Wyatt. Can I ask you something?"

"You can ask me anything you want."

"What did your mom mean? About talking you into going back to Ohio State?"

"Like I said, Clarke, dreams change." Wyatt wadded up his napkin and dropped it onto a plate covered in pizza crusts. "Hey, do you like video games? Looks like they have a pretty sweet arcade."

Wyatt pushed himself back from the table before CJ could even answer.

CHAPTER **FIFTEEN**

AVA NEEDED one more piece for her RISD portfolio. She'd read online that it was a good idea to paint something that showcased her personality, so she stared at the blank canvas and thought about the different qualities that made her who she was. As much as she wanted to, it would be a lie not to include her depression. She wasn't quite sure how to show that with paint and decided to try her hand at an abstract piece.

She was the only one in the art room that morning when she started. Ava mixed colors together until she'd made a shade of brown the color of her skin. She dipped her brush and swiped it across the canvas in quick, sharp strokes. She didn't have a plan. She painted quickly in order to stop herself from overthinking her choices.

"Hey," said a voice from behind her.

Ava jumped, and the brush flew across the canvas, leaving a long streak. She spun around to find Logan Diffenderfer standing there.

"Shit," he said. "Sorry."

"It's fine. It's..." She tilted her head and looked at the long streak of paint. "It's cool, actually. I like it." She turned and saw the heavy expression on Logan's face. "What?" she asked.

"I talked to the private investigator. To see if he'll take your case."

Ava nodded. She was ready to accept the answer no matter what it was. In fact, it would probably be better if he wouldn't do it. Her mom and her therapist were right. She wasn't in a good place for this. She wasn't strong enough.

"He'll do it."

Relief flooded through Ava like a wave. Her mind hadn't been ready to admit how badly she wanted this, but her body apparently knew. "Thank god," she said quietly.

Logan shifted. "Before I tell him to go ahead, I just want to make sure. I mean, make sure you're sure. Carl, that's the investigator, he was telling me how complicated these kinds of cases are. Not like it would be complicated to find her. But...emotionally. For you. He felt a little weird about doing this for someone so young."

Everyone thought they knew what was best for her.

Her mom, her therapist, and now Carl. "But he will? He'll do it?"

Logan nodded. "Yeah. But…" Logan shifted again. She'd never seen him so uncomfortable. "Ava, are you sure? This sounds like…a lot."

"And you think I'm not strong enough?"

"No. Not at all. I *know* you're strong enough."

His eyes met hers and she looked quickly away.

"I'm ready," Ava said. "This is what I want."

"Okay. I'll tell him."

Ava looked up and saw that Logan was staring at her canvas. She was suddenly embarrassed. The piece was beyond abstract. It was chaotic. Ava felt exposed and vulnerable. She didn't want Logan to see the frantic and crazy brushstrokes of her frantic and crazy mind.

"It's not done yet," she said. "I'm trying something new."

"It's cool, though. It's the jungle gym, right?"

Ava was confused until she looked at her painting. He was absolutely right. The brushstrokes had come together in a way that formed an abstract image of the jungle gym.

"I'll go call Carl," Logan said.

After he left, Ava stepped back and looked at her canvas for a long time. Her painting wasn't crazy at all. It was beautiful.

CJ picked up cones from the gym floor after an afternoon of indoor soccer.

"I think that went well," Wyatt said.

CJ nodded, though not particularly exuberantly. Dakota was a no-show that day.

Wyatt tilted his head to the side, and CJ got ready for him to say something sage about how they couldn't force Dakota and that CJ needed to stop being so hard on herself.

"I'm having a crazy thought," Wyatt said. "Do you have anywhere you need to be right now?"

She shook her head.

"Good. Because I'm thinking we should kidnap Dakota."

CJ laughed. Until she realized that Wyatt was serious. Then she sighed and got her car keys. Ten minutes later, they pulled up to Dakota's house.

"We're not talking about an actual kidnapping, are we?" CJ asked as she put the car in park.

"Next time you agree to a kidnapping, you should probably clarify all the details in advance. Rookie mistake, Clarke."

The house was small with chipping paint and a front deck that needed some serious work and a garden that was nice and obviously well loved. CJ got out of the car, set up Wyatt's wheelchair next to the passenger seat, and locked the wheels. She leaned down and he put his arm on her shoulder. "Okay," he said, once he was in his chair. "Let's get her."

The path to the door was smooth and new, put in to accommodate a wheelchair.

"I hate to be practical when it seems like you're really into the spontaneity of this," CJ said. "But do you have any idea what we're actually going to do with her?"

"Not a clue." He rang the doorbell.

"Have you at least thought about what we're going to say to her mom?"

Wyatt looked up and to the left. "Hmm. No. But I probably should."

The door opened before Wyatt could give it much thought. Margaret seemed surprised to see them. "Hi," she said.

"Hi," said Wyatt. "We're here to kidnap your daughter. I know this sounds strange, and we're not entirely sure—"

"Take her," Margaret said. "She's yours. Oh my god. Please. Take her." Margaret turned back into the house. "Dakota! Grab your coat!"

Once they had Dakota in the back seat and CJ had figured out how to stack two wheelchairs in the trunk, she backed out of the driveway. "Where am I going?"

"Wherever the road takes us," said Wyatt.

CJ looked over at him. "I'm driving this car to Baskin-Robbins unless someone has a better idea."

"I hate ice cream," said Dakota.

CJ glanced in the rearview mirror and met Dakota's eye. "I bet that's not true."

Dakota folded her arms. "It is true. I'm lactose intolerant."

Wyatt turned around to face her. "Jeez, kiddo. The chair and no dairy? You got dealt a rough deck."

"Hey, Dakota," CJ said. "I was wondering. *Why* are you in the chair? If it bothers you to talk about it, we don't have to."

Wyatt touched CJ's knee. She knew what the touch meant. He approved of the question. But she didn't know what it meant that she wished he'd keep his hand there.

Dakota uncrossed her arms. "I assumed my mom told you," she said quietly.

"No," CJ said.

Dakota looked out the window. It seemed like she didn't want to talk about it. It also seemed like she *needed* to talk about it. "I was born with something. Do you know what spina bifida is?"

"I've heard of it," CJ said. "But I don't know much. Can you tell me?"

"My spinal cord didn't form the way it's supposed to. It never hurt me, though, and I didn't have any problems. Then last year I grew a lot. I guess that does something or whatever. I was in PE and we were playing volleyball. All of a sudden, my legs felt weird and I looked down and...

um…I'd peed. Everyone laughed. *Everyone.* My best friend laughed. But it wasn't funny and it wasn't my fault."

"Of course it wasn't your fault," CJ said.

"I had to have surgery, and they told me that it would fix everything and that I'd be fine. But it didn't. It made it worse. Like a freak, terrible outcome. And it happened to me. It's not fair." CJ glanced into the rearview mirror. Dakota looked down and wouldn't make eye contact. "Sometimes I still pee when I don't mean to." Her voice got soft and timid. "I don't want everyone at Sensational Recreational to laugh at me."

CJ and Wyatt traded a look of deep empathy. They'd unlocked it. The reason Dakota wouldn't set foot, or chair, onto the court.

Wyatt turned around. "They won't laugh at you, Dakota. I'll make sure of it. Nobody will laugh at you."

But they might. CJ couldn't imagine what it was like to go through everything that Dakota had experienced, but she absolutely knew what it was like to be laughed at. She folded an arm over her stomach in a defensive reflex, a physical guard against a memory that would never go away.

"My best friend laughed," Dakota said. "She never even came to see me in the hospital. She hasn't said anything to me since I've been back at school."

CJ glanced into the back seat. "That's awful." CJ's friends never laughed. Ever. When Grayson said that she was so big that she must be a man, Jordan got in his face and whispered, "Jealous much?" The next time he said something like that, Martha punched him. And Ava, sweet, wonderful Ava, was always at CJ's side to tell her she was beautiful.

Dakota shrugged. "So are we going to do anything or are we just going to drive around like losers?"

"I really am sorry, Dakota," said CJ. "I'm not excusing it, but I bet your friend is probably really scared and really embarrassed. She doesn't know what to say or how to act, so she's on eggshells."

"And speaking of eggshells..." said Wyatt. "Let's egg her house."

"Yes!" Dakota shouted from the back seat.

"No." CJ looked at Wyatt. "Wyatt, no."

"Please, CJ." Dakota sounded more excited than CJ had ever heard her. "Please, please, pleeeeeease."

Wyatt joined in with her chorus. "Pleeeeease. There's a CVS right at the corner. If that's not a sign, I don't know what is."

"Wyatt...I'm not really a rule breaker. And this is... It's destruction of property...It's egging a kid. This is a terrible idea." But when she saw Dakota's hopeful face in the mirror, it broke her heart just enough that she put on her blinker and pulled into the parking lot.

"Yes!" shrieked Dakota.

Ten minutes later, CJ was alone in the CVS bathroom filling up water balloons. At least she'd managed to talk them out of eggs. There was a knock on the door of the bathroom, and Wyatt peeked his head in. "How's it going?"

"Fantastic," CJ said flatly. "I'm alone in here. You can come in."

Wyatt pushed the door the rest of the way open and rolled up next to her. "You hate this idea, don't you?"

"I'm not condoning her friend's behavior. At all. But...I get it. It's confusing. It's scary. And she's only eleven. How can she be expected to deal with this at eleven? I'm seventeen and I can barely deal with it." CJ felt the tears and tried to push them back. "Part of me wants to kill that kid. But part of me feels like I would have *been* that kid." The tears crept out. "I don't know if I would have handled it any better. I'm every bit as awful. You should throw the water balloons at me." CJ could feel the tears dripping down her cheeks. She was mortified. "I don't know why I'm crying. That's not fair either. She's the one in the wheelchair and I'm the one crying."

"Bend," Wyatt said.

"Huh?"

"You're too tall. I need you to bend."

CJ crouched until she was at his eye level. He took a bit of paper towel and used it to dry her tears.

"You're not awful, Clarke. You never would have laughed."

"How do you know?"

"I know."

They looked at each other for a long moment. His hand was still on her face. She was wondering what it would be like to kiss him. She was almost certain he was wondering the same thing. If she leaned forward, she could find out. But she didn't. She pulled away.

"Well," she said, standing up and shaking off the moment, "I guess we should probably get on with this."

Wyatt was staring at her, but CJ wouldn't meet his eye. She put all the water balloons in a bag.

"Don't worry, Clarke. We're not really going to throw water balloons at a kid. I thought we could just hurl them at trees or something. You on board with that?"

She nodded. Then she held the door for him and followed him out.

Jordan was driving Martha home when she got the text. Since her parents had made her sign an actual legal document swearing that she wouldn't text and drive, she asked Martha to check the message for her. She regretted it the second that Martha told her who it was from.

"It's from that political guy, Scott Mercer." Martha's voice was filled with surprise. "Why is he texting you?"

"I don't know. Weird." Jordan quickly reached for her phone.

They'd been texting a lot. Some of it was professional, but some of it was not. They texted back and forth about what TV shows they were watching. And their hopes and dreams. Casual things like that.

Martha held the phone out of reach. "Don't you want me to read it?"

"I'm sure it's nothing important. Don't worry about it." She made another grab for the phone and the car swerved as she jerked the steering wheel.

Martha eyed her. "Jordan. What the hell?"

"Nothing," Jordan said. "I don't know what he wants."

"Well, let's find out." Martha crammed herself against the window so Jordan couldn't grab for her phone. As Martha opened the message, Jordan felt an edge of worry. She honestly didn't know why Scott was texting.

"He says"—Jordan braced herself—"'Can you be at City Hall tonight? Can't tell you why over text, but you'll want to be here for your article.'"

"Oh," Jordan said. The text was professional. *Thank god.* "Interesting. Guess I should check that out."

"Guess so," Martha said. There was an air of suspicion in her voice. "So I guess we're not hanging out tonight?"

They were on their way to Martha's apartment to work

on their history project together. "I think I should probably follow this City Hall lead," Jordan said. "It sounds important. Don't you think?"

Martha turned and stared at her, deadpan. Jordan was pretty sure she was about to ask her what the hell was going on. But she shrugged instead. "Whatever. Can you drop me at the theater, then?"

"I thought you weren't working tonight."

Martha shrugged. "I'm not." She didn't elaborate, and Jordan was almost positive that Martha was doing it on purpose. If Jordan was going to have secrets, then so was Martha.

After she dropped Martha off, Jordan rushed home and changed clothes quickly. She grabbed her car keys, then thought better of it. Parking downtown would cost a fortune. She'd have to take the bus.

The bus took forever, and by the time it dropped her off, she was in a rush. Still, she took a moment to pause in front of City Hall and take it in. She'd been there once before. For a school field trip. She'd never seen it at night, all lit up like this. It was spectacular.

Jordan walked up the steps into the building. She didn't remember it being so grand and inspiring. An American flag fluttered high above her. Walking underneath it made her feel important and humble all at once. She found the elevator and pushed the button for the top floor. Scott was waiting for her when the doors opened.

"Hi," he said.

Jordan felt her heart pound. "Hi."

He leaned toward her and put his mouth close to her ear. For a minute, she didn't know what he was doing. He whispered, "Council chambers. It's at the end of the hall." His breath tickled against her hair. "The city council meeting starts in five minutes. You didn't hear this from me, but the mayor is planning to weigh in on the park. We don't know what she's going to say. The developer is nervous. So's my boss." He pulled away as someone approached. Jordan tried to look casual. "Go," Scott said.

Jordan walked briskly down the hall, and her entire body buzzed. Men and women in suits stared into their phones and looked important. Jordan's heels echoed across the floor. Inside the council chambers, Jordan paused. The mayor and every member of the council sat at a long dais. Jordan no longer felt important. She felt intimidated. She wasn't sure where she was supposed to sit, and she was too scared to ask so she took a spot in the back row where she wouldn't be in the way.

The council president started the meeting and introduced the issue of the minimum-wage increase. Jordan's ears perked up. This was an issue that Martha had been following closely. One of the women at the table (there weren't many), Councilwoman Morales, read a prepared statement and lobbied passionately for the increase. She was the youngest woman on the council and she wouldn't let the men cut her off. Jordan wished Martha was here to see this. She wished Ava and CJ were too.

After a few more agenda points, it finally came time to talk about the park. Councilman Lonner summarized where they were in the approval process. He talked about the environmental impact report and stated that nothing in it was concerning. Jordan wasn't sure if she was allowed to record or not so she took out her notebook and wrote as quickly as she could. She noticed that Councilman Lonner seemed worried as the council president handed the floor over to Mayor Wilhelm. The mayor leaned forward and spoke into the microphone.

"My concern," she said, with gravitas, "isn't the environment." She looked at Councilman Lonner. "It's the kids who play in that neighborhood. Do we have an impact report to evaluate what the park closure will do to them?" She paused to give him a chance to answer. "It wasn't a rhetorical question, Councilman. I'd like you to think about that."

The councilman rambled about looking into it and talking to his community. The mayor remained calm and completely firm. Scott sat a few rows in front of Jordan, and at one point, he turned and caught her eye. He raised an eyebrow as if to say, *This is interesting.*

After the meeting ended, Jordan packed up her things and went outside. Scott was waiting for her at the bottom of the steps. He wore a long wool coat and his hands were shoved in his pockets. There were still people from the meeting hanging around, so Scott jerked his head slightly, motioning Jordan around the corner to where it was private. Once they were out of sight, he spoke. "Well?" he asked. "What did you think of it?"

For the first time since all of this had started, Jordan felt hope. "Mayor Wilhelm seriously put your boy in his place. I think he heard her."

"No comment," Scott said with a smile. "Come on. I'll walk you to your car."

"I took the bus. You can walk me to the stop."

He shoved his hands deeper in his pockets. She could see his breath in the chill of the evening. "It's way too cold to wait for the bus," he said. "I'll drive you home."

"Thanks," she said.

They walked to his car, and he opened the door for her. CJ and Martha both thought that sort of thing was sexist and old-fashioned, but Jordan didn't mind. She thought it was sweet. She sat down and pulled the seat belt across her chest.

"So," Scott said, sliding into the driver's seat, "where do you live?"

Before the question was even out of his mouth, Jordan realized she had a major problem.

"Uh," Jordan said, starting to panic. "Um…" This was not good. This was not good at all. There was no way she could let him see where she lived. Unless she could come up with a really good explanation why a freelance journalist could afford to live in a very large four-bedroom ranch-style house.

"Address?" he prodded. His phone was out and his GPS was ready.

"Uh…um…my address…"

"Yes," he said, not understanding why she was being so weird. "Your address. That would be helpful."

If she told him the truth, it would ruin everything.

"Jordan? Is something wrong?"

"1558 Bader Court!" She blurted it out so forcefully that she almost felt like she should apologize. It was Martha's address. "1558 Bader Court," she repeated. This time more calmly.

He plugged it into his GPS. "On our way."

———

Martha watched with a bit of awe as Victoria carefully placed a gummy bear onto a stack that was already seven gummies high. Victoria pulled her hand back, careful not to let the charm on her bracelet knock the whole thing over. When it successfully held, she shouted out in her strange hybrid accent, "Boom, bitch!"

Martha was stunned. "That's not even architecturally possible. I think that actually violates the laws of physics."

"And yet there it is. Your turn."

The game was Victoria's invention. A way to combat the boredom of a slow evening. Martha took a fresh gummy bear out of the pack, licked it, and approached the tower slowly.

"Hey, can I ask you something?" Victoria said.

"Not if you're doing it to try to distract me."

"What are you doing here?"

Martha didn't turn away from the tower. "I told you. I misread the schedule. So stupid, right?"

"Did you really?"

Martha felt her cheeks go warm. She stuck the gummy bear and backed away. "Your turn."

"I didn't mean to embarrass you," Victoria said. "I'm glad you're here. I was just wondering if you were avoiding home for some reason."

"Oh," Martha said. "No. Nothing like that."

Martha watched Victoria take another gummy bear from the bag. She liked that Victoria wanted to talk about real things. "I love my home," Martha said. "It's just me and my dad, and we get along really well. Which is good, since I'm probably just going to go to Cleveland State next year."

"Really? I thought you wanted to go to MIT."

Martha had brought up MIT only once. Victoria was such a good listener.

"I mean, it's one of the best engineering schools. And Boston seems cool. I'm just not sure it would be worth it. If I go to Cleveland State, I can probably graduate debt free. Or close to it. I mean, why wouldn't I do that? The idea of all that debt. And leaving my dad. It's all so...terrifying." That final word just sort of slipped out. She hadn't meant to admit she was scared. Victoria stepped away from the stack to look at her.

"Can I say something?" Victoria asked.

Martha nodded.

"Do the thing that scares you. The best things in my life have happened when I've been scared."

She turned back to the stack and delicately lowered the bear. Victoria held her breath as the tower wobbled, then settled. Martha held hers too. "Your turn," Victoria said.

"Like what?" Martha asked. "What have you done that's scared you?"

Victoria smiled. "Oh, like telling someone I wanted

to kiss them when I wasn't sure if they wanted to kiss me back."

"And…" Martha asked. "Did they?"

Victoria laughed. "One time, yes. Another time, I got my heart broken. But I'm still glad I told the truth."

Martha noticed that Victoria didn't look away. She wasn't afraid to make eye contact. But Martha was. Flustered, she took her phone out of her pocket and cycled through all the usual distracting apps. She found a text that Jordan had sent earlier in the evening. Her face must have shifted when she read it because Victoria asked her if everything was okay.

"Yeah," Martha said. Jordan had texted to say that the park might not be dead after all.

"You sure you're okay?" Victoria asked.

Martha slid her phone into her back pocket. "Yeah. It's good news."

"Then why do you look…"

Martha sighed. "Because my friend is at this big-deal meeting. Trying to change the world." Martha gave a self-deprecating smile. "And I'm here. Building a tower made of movie-theater snacks."

"You say that like this is just any old tower," Victoria said. "I think we might be eligible for a world record."

Martha smiled. At least that would be one way to leave

her mark on the world. She knew it was stupid, but she still cared about carving her name into that jungle gym. Martha pulled a gummy out of the bag and licked it.

"You've got this," Victoria said. "For the world-record books. We'll be remembered together."

Right as Martha lowered her bear, her phone chimed from her pocket. Martha groaned. "If I move my hand, it's going to fall."

"Then we won't be in the record book. No pressure."

Martha mustered all of her focus. Her phone chimed again. Martha ignored it. She steadied her hand. Her phone chimed again. And again. Martha tried not to let it fluster her.

"Here," Victoria said. "I'll get it for you."

Victoria slid up behind Martha, and as gingerly as she'd lowered the gummy bear, she slid her hand into Martha's back pocket. Martha felt her body go rigid as Victoria carefully slid the phone—and her hand—up the length of Martha's butt. Martha longed to turn around. She wanted to slide her hand into Victoria's, and she wanted to tell her all her secrets.

Victoria pulled the phone out and looked at it. "It's your friend Jordan."

"Ignore it." Martha was going to let the tower topple. She was going to turn around, and she was going to ask Victoria if she was feeling the same thing Martha was. "I don't care about the park right now."

"Uh, it's not about the park," Victoria said. "I think you'd better look at this."

Scott put his blinker on and turned onto the freeway. Jordan typed a series of frantic texts to Martha.

Are you home?

Please tell me you're home.

It's a long story. I need you to pretend to be my roommate.

She knew Scott would insist on walking her to her door. He was that kind of guy. And she kind of wanted him to. She knew what it would mean if he offered.

WHERE. ARE. YOU?

Scott followed his GPS. It was a twenty-minute drive, and they chatted the entire time. Jordan kept a steady eye on her phone. There still wasn't anything from Martha when he pulled up to the cu   rb.

"Well," Jordan said, "this is me."

Scott glanced up at her building, then at her. "I'd better walk you to your door."

Jordan tried to imagine what would happen when they got there. How would she explain that she didn't have keys? She could knock. No, she couldn't. Martha's dad might answer. Now that he was working more normal hours, he was usually home at night.

"It's okay," Jordan said. "You don't have to. Thanks for the ride."

Jordan climbed out of the car and Scott did the same. "Jordan. I know the crime stats for this neighborhood. I'm walking you to your door."

She looked at him, and he misread the hesitation on her face.

"I hope that didn't come across as rude," he said. "I don't exactly live in a palace either." He eyed Martha's building. The one he thought was hers. "This is nicer than mine and I can barely afford my rent."

Jordan wasn't quite sure how to respond. "First apartments," she said. "Am I right?"

Scott laughed. "Exactly. I think it's like a requirement to have a place like this when you're in your twenties. If we're still living in shitholes when we're thirty, then we can worry."

They both turned when they heard footsteps.

"Hey, roomie," said Martha as she walked up to them. Jordan couldn't tell if she'd overheard them talking or not. "You just getting home too?" Jordan gave Martha a complicated look, imploring her not to ruin this and apologizing all at the same time. Martha turned to Scott. "Hi. I'm Martha. Jordan's roommate."

He shook her hand. "Nice to meet you."

"Thanks for getting her home," Martha said. "I got

it from here. We always walk together at night. You can never be too safe in these shithole neighborhoods." Jordan laughed awkwardly. Martha turned to her and destroyed her with her gaze. "First apartments, am I right?"

She'd heard it. She'd heard everything. Jordan felt awful. Worse than awful. She barely looked back at Scott. "Thanks for...everything. Good night."

"Night, Jordan," he said. "Nice meeting you, Martha."

Martha's voice brimmed with anger and hurt. "The pleasure was all mine."

Jordan waited until Scott drove away from the curb to say something to Martha. "I am so sorry. So incredibly, deeply sorry."

Martha shrugged. "Forget it," she said, voice cool. "I'm sure it was worth making fun of my home to save the park." She looked at Scott's car driving away and then back at Jordan. "Because this is all about saving the park, right?"

CHAPTER **SIXTEEN**

AVA SAT on the bleachers between Jordan and Martha, and felt the stiffness radiating from each of them. It was the final football game of the season and the first real snow of the year. The whole athletic field was speckled in white. The girls didn't usually go to football games—CJ was the only sports fan—but this was the last game of the season. It was the last game of their entire high school experience. So they wrapped themselves up in maroon-and-gold scarves, huddled in the stands under blankets, and kept their hands warm with paper cups of hot chocolate.

The football team must have done something good because the cheerleaders suddenly started high kicking and waving their gloved fingers in the air. Jordan clapped and shouted onto the field, "Go Bears!" Then she leaned over

Ava and touched a gloved finger to Martha's arm. "This is fun." She was trying so hard to make everything feel normal. "I wish we'd gone to more games when we had the chance."

"Do you even know who's winning?" Martha asked.

"Not a clue," said Jordan. "But that's not the point. It's nice to be here together."

"Well, we're getting our asses kicked," Martha said. "How much longer are we going to stay here? I have to go to work soon. You know, because I'm poor."

Ava and CJ traded a tense look as Jordan turned to Martha.

"I'm sorry," Jordan said. "I've said I'm sorry. I don't know what else to say—"

CJ's phone chimed, and she used it as an excuse to cut Jordan off. "Help," she said. She shoved her phone into Jordan's face. Jordan was the only one wearing gloves with sensor pads on the fingers. Jordan used her index finger to unlock CJ's phone. She knew the code because they all used the same one. 0809. August ninth. The day they'd met in the park.

The text message popped up and Jordan gasped. "Clarke Josephine Jacobson," she said. "Why is Wyatt No Last Name Provided sending you a dick pic?"

There was a mother with young children sitting in front of them, and she turned around and shot CJ a look. "I'm so sorry," CJ said to the mom. "It's not actually a…you know. It's a vase."

The mother turned back to her kids, and Martha and Ava both leaned over to see CJ's phone. Wyatt had sent her a picture of a bulbous piece of pottery.

"It's an inside joke," CJ said defensively. "His mom makes these vases."

"Nope," said Martha. "There is no way that's a vase. That is definitely a penis."

The mother whirled around again. "Hi," Martha said casually. "How's it going? Enjoying the game?" The mom gave an annoyed warning glance before turning back to her kids.

CJ shrank down, looking mortified. "Please kill me now."

Ava laughed. Even though CJ really did look like she wanted to die, she was also smiling. "You and Wyatt certainly have a lot of inside jokes," Ava said, teasing.

CJ talked about Wyatt all the time. She told funny stories about him that weren't even really that funny. She found ways to bring up his name.

"Anyway." Martha said, "I really do have to go."

CJ put her phone away. "Okay. How about we meet you at the theater after the game? We still need to figure out our next move on the park."

They were encouraged by what the mayor had said. CJ felt that now was the time to make a push. Ava agreed.

They just didn't know what that push should be. Jordan was reluctant to publish anything. She didn't want to out herself as a high school student. Ava didn't really understand why that mattered.

"What's there to talk about?" Martha said. "If Jordan doesn't want to do anything..."

Jordan stiffened. "I *do* want to do something. I just don't think publishing a boring article will solve anything."

"Then don't write it boring," Martha said.

"You know what I mean. It's not worth burning my source yet."

Martha rolled her eyes. "Yeah. Okay. Whatever."

"No. Don't keep saying 'whatever.' If you want to yell at me, then yell at me."

"Okay," Martha said. "I'll yell. No. I'll say it calmly. Who cares about your dumb source? Scott's a jerk."

Jordan brushed the snow away from her eyelashes. "He's not a jerk. He's been incredibly helpful. He gave me the scoop on that meeting because—"

"Because he wants to get in your pants!" Martha shouted. "He just wants to sleep with you."

The mother whirled around again. Just as Jordan opened her mouth to say something, CJ stepped in. "Yep. You're right," she said to the mother. "We're taking this out of the stands. Ladies."

CJ stood and so did Ava. Jordan crossed her arms. "No.

I'm staying. We came to see the last McKinley High School football game we'll ever see. I'm not missing it."

Martha got up. "Great. Let me know if you figure out which side is ours."

She stormed out of the stands. CJ looked down at Jordan. "Come on. Let's all go talk about this."

Jordan crossed her arms even tighter. "There's nothing to talk about."

Ava turned to her. "Come on, Jordan. Please."

Jordan shook her head. "I'm staying."

Ava and CJ gave her a minute to change her mind. When it was obvious that Jordan wasn't budging, they walked off to find Martha. Ava looked back once. Jordan sat with her arms folded, letting the snow fall on top of her.

———————

Martha descended the city bus stairs, headed for the movie theater. She stepped onto the street and right into a hidden puddle. She was already mad at Scott and mad at the world and now she was mad at the puddle too. She wanted to be mad at Jordan, but the truth was, she wasn't. She was just hurt. She wished Jordan could understand how awful it had felt. To be sized up and disregarded like that. For something totally beyond her control. Martha stopped. She squeezed water out of the cuff of her jeans and felt like an asshole. Because of course Jordan knew what that was like.

She knew it better than any of them. Martha went back to being mad at the world. And Scott.

When she reached the theater, she tugged the door open. She felt a rush of warm air and then a rush of relief when she saw Victoria. Martha wondered if Victoria would know right away that something was wrong. Probably. Maybe she'd even hug her again. Martha hoped so.

But Victoria wasn't alone. She sat at one of the concession tables with Logan Diffenderfer. They appeared to be deep in conversation.

"Hey," Martha said.

"What's wrong?" asked Victoria.

A minute ago, Martha had felt desperate for Victoria to say those words. Now she only shrugged. "Nothing." She took her coat off and stomped the snow out of her boots, making a pile by the door.

"You sure?" Logan asked. "You seem..."

"I seem what, Diffenderfer?" Martha asked defensively.

He held up his hands as if in surrender. "Okay. I was just asking." He turned to Victoria. "Anyway, I should go in. I don't want to miss the beginning. Seriously, though. Check out *Blue Velvet*. It's weird, but I think you'll like it."

Victoria nodded. "I'll add it to my list."

As Logan ducked into the theater, Martha walked behind the concession stand and shoved her damp coat into one of the cupboards. She kicked the door closed with a *bang*.

"Seriously," Victoria said. "What's wrong?"

"I'm fine. You can join Logan if you want. I can take care of the concession stand. You guys can keep talking about movies. Or whatever." She'd been saying "whatever" a lot tonight.

Victoria leaned across the counter. "I don't want to watch the movie. I want to know why you're being weird."

Martha didn't even know where to begin. The fight with Jordan wasn't what was bothering her. Not really. She knew that part would get resolved. She didn't doubt that Jordan was sorry. She was sorry too. For picking and picking and not letting it go. She knew those feelings would eventually fade away. A year from now, neither of them would even remember it. Jordan would probably be at Northwestern in her dorm room or at the campus newspaper office, and it would be just an insignificant thing that happened to her in high school. Martha wondered where she'd be. Probably right here, in this exact spot, stomping her boots out onto the same carpet and shoving her coat into the same cupboard. "Have you ever felt...I don't know...not worthy?"

Victoria nodded gently. "Of course. Everyone has."

Martha never cared that she didn't grow up with money. She was proud of her dad and how hard he worked. She loved the tiny apartment with the gray carpeting. That's why what Jordan said had hurt so much. When Scott, with his preppy button-downs and his idealistic job, had insulted her home, Jordan didn't stand up for her. She didn't tell him that he had absolutely no idea how hard it is when plants close, and production moves overseas, and life as you know it gets ripped out from under you. Scott didn't understand the price of progress.

"You are, though," Victoria said. "You are worthy. I don't know who made you feel like you're not. But they're wrong."

Tears leaked out of the corners of Martha's eyes. Victoria reached out and took Martha's hand. "Hey," she said, giving it a squeeze. "You are."

Martha nodded. She wasn't thinking about Scott anymore. She was only thinking about Victoria and how good it felt to stand there with their hands together. "Victoria... I want to tell you something."

Suddenly, the theater doors slammed open. Startled, they both dropped their hands and turned. Logan was walking up.

"God, Diffenderfer," Martha said, quickly wiping her eyes. "Learn to open a door."

Logan rushed over without apologizing. "Do you know where Ava is?" he asked.

"Why? What's wrong?"

Logan turned his phone around and showed her something that was on it.

"Oh my god," Martha said.

"I know," said Logan. "Is she home?"

Martha pulled out her own phone. "I'll find her."

Victoria looked back and forth between them. "Is everything okay?"

Martha nodded. "Yeah. It's a long story. Ava's been looking for her biological mom—"

"I know," Victoria said.

Martha looked up with surprise. "You do?"

"Logan told me about it."

Martha didn't have time to think about it or fully absorb just how much Logan and Victoria had been talking lately. She looked up from her phone and turned to Logan. "Ava's home. AirDrop me the file."

He hesitated. "Shouldn't I...?"

Martha leveled her eyes at him. "I know you have the best of intentions here. But I think it would be better if she heard this from me. And CJ and Jordan."

To his credit, Logan didn't argue. "Yeah, okay. You're probably right."

He selected the file, and Martha waited for the electronic beep that told her it had come through. "Thanks." She turned to Victoria. "Can you cover the theater?"

"Sure. Of course."

Martha grabbed her coat from the cupboard. She pulled it on as she walked. When she got to the door, she paused and looked back. Victoria gave her a small wave and a look that was impossible to read.

_____

CJ had never just shown up unannounced at Wyatt's house before. She regretted it the second she knocked on his door. She hoped nobody was home.

The door opened a second later.

"Clarke," Wyatt said. "What are you doing here?"

"I have no idea. And you're probably in the middle of something."

"I am, actually."

"I'm sorry. I'll go."

"Clarke, wait. It's the kind of something you can join in on."

He opened the door wider. She entered but kept her coat on. She didn't know how long she'd be staying. The house was warm and quiet. He led her into the dining room, and she saw that the table was covered in a thousand puzzle pieces. She laughed. "A puzzle? That's what you're doing?"

"Clarke. I did not invite you into my home to be mocked. Now sit down and help me. When I'm done, it'll be a kitten scaling a set of drapes. I believe it also contains an inspirational message, but I lost the box top."

CJ sat and started to look for edge pieces. She thought

that's how everyone in the world did puzzles, but Wyatt had started with the center. It was positively barbaric.

"So..." Wyatt said, scanning the table for the piece he needed. "What brings you out on such a blustery night?"

CJ connected two edge pieces together. "I was heading home from a football game, but I realized I didn't feel like going home. So I was just driving around and...ended up here. But if you want me to go..."

"Clarke. I don't want you to go."

CJ reached for a puzzle piece, but it was the same one that Wyatt wanted. Their hands overlapped. CJ felt the same zing she felt every time they touched. She pulled her hand back quickly. "Sorry," she said.

"I forgive you."

She liked him. She was sure of it now. She also knew why she pulled her hand back every time. It was the wheelchair. She wasn't proud of it. It was just the truth. She knew that it shouldn't matter. If she was a good person, it *wouldn't* matter. She wasn't a good person, though. Because she couldn't stop herself from thinking about all the complications. All the places they couldn't go together. The things they couldn't do. She didn't even know if he could have sex or not. She was still a virgin. She'd barely even made it to third base, and yet she was always thinking about sex when she was near him.

"What are you thinking about?" he asked.

"Nothing."

"Clarke. You were thinking about something. Tell me."

"Oh god. Please don't ask me again."

"Clarke."

"I was wondering if you can have sex."

Wyatt's hand hovered over a puzzle piece. She'd probably offended him. Of course she'd offended him. It was an offensive thing to ask. But when he looked up, he was smirking. "Clarke Jacobson. Are you propositioning me?"

"No. Of course not." Her eyes immediately darted back to the table. "I'm so embarrassed. I should have never asked—"

"Yes."

She looked up. He nodded, slowly, carefully, and deliberately. "I can. Is there anything else you'd like to ask me?"

CJ felt her face get warm. "Have you?"

She wanted to look away. She didn't want to look away.

"Yeah. Not since the chair. But, yeah, I have."

"Oh." CJ went back to the puzzle and fumbled for another edge piece. She didn't like thinking about Wyatt with another girl. She was probably beautiful. She was probably a normal height and totally unselfconscious.

"I had a girlfriend before the accident. We didn't break up because of what happened to me or anything. We made a mutual decision to end things when we both left for college. So you don't have to hate her."

"Can I still hate her?"

"I would love for you to hate her."

CJ escaped into the puzzle again.

"Okay, Clarke. Now I get a question."

She suddenly became very focused on looking for the puzzle piece she needed. "Sure," she said. "That seems only fair."

"Okay, my question is why did you ask that question?"

CJ found the puzzle piece she wanted. *Tell him. Tell him that you have feelings for him.* She turned it over in her hand. *Tell him that you've never felt this way about anyone before.* She put the puzzle piece back down. *Tell him everything. Tell him!* CJ looked up. "I was just curious."

She watched him nod. He betrayed nothing. Then he went back to the puzzle. CJ connected a few more edge pieces and wished she were a better person. That's when her phone buzzed with a text from Martha.

———————

Jordan paced the sidewalk in front of Ava's house. The snow had lightened up for a while, but now it was coming down hard. She turned when CJ's car pulled up, and when she saw that Martha was in the passenger seat, she immediately felt awkward and awful.

"Hey," Jordan said sheepishly, as both of her friends climbed out of the car.

Martha responded in kind. "Hey."

It was hard to tell who made the first move. Jordan only knew that one minute they were standing there kicking at the snow and the next minute they were hugging.

"I am so sorry," said Jordan, pulling back from the hug. She found Martha's eyes and said it again. "So, so sorry. I should have told Scott to shut up. I wish I could take it back."

"It's okay. I know you didn't mean it."

"Do not let me off the hook. I feel horrible."

"I know you do. And I feel horrible too. Because I know you've dealt with stuff like this times a million and—"

"This is not a privilege-off. I love you, Martha."

"I love you too."

They hugged again. This time neither one of them pulled away until CJ cleared her throat and said, "Um, guys?"

Jordan told CJ that she'd already tried the front door. She'd slammed her palm against the side window like an octopus so Ava would know it was her. "No answer."

"She must be in the shower. Or asleep," CJ said.

Fortunately, they knew another way in.

The night was bitterly cold, and their breath came out in steaming clouds as they walked around to the side of the house where Ava's bedroom was. CJ found the flower-pot that they could turn over and use as a step stool. It had been almost four years since they'd climbed through Ava's bedroom window. Back then, they didn't know what was wrong with her. They only knew that sometimes she couldn't seem to get out of bed. They thought they were helping when they encouraged her to try harder. They thought they were doing the right thing when they tried to drag her out. Everything they did only made Ava want to burrow in deeper. It also made her lock the door. But that's the thing about best friends; they'll always find a way around a lock. Jordan would never forget the night they broke into her bedroom. Ava was so tired that she didn't even roll over. She directed her words at the wall. *I'm not getting out of bed.* CJ was the one who responded. *You don't have to. But we're coming in.* And then they did. All three of them. They climbed in and surrounded her. One of them—there would forever be a disagreement about who it was—took Ava's hand and gave it a squeeze. "This means I love you," she said. Whichever one of the shes it was. "If you love me back, you don't have to say it, just squeeze twice." Ava's hand was weak, but she did it. Two squeezes.

The snow fell in thick flakes as the three of them congregated outside Ava's window for the first time in years. CJ balanced on the flowerpot and worked her fingers into the small opening at the base of the window. She pushed up and it opened easily. Ava never told her mom that her friends had broken the lock, so she never knew it needed replacing. The first thing Jordan noticed was the music as it flowed outside. Tinny and hollow. Like it was coming from a pair of earbuds that were cranked up way too loud. Which is exactly what it was.

Ava was at her easel, lost in music and lost in her work, but as soon as CJ thrust the curtains open, she screamed. She was so startled by the faces of her three best friends that she hurled her paintbrush at the intruders. She hit CJ square in the middle of the forehead.

"What the hell?!" shouted Ava.

CJ wiped brown paint off her face.

Ava tried to catch her breath. "What the actual hell?"

It was Martha who answered. "We have the name of your birth mother."

Ava pulled the earbuds out of her ears.

A few minutes later, all four girls were sitting on the floor of Ava's room, their muddy shoes in a pile by the window. Ava's mom was away in Chicago for a conference, and Ava would always remember how empty and quiet the house felt that night.

"I can't do this," Ava said. She was holding Martha's phone. The file was just waiting for her to open it. "I can't. Someone else do it."

She held the phone out and CJ took it from her. Ava shut her eyes as CJ clicked the attachment open. Then all three of the girls with their eyes still open uttered some version of "Whoa."

"What?" Ava kept her eyes shut tight. "What's happening?"

"Um...she's..." The voice sounded like Martha's. But it also sounded like it was tearing up. So it couldn't be Martha. Martha didn't cry. "She looks like you, Ava."

Ava opened one eye slowly. Then the other. CJ handed her the phone, and Ava gasped when she saw the picture. "Oh my God. Is that...is that me? With my—" Her voice cracked before she could say the word.

The photograph showed her birth mother lying in a hospital bed looking wide-eyed and terrified but also overcome with love. There was a baby in her arms. Baby Ava.

"Wow," Ava said to the picture. The image was clear and focused. This woman would never be a fuzzy image again.

"Isabel Castillo," Martha said. "That's her name."

"Ava Castillo." Ava said it like she was trying it on. The name felt clunky and awkward in her mouth. "But I guess I would have had a different first name too."

Ava read through the rest of the information. Isabel Castillo lived in California. There was an address in East Palo Alto. There was even a phone number.

"It's still early enough there," CJ said. "They're three hours behind in California if you want to call."

Ava didn't need to think about it for long. She shook

her head. "No. I can't." Ava had never intended to get in touch with her biological mom. She only wanted to see her, to have some sort of image to put in that blank space. And now she had it. That was enough. It was more than enough. "Thanks for coming by," Ava said. "But I kind of want to be alone."

Her friends understood. They gave her long and lingering hugs, and said they'd keep their ringers turned on all night if she needed anything. Ava honestly didn't know if she would or not.

After her friends left, Ava stared at the canvas she'd been working on. She'd decided to paint the park. Not abstract this time. She was painting from an old photograph taken when the girls were fourteen. It was one of the best summers Ava could remember. Though looking back now, she didn't know if the summer was truly that special or if it was because it was the last one before depression. Before Dr. Clifford, before Lexapro, and before Logan Diffenderfer had called her stupid.

She knew she needed to call him. He'd found the information for her. He'd given her the gift of a picture. She needed to at least say thank you. Every time she picked up her phone, she couldn't do it. She sent him a text instead.

Thnx.

Logan was weird when she saw him at school on Monday. Well, not weird, exactly. Cautious. He asked her how she was doing, in a way that was loaded and full of meaning. She knew what the question meant. How was she doing now that she knew what her mom looked like?

"Fine," Ava said.

Only she wasn't fine. When her mom had come back from Chicago on Sunday night, Ava had been weird and jumpy. She was angry at her mom—her adoptive mom—for keeping this information from her. But she also felt horrible for seeking it out on her own. She felt both betrayed and like the one who was doing the betraying.

It turned out that having the tiny taste of a biological mom was worse than having no taste at all. Every time Ava stared into the mirror, she would see the face of Isabel Castillo staring back at her. It was there when she walked past windows, and it startled her when she glanced in the mirror. She even saw it in the puddles that filled the sidewalks when the temperature spiked that Wednesday and all the snow melted at once. Logan was early to art class that day. He'd been early every day that week.

"How are you?" he asked in his new heavy way.

"I'm okay."

It was his idea to look up Isabel's address in Google Maps. Ava just wanted to see where she lived. To get some small clue about what her birth mother's life was like. Maybe she was poor. But maybe she was rich. While Logan plugged the address in, Ava caught herself silently singing "Maybe" from *Annie. Maybe far away or maybe real nearby.*

Ava leaned over Logan's shoulder and watched while the address came into focus. The apartment building was blank and ordinary and frustratingly nondescript. Facebook and Instagram were their next stop, but there were so many Isabel Castillos that it took the entire art period and all of their lunch hour to look them all up. None of them were *her* Isabel Castillo.

The next day, Logan showed up early to art class again. "I think I know a way you could fly out to California to see her."

Ava shook her head. "She doesn't want to meet me."

"I'm not saying you have to *meet* her. Just *see* her. Wait for her outside her apartment until she comes out."

"Like a stalker?"

"Like a daughter who just wants to know something."

Ava shook her head. "No way. Hard no."

"Can I just tell you my idea?"

"No means no, Logan."

At lunch time, Jordan showed off the new dress that her grandmother had helped her make, and that stupid song from *Annie* popped into Ava's head again. She had to duck into the bathroom so nobody would see her cry.

After school, she found Logan. "Hypothetically, let's say I'm not totally opposed to stalking my mother. You said you had an idea to get me to California?"

Logan showed her on the map how East Palo Alto was only about a fifteen-minute drive from Stanford. "Tell your mom you want to apply to Stanford."

"But I don't want to apply to Stanford."

"Tell her you might. And that you want to see the campus to help you decide. There's a prospective-students' weekend a little after Thanksgiving. You could fly there, and then it's only a short bus ride to your birth mom's."

Ava looked down. "I don't know." It didn't feel right. Tricking her adoptive mom into paying for a flight so she could see her biological mom.

"I could even go with you," Logan said. "I've already seen the campus. But I'm sure my parents would say okay. They're pretty desperate for me to go there."

Ava stared at her toes. "I'll think about it."

CHAPTER **SEVENTEEN**

WHEN THANKSGIVING break came, CJ drove the three hours to Ann Arbor with her parents to eat dried-out turkey at her oldest sister's house like they did every year. She called Wyatt when they got there. "Just reminding you that my family left early for Thanksgiving break," she said. "So I won't be there tomorrow."

She'd already told him. Several times.

"You're just calling to rub it in, aren't you? Since I'll be stuck in the Cleve."

"Won't most of your friends be back from college? That should be fun, actually."

Wyatt sighed dramatically. "Define 'fun, actually.' "

"I feel like that doesn't need a definition." Her niece was racing through the house in a pink tutu and fairy wings. She was petite and feminine, a mirror image of CJ's oldest sister. She stopped in front of CJ and did a cartwheel. CJ gave her a big thumbs-up.

"Yes, it will be fun to see them," he said. "It will also be fraught."

"Fraught?"

"Complicated."

"I know what it means. I actually have a pretty good vocabulary. Don't let my mediocre SAT score fool you."

"Clarke," he said in a bright way. "You made a joke about your own inadequacies. This feels like progress for you."

"Thanks." She watched her niece do pirouette after pirouette. "But don't change the subject. Why is it fraught?"

Wyatt sighed again. This time it wasn't dramatic. It was real. "Most of my high school friends are from cross-country and track. A lot of them are running at college. It's hard to hear about it." There was a long pause. Her niece spun around faster and faster. "I miss running," he said. "God, do I miss it."

"I'm sorry." She thought about her own running shoes packed carefully in her suitcase. She was going to run the Thanksgiving Turkey Trot with her dad. It was one of her favorite traditions.

"Thanks. It'll be good to see them, though. We're going to celebrate my birthday."

"When's your birthday?"

"Not until next Saturday." CJ made a mental note. "But since everyone is in town, we're going to rage. And by rage, I mean they're going to come over and my dad will make his famous baked ziti."

"That's adorable," said CJ.

"I know you're making fun, but it actually is. It's my grandma's recipe. It's one of my favorite foods ever. And speaking of favorite foods ever. Top three Thanksgiving side dishes. Go."

CJ's niece spun herself into dizziness and collapsed in her lap. CJ smoothed her hair back and kissed her head. "Stuffing. Green bean casserole. And corn bread. You?"

"Pumpkin pie. Pecan pie. And any third variety of pie."

"A pie isn't a side dish. It's a dessert."

"It's a dessert and a side dish."

They stayed up until midnight debating it.

The next day, he called her. "My friends are out doing a big trail run together. Distract me. What are you doing?"

CJ was on the floor with her laptop in front of the fireplace. "I'm trying to write about a time I've had a transformational experience."

"That sounds horrific. Why?"

She told him about the Stanford application essay topic and read it for him. " 'Describe a transformational experience and how it has shaped you into the person you are today.' "

"That's a terrible topic, Clarke." Wyatt breezed on to the next thing without elaborating. "Now, tell me why you want to go to Stanford. I've never asked."

The logs in the fireplace shifted and a cascade of sparks fluttered and settled. "You'll laugh."

"I would never laugh."

CJ grabbed the fireplace poker and jabbed at the logs. "I want to go to Stanford because I want to make the world a better place." She stopped poking. "Are you laughing?"

"Not at all. But I do have a sub-question. Why does making the world a better place require a Stanford diploma?"

She shrugged. "It doesn't. It just gives me some validity, you know what I mean?"

"No. I don't know."

"It was a rhetorical question."

"I don't think it was."

"I want people to take me seriously, Wyatt."

The confession was vulnerable. His response was forceful. "Then make them."

CJ stopped poking at the logs. What he'd said hit her hard. So hard that she had the sudden urge to make a joke. "Oh, and also the weather. I'm sick of Cleveland winters. Stanford is sunny."

"Fair enough," he said. "That I can support."

"Why did you want to go to Ohio State?" she asked.

"I had a track scholarship."

"Wow," CJ said.

"Yeah. It *was* pretty 'wow.' I was excited."

CJ watched as the fire dimmed. "When do you think you'll go back to school?"

He didn't say anything for so long that she looked at her phone to make sure she hadn't lost him. "You still there?" she asked.

"I'm still here." There was another stretch of silence. "I don't know. It's going to be so...different. I had this vision of college...I don't know what it'll be like now."

She thought about what he'd said to her at the mini-golf course. *Dreams change.*

His demeanor shifted. "Anyway, my mom just got home. I've gotta jet. Bye, Clarke."

"Bye," she said.

———————

It was while eating a rotisserie chicken from Whole Foods on Thanksgiving Day that Ava decided she wanted to fly to California to see her birth mother. Ava and her mom were sitting across from each other in the dining room. Even though it was just the two of them, her mom always put together a centerpiece and Ava made place cards. It was tradition.

Ava moved her food around on her plate. She hadn't had much of an appetite the last few days.

"How's your RISD portfolio coming?" her mom asked.

Ava stopped pushing her food. They hadn't talked about RISD since that awful day in the college counselor's office. "It's...it's okay."

"I'm trying to keep an open mind," her mom said.

"Thanks." Ava dragged her fork through the stuffing and wondered why Whole Foods put raisins in it. It seemed criminal.

"I just want you to be happy."

Ava looked up. Her mom was trying. It wasn't her fault that no amount of trying could ever make up for the fact that there were certain things that she would never understand. Her mom would never know the ache of desire to put paint onto a blank canvas. She would never know what it was like to be the only brown face in a sea of white ones. She would never know what it felt like to be leveled by depression. "Actually," Ava said, "I'm trying to keep an open mind too. I'm thinking of maybe applying to Stanford."

Her mom looked up. "Really? That's fantastic."

The exuberance in her mom's voice almost broke Ava's heart. "There's a prospective-students' weekend. To see the campus. Do you think maybe I could go?"

"Yes. Yeah. Oh my gosh. Of course." She was beaming. "We can book our flights tonight if you want."

"Oh," Ava said. "You don't have to...I know how busy you are with work and..."

"Ava. I'm not too busy for this." Ava looked down at the table. She hadn't even touched her chicken. "And the idea of you flying all that way on your own. I'll be honest, it worries me a little."

Ava looked back up. She could fly on her own. She could do all sorts of things that her mom didn't think she was capable of doing. "Mom. I'll be fine."

"It's the other side of the country."

"Please, Mom," Ava said. "I..." Her voice cracked slightly. "I need to do this."

Her mom still looked nervous.

"What if I'm not the only one going? If a friend goes with me...then can I go?"

Her mom considered. "I suppose that would be okay."

Ava almost called Logan Diffenderfer that night. Almost. She called CJ instead.

"So..." CJ said, after Ava laid out the plan. "You want me to go visit Stanford for the weekend with you so we can stalk your birth mom."

Ava was curled onto her bed, the postcard from her birth mom in her hand. "You've never actually seen the campus. So I'm thinking you could convince your parents."

There was an inordinately long pause.

"CJ?"

"Processing." Another pause. "Okay, I've processed. No, I haven't. Still processing. But, yes. I would walk through fire for you. So I will figure out a way to get the money."

Ava set the postcard down and sat up. She hadn't even thought about how much money this would cost and how hard that would be for CJ. "Shit. CJ, I didn't even think. Just forget the whole thing. It's a terrible idea."

"Wait," CJ said. "I just remembered something." She laughed slightly. "The SAT course I took this summer has a money-back guarantee. Either your scores improve, or you get a full refund."

"Don't waste the money on me," Ava said. "Spend it on yourself. Spend it on something important."

"This is something important," CJ said.

––––––––––

"I hate to be the one to point out the obvious," Martha said that following Monday. "But I'm going to point out the obvious." She stared incredulously at Ava from across the cafeteria table. "You can't go to Stanford that weekend."

Ava picked at the plastic label of her water bottle. "I have to." It was chicken nugget day, and a pile of them sat untouched on her plate.

"I don't know," said Jordan. "If she doesn't go, she's always going to wonder."

"Exactly what I said." CJ picked one of the nuggets off Ava's plate and held it up. "Are you not eating?"

Ava shook her head. "You can have it."

"No. I mean..." She lowered her voice. "Are you not eating?" The question didn't require the loaded tone. They all knew what it meant. Ava stopped eating when she was depressed.

"It's just a hard week," Ava said. "I'm overwhelmed. But I'm okay."

"You promise?" CJ asked.

Ava shrugged.

Jordan pulled out her phone. "That settles it. I'm going too. You need all the emotional support you can get. What weekend is it?" She opened her calendar.

"The one after next," Ava said.

Martha was getting impatient. "That's my point," she said. "And what else is that weekend?"

Ava kept picking at her water bottle. It made a frustratingly repetitive sound. "I don't know."

Martha reached over and took the water bottle away from her. "Ava. Your art show."

Ava looked up. "Oh my god. I can't believe I forgot."

They were planning on going together. All four of them. Martha had already asked to get the night off from work.

"Shit," Ava said. She looked at each of her friends. "Someone tell me what to do. I need someone else to make the decision for me."

"No, you don't," said CJ. "What do you want? We're with you no matter what."

Ava stared at her nuggets. The coating was starting to turn white and rubbery where the fat was congealing. "I have to do it," Ava finally said. "Jordan's right. I'm always going to wonder."

Martha couldn't help but feel like this was a terrible idea. There was a good chance that it would make everything worse, not better. She knew she couldn't say that, though, so she reached across the table and took Ava's hand instead. She squeezed once. Ava squeezed back twice. Her grip was strong and it made Martha feel less worried. Only slightly, though.

CHAPTER **EIGHTEEN**

WYATT WATCHED out the window of CJ's car as the trees became thicker and the scenery grew more and more unfamiliar. "You're taking me into the woods to murder me. That's the surprise, right?"

"Happy birthday," she said.

"Well, even that would be better than the celebration with my friends last week. So I say cool. Let's do it."

"Why?" she asked. "What happened?"

"Oh, nothing terrible," he said lightly, as if to brush it aside.

CJ turned the car down another densely wooded road, and he glanced back at her.

"Seriously. Where are you taking me?"

"I told you," CJ said. "It's a surprise. What happened with your friends?"

He gave a noncommittal shrug. "It was fine. They all tried very hard to say all the right things. It was very polite."

"Oof." CJ had spent enough time around him now to know that the politeness was the worst. No matter how people intended it, Wyatt always read it as an expression of pity. She looked over at him and he smiled warmly, distracting her so much that she almost missed her next turn. "Sorry," she said as she took the corner a little too quickly.

They were so far outside the city that some of the streets didn't even have signs. CJ eventually turned onto a long gravel road. She looked over and found Wyatt staring at her. "Thank you," he said.

"For what?"

"For this. Even if you are taking me into the woods to murder me. Thank you."

CJ was positively giddy about the present she'd found for him. She'd originally bought him a book about Franklin Roosevelt, *The President in the Wheelchair*. But she was thankful that she'd skimmed it before giving it to him. She thought it would be empowering, but it turned out that her history class had gotten the legend of Roosevelt wrong in a lot of ways. He was a man who was very much not at peace with his limitations, going to great lengths to hide what he saw as a weakness. The prologue went so far as to say that in today's world, a man in a wheelchair would likely never be elected. CJ wanted to burn that book.

Loose gravel crunched underneath the tires until they reached the end of the road. She turned into a dirt driveway. At the end of it was a rustic red barn. "We're here," she said.

Wyatt read the white letters that were painted across the barn. "Cross Creek Ranch Stables?"

"It's an adaptive horseback riding facility. Surprise!"

He seemed confused. "For the kids?"

"No," CJ said. "For you. Happy birthday." She turned off the car and faced him. "I heard you when you said that you missed running. I get it. I get it on such an insanely deep level. Anyway, I was doing some random googling and I stumbled onto this."

Outside, a handler was leading a chocolate-brown horse into the ring. The horse was outfitted with a saddle, but not like any CJ had ever seen.

"I read online that a horse's hips mimic the motion of running for humans. A lot of people in wheelchairs say that riding horses gives them the sensation of being able to run. So that's your gift. The gift of going running again."

Wyatt didn't say anything. He was staring at the horse with an intensity CJ wasn't used to seeing from him.

"You ready?" she asked, somewhat cautiously.

Wyatt turned to her. Or more accurately, he turned away from the horse. "The gift of running again? Clarke. I'm never going running again."

"You know what I mean."

"No. I don't."

His brusqueness flustered her. "Maybe I should have told you first. But I wanted it to be a surprise."

Outside, the handler waved to CJ and Wyatt. CJ waved back. Wyatt did not. CJ put her finger up in a "give us a sec" gesture.

"The testimonials were really incredible. And the lady I talked to was so nice. Maybe if you just talk to her for a minute. Get some more details. She said there are lots of trails up here, and once you get comfortable in the saddle, you can go wherever you want. I was thinking I could bring my running shoes and we could go running together."

Wyatt scoffed. It was a terrible sound. "Don't you get it? We're not going to go running together, because I'm never running again!"

CJ looked down. She felt awful. "Wyatt. I'm sorry. Everything I'm saying is coming out wrong. Please. Just try it."

"I don't want this, CJ!" He'd never called her CJ before. "God," he said. "How could you ever think I would ever want this?"

"I...I'm sorry."

"Get me out of here," he said. "Please. Get me out of here."

CJ started the car and pulled away, leaving a spray of dust and a very confused horse handler in their wake.

Neither one of them said anything until they were back on the highway. CJ was relieved when he broke the silence. "Can I ask you a question?" He didn't look at her when he asked.

She nodded. "Anything."

"Was this for you or for me?"

She looked over at him. Her eyes showed that she didn't understand the question.

"Clarke, I'm never going to be able to do everything that you can. And I guess I'm just wondering, will that ever be enough for you?"

She took her eyes off the road. "Of course," she said. "Wyatt, I don't care that—"

"Then why didn't you kiss me?"

His question shocked her back into silence.

"The day with the water balloons. You wanted to. I wanted you to. But you didn't. And the day with the puzzle and all those questions. Why did you ask?"

She looked at him and decided to answer honestly. "I did want to kiss you. I didn't because...because I was scared."

"Of what?"

CJ looked back at the road. "You know what. It does make everything complicated. We can pretend like it doesn't, but it does."

"Thank you for your honesty." There was an edge to his voice.

CJ made a decision in that moment. She was tired of being scared. She put her turn signal on. She turned onto a small road, slowed to a stop, and put the car in park. She unbuckled her seat belt. Then she leaned over and kissed him. As their lips touched, she felt his hand tighten around her arm. His grip was so strong and sure that it took her a minute to notice that he wasn't pulling her closer. He was pushing her away.

"I'm not here so you can prove something to yourself, Clarke."

The butterflies in her stomach turned into caterpillars. Dense and writhing. "That's not why—"

"You want to be able to tell everyone about the time you kissed a guy in a wheelchair. How you learned a valuable lesson about yourself. How it was a transformational experience." He shook his head. "No way. I'm not that guy."

They barely spoke on the car ride home. She dropped him off and helped him into his wheelchair. Then she stood there hoping that he'd speak first. He didn't.

"Wyatt..."

"Don't worry, Clarke. This won't change things at the rec center. At least I don't want it to. You're too good with the kids."

"Thanks," she said. Because what else was there to say? "I'll see you on Monday."

She walked around to the driver's side door, then paused when she remembered. "Wyatt. This is terrible timing, but I meant to tell you earlier that I won't be there on Friday."

"Are you going somewhere?"

"To Stanford. To see the campus."

He nodded. "No problem. I hope it's everything you dreamed it would be."

Ava leaned over Jordan and watched as a large machine deiced the wings of their plane. If they didn't die, it would be seventy degrees and sunny when they landed in California.

"I'm nervous," Ava said.

"Don't be," said Jordan, who seemed nervous herself. "It's totally normal. Wings get covered in ice all the time. We'll be fine."

Ava shot her a look. "I'm nervous about seeing my birth mom."

"Don't be," CJ said from the aisle seat. "Adopted children observe their biological mothers from a safe distance every day. You'll be fine."

Ava turned to CJ and shot her the same look she'd just given Jordan.

Outside, there was a loud whirring sound as the machine blasted the plane wing with some kind of chemical.

"Okay," Ava said. "Now I'm nervous about the plane. I should have brought a magazine or something."

"Oh," CJ said. "I almost forgot. I have something for you."

It took a little maneuvering for CJ to bend her tall body enough to reach her backpack under the seat in front of her. She pulled a book out of it and handed it to Ava.

"A biography of Franklin Roosevelt," Ava said, running her hand along the cover. "Thanks?" She opened it and found an inscription on the front page. "A little inspiration in case you ever decide to run for president. XOXO, Clarke."

CJ reached over and shut the book. "I forgot I wrote that. Sorry. It was originally supposed to be for Wyatt."

Jordan peered at the book. "This is an incredibly weird thing to regift, *Clarke*."

"Just trust me," CJ said. "You can skip the parts on Franklin. Read up on Eleanor. I think you'll find it interesting."

Ava set the book in her lap. The deicing truck was backing away from the plane. A flight attendant's voice crackled over the PA and told them that they would be departing shortly. There was no turning back now. Jordan and CJ each took one of Ava's hands and squeezed.

The takeoff was bumpy but they soon leveled off, and once the threat of death was behind them, CJ and Jordan fell asleep almost immediately. There was no way Ava could sleep. She was too anxious. She looked out the window, and the clouds brought back a memory of sitting next to her mom on a flight like this one. A million memories, actually. Her mom had traveled a lot for work when Ava was young and she'd always brought Ava with her. Ava would spend every flight staring out the window, sure that her mom had the coolest job in the world.

Ava shifted in her seat and tried to shake off the memory. She could feel the guilt creeping in and was worried that it might make her lose her nerve. With her phone off and CJ and Jordan both passed out next to her, she picked up the book CJ had given her as a distraction. As instructed, she skipped the parts about Franklin Roosevelt and dropped right into Eleanor. Ava already knew a lot of the information from AP US History. She knew that Eleanor had essentially redefined the role of the first lady and that a lot of historians even thought that Eleanor might have been president herself had the world not still been a raging ball of sexism at the time. Her list of accomplishments was certainly impressive. Was this what CJ wanted her to see?

Ava really didn't care about an impressive woman doing impressive things. Stories like these always made Ava feel inadequate. But since the only thing she feared more than not living up to her potential was being alone with her thoughts, Ava kept reading. After another couple of pages, she learned what she had never been taught in history class. Eleanor Roosevelt suffered from depression.

How did Ava not know this? Why didn't anyone ever teach her this? She devoured the chapter. Eleanor Roosevelt was a timid wife when her husband pushed her into the spotlight. It was only because she was forced to, that she found her voice. But, boy oh boy, did she find it. It wasn't just that she had depression. She wasn't ashamed of it. The first lady of the United States of America was open and honest about her struggles. She even gave her dark periods a cutesy nickname. She would tell family and friends that she was "in one of her Griselda moods." Ava loved it. Griselda moods. Somehow the name made it sound so much more dignified. And so much less terrifying.

By the time she was done with the book, Ava was sure of two things: (1) Their history teacher had never taught them any of the really important stuff, and (2) it was an absolute shame that the world was a raging ball of sexism at the time, because Eleanor Roosevelt would have been one hell of a president.

Ava flipped to the front of the book and reread CJ's inscription. *A little inspiration in case you ever decide to run for president.*

She closed the book and shook Jordan and CJ awake. "We're here."

————————

Martha wasn't exactly jealous that her friends were in California without her. It's not like they were there for a rocking good time or anything. Still, she wished she was with them. She'd thought about trying to buy a ticket. She'd even looked at flights. The cheapest one was almost four hundred dollars. She wouldn't even let her brain calculate how many hours she'd have to work at the movie theater to pay for that.

So instead of accompanying her friends on an emotional journey that they would no doubt remember for the rest of their lives, Martha boarded the smelly city bus that would take her as close to her mom's house as she could get with public transportation. Her mom still hadn't given her the financial aid form. Her dad's had been a mess, but at least he'd done it. Her mom, on the other hand, had given her nothing but excuses. Martha decided that the only way she was going to get it was to show up and stand there while her mom filled it out.

The bus ride was long and Martha picked at her nail polish, letting it fall to the floor in little flakes. Her mom was waiting for her on the sidewalk when the bus dropped her off.

"It's freezing," Martha said as she came down the bus steps. "You could have waited in the car."

Martha wished her mom had waited in the car. She wanted to be mad. It was easier to be mad when her mom didn't do kind things.

"It's good to see you." They stood there awkwardly for a second, and Martha wondered if maybe they should hug, but the moment passed. "Come on. The car is this way."

Twenty minutes later, they pulled into the poorly shoveled driveway of the house. Martha's mom told her, with some level of amusement, that the twins had done the job for twenty bucks apiece and wasn't that adorable?

"Adorable," Martha said. It was more than twice her hourly wage. The house was obnoxiously warm and smelled like cinnamon. Her mom offered her tea, and Martha said okay even though she didn't really like tea all that much.

"So," her mom said as she set the kettle on the stove, "how's your dad?"

"He's good. He's on a much more normal work schedule."

"Good for him."

Martha shifted on the Pottery Barn stool and drummed her fingers against the marble countertop. "I need those forms, Mom. The financial aid ones."

Her mom sighed. "I know. We're working on it."

"Mom. I really need them. Like now. Like two weeks ago, actually. But I'll settle for now."

Her mom grabbed two tea bags from the cupboard and dropped them into matching mugs. "Roger is the one with the information, and I can't make him move any faster."

"Well, can I talk to him, then?" Martha never knew if she should call him Roger or Mr. Russell. She got around the whole thing by only ever referring to him as a pronoun.

"I've spoken with him, Martha. He's working on it."

Martha kicked her feet into the white baseboards of the counter. It would leave scuff marks and drive her mom crazy. She didn't care. Or maybe she did care and that's why she was doing it.

When the teakettle whistled, her mom poured hot water into their mugs and set a timer for two minutes. It was a tea timer. A small silver device with only one purpose in the world. To properly time tea. It made Martha almost as irate as the poorly shoveled front driveway.

"Mom. If I don't get those forms—"

"You will get the forms. It's complicated."

"Why is it complicated?"

Her mom set the kettle back on the stove with a bit too much force. "It's adult stuff. Not your problem to worry about." She sat on the stool next to Martha. "Now. Tell me what's going on with the park."

"Nothing is going on." After Ava's birth mother had entered her friends' thoughts, the park had faded from them. She didn't even know why her mom was asking. Maybe she wanted her steak knife back.

Her mom blew across the top of her tea. "I'm sorry you and your friends won't get to leave your names behind."

Martha shrugged. "It's fine." She thought again of the knife. It seemed so strange that her mom would have kept it for all these years. "So I guess it was a big deal. Carving your name in?"

Her mom smiled. "It was a special night." She had a faraway look, like she was remembering something. "It felt like we had our whole lives ahead of us. In this really exciting way."

Martha looked down at her tea. "Do you ever regret not going to college?"

"Of course not."

"Mom. It's okay. It's not going to bother me if you say yes." She knew she was the reason her mom didn't go to Indiana State like she was planning. "I'm almost an adult. You can tell me."

Her mom tapped her nails against the mug. They were perfectly polished. "I don't regret it," she said. "I really don't." She looked up and Martha could see that she was emotional. "Okay, maybe a little. It's impossible not to wonder how things might've turned out differently." Her mom looked down at her tea. She was staring at it so hard that Martha thought she might fall into her mug. "Martha.

Roger is really doing his best with those forms. Money is complicated. Having it is actually more complicated than not having it."

Martha seriously doubted that.

"He's talking to his accountant about the best way to proceed. But like I said, it's complicated. His income is high, but so much of it is tied up in the business. It's not accessible."

Martha wasn't sure where this was going. She sipped her tea. It tasted like an apple orchard.

"When the twins were born, Roger set up college funds. It's just what you do. I assumed your dad had done that for you. I never handled the money."

As her mom continued talking, it was hard at first to process what she was saying. Then it came into focus. Clear and sharp and certain. The reason her mom hadn't given her the forms yet wasn't out of laziness. It was because her stepfather made too much money. Martha wasn't going to be eligible for financial aid.

"So...what do I do?" Martha asked. She'd never asked her stepfather for money in her life; she hated the idea of it, but maybe her mom would offer. Maybe this would still be okay.

"I don't know, Martha. I'm so sorry." Martha felt her world close in on her. "I should have paid more attention. I just thought your dad—I just assumed he'd have his act together by now."

Martha set her tea down. She wouldn't let her mom blame her dad for this. She didn't yell or scream or cry even though she wanted to do all of those things. She simply asked for a ride back to the bus stop. On the bus, she typed out a frantic message to her friends. Then she deleted it. She didn't want Ava to have to think about this in the middle of her emotional weekend. She considered texting just CJ and Jordan, but they were busy being there for Ava. Martha didn't feel bitter about it, exactly. She just wished that someone could be there for her too. Martha stared at her phone for a long time. Finally, she thought of someone she could call. Victoria picked up after the second ring.

"Hello," she said.

"Hi," Martha said.

"What's wrong?"

Martha loved that Victoria could tell that something was wrong just by hearing a one-syllable word. "Everything. Any chance you'd want to hang out tonight?"

She could hear Victoria doing something in the background. She could also hear the moment she stopped. Victoria shifted all of her attention to Martha. "I can't. I'm on the schedule tonight."

"That's right." Victoria was covering Martha's shift for her. "I forgot. And I have my friend's art show. Don't worry about it."

"No, wait. I can talk now. What's going on?"

Martha felt like she was going to cry. She didn't want to cry on the bus. There was a guy sitting across the aisle from her and he was staring. She felt like shouting, *Mind your own business!* She turned her back to him. "Never mind," she said to Victoria. "Don't worry about it."

"Martha."

"Seriously. I'll talk to you later. Bye."

She hung up quickly. Almost immediately, her phone buzzed with Victoria calling her back. She sent it to voice mail and stared out the window. She'd be fine. This was all going to be fine. She'd figure out a way to handle this on her own. She always had before.

CHAPTER **NINETEEN**

THE STUDENT tour guide walked backward and used her hands a lot. CJ hated her. It's not that her exuberance wasn't appreciated; it's just that she was really dragging this tour out and Ava already looked like she was going to leap out of her skin. She hadn't said much since they'd gotten to California. She didn't have to. Her terror was visible.

CJ had hoped that seeing Stanford would be disappointing. It would have made it easier when they inevitably rejected her. Unfortunately, it was stunning. Even more beautiful than the version of it she'd dreamed. The tour guide pointed out Hoover Tower, the famous (and famously phallic) building at the center of campus. It made CJ tear up. She couldn't help it. The tower reminded her of the vase that Wyatt's mom had given her. She loved that vase with all its imperfections. In a lot of ways, it reminded her of herself. A giant mess with a huge heart. She wished Wyatt was here now. She felt increasingly like a fraud as they walked across campus. He would say something to make her laugh and remind her that she didn't need an acceptance letter to know she was valuable.

As soon as the tour was over and they'd adequately instagrammed it (Ava's mom followed her on social media and they figured she'd be checking in), they asked the tour guide to point them toward the bus stop. The three of them squeezed into one row and didn't say much as the bus drove them across town. CJ peered out the window, watching as the scenery evolved from mansions to small houses and apartment complexes.

The bus let them off just a few blocks from Ava's mother's apartment, and they walked the rest of the way there. The apartment building was one of the nicer ones on the block, and CJ looked over to see how Ava was reacting. She was blank. She'd been blank all day. She'd also barely eaten. "You ready?" CJ asked.

Ava nodded. The movement was so slight, it was almost imperceptible.

Jordan took off her backpack and pulled out a box of candy bars. The plan was for her to knock on the door and say that she was selling candy to raise money for her school. They'd already looked up the name of the local high school— Menlo-Atherton—and Jordan had memorized the mascot and even a couple of teachers' names in case it came up.

"Okay," Jordan said. "I'm going in."

As Jordan walked across the street, CJ felt Ava's hand reach for hers. They watched Jordan knock. Then they watched her knock again.

"Maybe she's at work," CJ said.

Ava said nothing.

The woman who lived next door to Ava's mom came up to her door with bags of groceries, and CJ could see Jordan say something to her. She squinted to try to read their lips, but it was too far and CJ couldn't read lips anyway. A minute later, Jordan took one of the grocery bags from her and disappeared inside the apartment.

"Um…" CJ said. "What do you think is happening?"

Ava said nothing.

A minute later, Jordan reappeared without her box of candy. She jogged back and CJ pounced on her. "What happened? Who was that? Where's your candy?"

"She bought it all," Jordan said. "She was so nice. We have to donate this money to the school or something. I felt horrible lying to her."

Ava's voice was tiny next to them. "Did she say anything about Isabel?"

"I didn't want to sound creepy so I kept it really general. I asked if she knew if the woman next door would maybe buy some candy, but she said she's not around." Jordan paused. "She said that Isabel is in the hospital."

"Did she say why?" Ava asked.

Jordan shook her head. "No. But I was like, Stanford Hospital, and then she was like, no, the junky one up the road."

"The junkie one?" Ava repeated. "Like she's a junkie?"

"Let's not make any assumptions until we get there," said CJ.

"I don't know if I want to go there," said Ava. But a second later, she spoke again. "I have to go there."

CJ grabbed a Lyft and it dropped them off in front of a small hospital. It was pretty obvious that if this is where Isabel was getting treatment, it wasn't for anything good.

CJ and Jordan followed Ava inside, and stood on either side of her as she walked up to the nurse at reception. The nurse greeted her in Spanish and Ava had to shake her head.

"I'm sorry, I don't speak—"

"How can I help you?" the nurse barked in impatient English.

"I'm looking…" Ava said in a meek voice. "I'm looking for a patient. Isabel Castillo."

The nurse seemed very confused. "A patient?"

"Yes," said Ava.

Right then, there was a loud crash. Everyone in the room turned and stared at the woman who had just dropped a mug of coffee on the floor. She stood there in her white lab coat surrounded by spilled coffee and ceramic shards. She was staring right at Ava. She was staring so hard it was uncomfortable. There was something familiar about her, but CJ couldn't quite place her. It all clicked into place when CJ saw the name on her security badge. DR. ISABEL CASTILLO. This was Ava's mother.

Martha was completely underdressed for the Coventry Art Gallery. Her jeans and faded black Converse stood out in a room of polished blazers and Chelsea boots. She hadn't even bothered to put makeup on. She felt stupid for not realizing that this would be a fancy affair.

A woman wearing the coolest pair of knee-high boots that Martha had ever seen walked up to her. "I can check that for you," she said, motioning to Martha's coat.

"Oh, that's okay. I can just hold it." Martha had to raise her voice to be heard over the music that seemed to be coming from everywhere.

"We're requiring everyone to check their coats tonight." Martha hesitated and the woman shifted, impatient. "It's to prevent people from bumping into the art. And there's no charge." She added that last part with an inflection that seemed condescending.

Martha peeled off her coat and handed it to the woman. "Oh, wait." She took off her hat and shoved it into the pocket. "Thanks."

Martha walked through the gallery, feeling small and foolish among the chic crowd. She wondered what Martha Washington would think if she could see this. She'd probably be embarrassed and disappointed that her offspring was such a misfit. The paintings of Martha Washington always showed her as a matronly old lady in a bonnet, but that was only because the history books liked to portray her that way. A simple woman, happy to stand in the background and let her husband shine. The truth was, Martha Washington was legendary for her style and her wealth. None of which came from George. The money was all hers. Of course, so were the slaves. That was the other thing the history books liked to gloss over.

Martha (the current Martha, not the long-dead racist) walked into the next room and heard someone call her name.

"Martha."

She turned. It was Logan. She'd never been more relieved to see anyone in her life. "Hi," she said. "Please tell me you know where her painting is?"

He motioned behind him. Martha felt an immediate surge of pride when she saw it. She'd seen this painting before, but not like this. Not on the wall of a gallery with proper lighting and a crowd of impressed onlookers.

"Oh my god," Martha said.

"I know. I've been through the entire gallery. The whole collection is good. But hers…"

Martha nodded. She knew exactly what he meant. It stood out. You couldn't take your eyes off it. "I wish Ava was here to see this."

"Me too." He paused, then shifted. "Have you heard from her? I texted." He shifted again. "She never responded."

Martha shook her head. "Not from her. But Jordan and CJ have been sending me updates."

"And?"

Martha shared the last information she'd heard. They were on their way to a hospital where Ava's mom was possibly a patient. Logan processed it. "Thanks. Keep me posted, would you? I just want to know that she's doing okay."

Martha nodded and said, "Yeah, sure," and she must have looked as torn up as she felt because he tilted his head slightly to the side and asked, "Are *you* okay?"

"Yeah," she answered by rote. Then she shifted almost immediately. "No, actually. I'm not." Martha was so desperate to unburden herself to someone. Anyone. She wanted to tell him the truth. *Needed* to. "I'm not okay, Logan. I'm not okay at all."

The volume of the room rose at that exact moment with a burst of conversation and laughter. The voices echoed off the walls and the sound felt personal. Like it was trying to swallow her up and drown her out. Logan moved closer so she could hear him over the din. "What's going on?" he asked.

She leaned closer. Their arms touched. She told him about the long bus ride and the tea that tasted like an apple orchard and the moment she found out that she wasn't eligible for financial aid.

"Shit," Logan said.

"I'm scared. I don't know what I'm going to do."

The entire room seemed to be laughing. She knew they weren't laughing at her, but it felt like it. She looked back at Ava's painting. The crowd was enamored with it. Martha had never been jealous of her friends before. Not once. The girls always existed as a singular unit, and their successes felt like they were hers too. Tonight something shifted. She didn't want to drift into the background while they shined. She wanted to do something remarkable with her life too. But how was she supposed to do that when she couldn't even pay for college? The tears sprang to her eyes. She quickly wiped them away with the back of her sleeve. "Oh my god. Sorry. I don't know what's wrong with me."

Logan grabbed her hand. "Martha. It's okay." It was a friendly gesture. Just a kind thing. But she needed a kind thing right then. She needed it so badly. He squeezed her hand, and by instinct, she squeezed back. Twice.

She stared up at Logan and didn't let go. Her hand was

still in his when she realized they were being watched. Victoria stood in the doorway. She looked gutted.

Martha woke up from wherever she'd been and dropped Logan's hand immediately. "Victoria."

Victoria turned and walked away.

The crowd was so thick that Martha had a hard time catching up to her. By the time she reached the lobby, Victoria was gone. Martha didn't pause to find the coat-check lady. She didn't pause for anything. She sprinted right out the door and chased after Victoria. It had started snowing and thick white flakes fluttered all around her. Martha shivered and ran faster. Thank god Victoria's legs were so short or Martha would never have caught up to her. "Victoria!" Martha shouted.

The girl who was named for Queen Victoria but wasn't related to Queen Victoria whirled around. She seemed surprised to see Martha standing there. She was especially surprised to see her with no coat and no hat. "What are you doing?" Victoria asked. "You'll freeze to death."

Martha didn't answer. "I thought you were working tonight."

Victoria's smile was conflicted and hurt. "I asked my uncle to cover for me. You sounded so…" Victoria shifted. "You sounded like you needed a friend. I didn't mean to interrupt."

"You weren't interrupting anything."

"It's fine. I don't want to get in your way. I didn't realize that...So you and Dinglehopper, huh?"

"No. No, no, no. He was just comforting me." Martha was absolutely freezing. She blew on her hands and shoved them into her pockets. "Please come back. We can talk."

"About what?"

The snow was coming down hard, and Martha had to squint to keep it out of her eyes. Victoria was squinting too. It made everything so much more confusing. It was so hard to read the emotion on her face.

"Just come back. It's cold." Martha shivered hard.

"I know. I'm going home. Go back to the gallery. You're going to freeze out here."

"I'm fine. I'm totally fine."

"No, you're not." Victoria took off her hat and offered it to Martha.

Martha shook her head. "I'm not taking your hat."

Victoria didn't take no for answer. She put it on Martha's head and pulled it down over her ears. "I'm not mad or anything," she said. "I'm just hurt. I misread something. But that's not your fault."

She turned and walked away, leaving Martha to wonder: *Are you hurt because you have feelings for Logan? Or are you hurt because you have feelings for me?*

The snow swirled around her and Martha shivered. She

was too cold to do anything other than walk back to the gallery to retrieve her coat.

———————

"Do you like bagels?"

This was the first thing Ava's birth mom said to her after CJ and Jordan left and it was just the two of them staring at each other.

"The cafeteria here isn't great, but they have bagels. We can grab a couple and talk. Or just coffee. Or water."

"I'm fine," said Ava.

They sat across from each other at a long table under bright fluorescent lights. The room was packed with people, but everyone was in their own world and nobody looked twice at Ava and Isabel.

"I guess you have a lot of questions," Isabel said after a little bit of silence. "Ask me anything you want."

Ava knew exactly where she wanted to start. "How did you know what I look like?"

The cafeteria was loud enough that their conversation felt private. "Your mother sends me a letter and a picture every year. On your birthday."

Ava felt her body go numb. She set her hands on the table because she was afraid she might collapse. "I didn't know that."

"I'm the one who asked for those terms. Lynn was just following my wishes."

"Why?" Ava's voice had an edge of anger.

Isabel sighed in this huge weighty way that was filled with so many complicated emotions that Ava couldn't even begin to define them all. "A lot of shame. A lot of embarrassment. I thought it might be harder for you if you knew." Isabel shook her head like she wanted to back up. "Not true. I convinced myself of that for a long time. But the truth is, I knew it would be harder for *me*. I didn't want you to know my face. I could handle you hating me if I was just this abstract idea of a mother. But if you knew me..."

"I don't hate you."

Isabel grabbed the table in the same way Ava had just done.

"I don't," Ava repeated.

"Would you like to know why I made the decision I did?"

Ava nodded.

"I don't know if this will be a good thing to hear or the opposite. But I came very close to keeping you. *Very* close. I'd already applied to medical school when I found out I was pregnant. But then the rejections started coming in and I thought it was a sign. Medical school had always been my dream, but maybe it wasn't meant to be. It seemed like the universe had another plan for me. I thought maybe that plan was you."

Ava looked down.

"Things with my boyfriend weren't great, but they weren't terrible. It was a life that I could see. I'd been wait-listed at Stanford and never in a million years thought I'd get in. But then the letter came. I was standing there seven months pregnant holding a letter telling me that I'd gotten my dream. My mom, your *abuela*, used to light a candle in her church in Mexico City and pray that she could give me a better life. She risked so much to come to the United States, and that acceptance letter felt like everything she'd fought to give me. I know that sounds like I'm using her sacrifice to justify what I did. But I'm not. In a lot of ways it made it harder. My mom would have been so disappointed with me if she knew what I did."

Ava looked up only to find that Isabel was the one looking away now. It was too hard for her to make eye contact.

"She died a couple years before you were born. I knew she would have wanted me to keep you. But I would have been living my life for her. I had to live it for me."

There was regret in her words, but also strength.

"The adoption agency sent me a lot of letters from different families. When I read Lynn's…" Isabel coughed and Ava knew it was to cover the emotion. "She wanted you so badly. And I wanted you to have that kind of life. A life where you were…" Another cough. Isabel took a deep breath. In and out. "I wanted you in the arms of someone who was ready for you."

"I understand," Ava said. "At least I think I understand."

"It's okay if you don't. I should have explained earlier. I should have agreed to meet you four years ago."

Ava looked up. "What do you mean?"

"When Lynn contacted me." Ava stared at the table. She didn't want Isabel to know that she wasn't aware of this part. "She said you were asking. I thought about it. I really did. I just couldn't. I don't have a better answer than that. I just couldn't."

Ava remembered back to the day when her mom told her that she'd decided Ava wasn't ready to meet her biological mom. It was a lie. A beautiful one. One that protected her from feeling rejected at a time when she needed to feel loved.

"What other questions do you have?" Isabel asked.

"Do you hate cilantro?"

Isabel laughed. "That one is much easier to answer. I hate it with a passion."

"Me too. I thought I was the only Mexican in the world who didn't like it. Do your thumbs bend back?"

Isabel held out her thumb and bent it into a weird angle. Ava raised hers and did the same.

"Are you artistic?"

Isabel smiled like the question brought up something bittersweet. "Not at all. That you get from your father."

Her father. Ava had wondered about him before. Though never with the same intensity that she thought about Isabel.

"I haven't talked to him in more than a decade. Last I heard, he was working as a graphic designer at Electronic Arts. He's so talented. But nothing like you. Lynn has sent me a lot of your work."

Ava could feel the emotion in her throat. Like a giant ball. She steered the conversation to something safe to keep it from leveling her. "Favorite subject?"

"Science and math."

Ava shook her head. "Not me. Art and English. And history."

Ava asked a few more questions that didn't really matter. She was working her way up to the big one, the thing she really wanted to know. "Do you get sad sometimes?"

Isabel put her hand to her heart. "Oh, Ava. Oh god. Yes. Not a day goes by that I don't feel sad about the choice I made."

Ava looked down. "Oh. I didn't mean...I mean, thanks. But I mean do you ever get sad. Like...for no reason."

Isabel took the hand that had been on her heart and set it down on the table. She drew small circles with her index finger. "I guess you got a lot more from me than just your eyes." Isabel sighed again. This one was the most complicated of them all. "Yeah. I have depression. It's a lot better with medication. But I still have bad days."

"Me too," Ava said.

"I'm really sorry you got that from me."

"It's okay. I think I got some good stuff too."

Isabel looked over Ava's head, and Ava could tell that she was looking at the clock.

"I guess you probably have to go."

Isabel nodded. "I work out of two hospitals, and I have a second shift starting pretty soon. I volunteer here because it's my community. They're really underfunded. That's why it doesn't look like much."

"The junky hospital," Ava said.

Isabel eyed her curiously. "Yeah. That's what my neighbor calls it. How did you…? Actually, back up even further. How did you find me?"

"A guy at school helped me out."

"Wow. Nice guy."

"Yeah. I think maybe he is."

"Well…" Isabel stood. "I'm not really sure how we end this. If you want, it doesn't have to be the end. You can contact me with more questions or anything else."

"That would be nice."

The table was between them so a hug seemed awkward, but everything about this had been awkward, so they leaned over and gave it a shot anyway.

Isabel left and Ava waited until she was gone to text Jordan and CJ. They walked through the door of the cafeteria thirty seconds later.

"We were right outside," Jordan said.

"You okay?" CJ asked.

Ava could tell that her friends were trying not to pounce. She could also tell that they really wanted to. "Yeah," she said. "I'm okay. I'm...good. Let's get out of here. I'm ready to go home."

CHAPTER **TWENTY**

THE GIRLS returned from their Stanford trip late in the evening on Sunday. The next morning, Ava woke up in one of her Griselda moods. The emotion of the weekend combined with the exhaustion was simply too much. She wasn't scared this time. Well, not *as* scared. She knew she would get through it. She also knew that she needed to ask for help. She found her mom in the kitchen and said that she couldn't go to school today and that she needed to see Dr. Clifford. Everything else tumbled out pretty quickly after that. Logan Diffenderfer's offer. The real reason for the Stanford weekend. Isabel Castillo.

Her mom's eyes got pretty wide, but she didn't freak out. At least not on the outside. She told Ava that she would call the school and let them know she was sick and then she'd call Dr. Clifford to book an appointment for as soon as possible. She did suggest that they make it a family session and Ava thought that seemed like a good idea. Ava crawled back into bed while her mom made the calls.

Not long after that, there was a light knock on the door. "Can I come in?"

Ava said yes.

Her mom sat down at the edge of the bed. "Dr. Clifford can see us later today."

Ava turned toward her mom. "Don't you need to go to work?"

Her mom smoothed the hair out of Ava's face and tucked it behind her ear. "I called in sick too."

"You didn't have to do that."

"Oh, Ava. We're in this together, okay?"

Ava nodded again. It was the only thing she had the energy to do.

"I know it's not as good as having your friends here, but if you want, I could lie down with you for a little while. Unless you want me to leave you alone?"

Ava shook her head. "No. Stay."

Ava's mom crawled into her bed and nestled next to her. She didn't say anything, but Ava felt safer having her there.

"I'm sorry, Mom. I'm so sorry I didn't tell you."

"I'm sorry I didn't tell *you*. About Isabel. About the letters."

"You couldn't. I get it. Thank you for writing them. And, Mom?"

"Yeah, hon?" she said, rubbing Ava's back.

"Thank you for fighting for me to stay in my advanced classes."

Her mom's expression changed. "You deserved to be there. Depression is not your fault, and there was no fucking way I was going to let them punish you for it."

Ava had never heard her mom swear before. She liked it. Next to her, her mom stared at the ceiling. "I'm sorry for not understanding right away."

"What do you mean?"

"When all of this first started. I thought you were just moody. It seemed like normal teenager stuff. Then it got bigger and I still thought we could handle it ourselves. I read this article online about cutting out gluten. That was a fail. Then there was this research that said endorphins helped. I thought if I could just get you out the door and exercising."

Ava turned to face her mom. "That's why you were always trying to get me to jog with you?"

"I know. It was ridiculous."

"No. It's... You were trying. You didn't know. You were doing your best."

"I think I just made you feel worse. It helped me, though.

I was feeling so scared and overwhelmed back then. Jogging really did make me feel better."

"I'm glad."

"We're going to get you back in a better place too. We're going to figure this out." Her mom cozied into her and held her tightly. "I'll be right here. As long as it takes. I'll be right here."

Ava closed her eyes, and for the first time in a long time, she felt that everything was going to be okay.

———

Jordan hadn't spoken with Scott or even exchanged a single text with him since that night in front of Martha's. That's why she was so surprised to find a voice mail from him when she turned on her phone after their flight from San Francisco landed back in Cleveland.

Uh, hey. It's Scott. Mercer. Anyway, can you call me back?

He'd sounded nervous. Which made her nervous. It was too late to call him then, and she'd planned on phoning him first thing in the morning. That was before her little brother came to her in a state of complete panic because he'd just remembered that he was supposed to be giving an oral presentation on the Great Depression. The only thing he currently knew about it was that it had happened in the United States and that it was depressing. Jordan gave him a crash course and helped him put together note cards so he could remember everything.

Then she was going to call Scott on the way to school. Her phone rang just as she was about to dial. It was CJ. "Did we know that Martha's mom totally screwed her on financial aid?" CJ was somewhere that echoed.

"No. What happened?"

"I don't have the whole story. Diffenderfer told me about it. I met up with him in the cafeteria this morning so I could get Friday's history notes."

"I'm almost to school. Let's grab Ava and we can all corner Martha. With love, I mean."

"Didn't you see Ava's text?"

"No. What's it say?"

CJ read it. " 'In a Griselda mood and staying home today. Mom's here with me and she's being awesome so don't worry. I'll be okay. *Double hand squeeze.*' The double hand squeeze is in asterisks. Like it's an action."

"Yeah. I get it," said Jordan. "What's a Griselda mood?"

"Just get here. I'll find Martha."

Martha told them about the terrible conversation with her mom. She seemed okay, though. Weirdly okay. They asked her what she was going to do, and she said, "I don't know. Cleveland State, I guess. Even if I get only a partial scholarship, I can still make it work, I think."

Martha may have been okay with it, but Jordan wasn't.

She was furious all day. It wasn't fair that anyone should have to miss out on their dream college because of something as stupid as money. Martha deserved better. She was still pissed off about it after school when she was walking to her car. Her phone rang. It was Scott. She'd completely forgotten about him.

"Hi," she said, cringing as she picked up. "Sorry I haven't called back yet."

"You're avoiding me, aren't you?"

"No. Things keep coming up." She climbed into her car and turned on the heat as quickly as possible. It was freezing.

"I was worried you'd figured out I was calling for inappropriate—"

Her phone switched over to Bluetooth, and she completely missed the rest of his sentence in the transition. "What?"

"What do you mean what?"

"I lost you for a second. You cut out at"—her heart was beating fast now—" 'inappropriate.' "

"Maybe it's good I cut out."

"Why? What were you going to say?"

"Never mind. How are you? So you were out of town this weekend?"

Jordan's windows fogged up as she sat there. "Yeah. A quick trip with my friends."

"Cool. Where'd you go?"

"Uh...California."

"Whoa. Big trip. Weather must have been nice."

"It was." Jordan was confused about where this conversation was going. He didn't seem to be calling about the park. And if he wasn't calling about that, then what was he calling for?

"Hey, Scott. What were you going to say before? When you cut out?"

He coughed slightly, and she could tell he was embarrassed. "Nothing. Forget it."

Her windows were completely covered in steam now. She couldn't see anything outside the bubble of her car. "Please tell me."

He sighed, like he was mustering his courage. "We hadn't talked since the night I drove you home. But I've been thinking about you. A lot."

Her windows got even steamier.

"Right before your roommate walked up, I was thinking how cool you are and..." He laughed at his own awkwardness. "Oh, screw this. Jordan, do you want to grab dinner this weekend?"

Jordan swallowed. Hard. "Like a date?"

"Yeah. Like a date."

Jordan had never been asked out on a date before. Not in any real way. With Logan, things had happened slowly.

Months of simmering tension until that one day when he looked over at her and wondered if he could hold her hand.

"I can't," Jordan said.

"Oh."

It was almost painful to say no. She had to, though. Didn't she? Even though they weren't that far apart in age, she was at an age that mattered. She didn't feel like a kid anymore, but technically and legally she still was. That's when she remembered something. "I mean, I can't go out this weekend. But I could in a few weeks."

"Oh," he said, relaxing.

"Yeah. I'm busy with something right now. In three weeks, I'll be...not busy." She gave him an exact date.

He told her he'd put it in his calendar, and she said she'd do the same. She didn't need to, though. It wasn't a date she'd forget. It was her eighteenth birthday.

After they hung up, Jordan sat there for a second. Her entire body felt like it was on fire even though her car's heater was struggling against the cold. She let her mind run away with the fantasy of Scott. His beautiful blue eyes and his important suits. The fact that he was an adult and that he made her feel like she was one too.

Suddenly Jordan's passenger's side door flew open. She was so startled, she actually screamed.

Martha hopped in. "Sorry." She rubbed her hands together frantically and blew on them. "It is f'ing freezing out there. Will you drive me to work?" Martha turned and made her hands into a begging gesture. "I'm worried I might literally die if I have to wait at the bus stop."

Jordan nodded. "Sure. Yeah. No problem. Not a problem at all."

"Is something wrong?" Martha asked, still blowing on her hands.

"No. Nope. Everything's good. Great. How are you?"

"God, it's steamy in here," Martha said.

Jordan turned the ignition. Then she looked over at Martha. "Is that a new hat?"

Martha touched the knit cap. It was pink and frilly, not at all Martha's style. It looked good on her, though.

CJ sat in her car for a full ten minutes before going into the rec center. She wanted to tell Wyatt everything about the weekend. About how seeing Stanford was weirdly painful and made her feel like she wasn't good enough. About how strong Ava had been and how proud she felt. About how much she missed Martha and how it made her realize they would all be somewhere different next year. She wanted to tell him that she was overwhelmed and scared.

When she finally worked up the courage to walk inside, they exchanged an awkward hello.

"Hi, Clarke. How was Stanford?"

"Great," she said.

She wanted to tell him a million things. But she couldn't. Because she'd screwed up everything.

Dakota wheeled herself over excitedly.

"CJ. CJ! My ex-friend got a herpes."

"Dakota!" Her mother was right behind her. "What did I say?" Margaret turned to CJ to explain. "Her friend, former friend, has a cold sore." CJ could tell that Margaret was trying to be adult about the whole thing, but it was impossible to miss the tiniest hint of a smile on her face. "It's a bad one."

"Everyone was making fun of it." Dakota's voice was quaking with excitement. "It was the best day ever. I believe in karma now."

"I feel like maybe we didn't learn the right lesson here," said Margaret.

"What? I didn't laugh. I just felt happy that everyone else did."

Margaret shrugged and CJ turned to her. "Do you mind if I talk to Dakota alone for a minute?"

"Please do."

Margaret gave the two of them some space. CJ knelt down so that she was at Dakota's eye level.

"Are you going to lecture me about making fun of people?" Dakota asked.

CJ shook her head. "No. I wanted to let you know that

we're starting volleyball today. I know that was the sport you were playing when…" The sentence didn't need to be finished. "I think it's going to be really fun. But I also know you don't have very good memories of it. So if you need a little extra time getting out there or if you wanted to talk a little before you play, I'm here. Okay?"

Dakota nodded. "Okay."

"I think you've got this." CJ put her fist out. Dakota put hers out to meet it. They blew it up.

Dakota didn't play aggressively that day, but she did play. CJ was proud and wished she could share it with Wyatt. She looked over at him and smiled. He didn't smile back, but he didn't look away either. He gave her a small meaningful nod. It gave her hope.

When the session was over, CJ hung around. She wanted to talk to Wyatt without any of the parents or kids.

"Hey," she said, walking up to him.

"Hey," he said. "Today was good, I think."

"I think so too."

She thought about everything she wanted to say to him. How he was the kindest, most hilarious, and most wonderful person she'd ever met. How she couldn't stop thinking about him.

"I…I…" She started and stopped. Started and stopped. "I'm really glad that Dakota had a good day."

"Me too," he said.

Ava's mom tapped on her bedroom door. The light was gray outside, and at first, Ava wasn't sure if it was night or morning.

"Your friend from school is here to drop off your homework."

Ava looked at the time on her phone. Night. It was nighttime. The appointment with Dr. Clifford had been short. She'd adjusted Ava's medication and given her a prescription for Ativan to help with her anxiety. She also suggested that they meet again for a longer session in a few days. While Ava's mom went to the pharmacy, Ava crawled back into bed. She'd slept the entire afternoon.

"I told him it's probably better that he just drop it off, but he asked if he could say hi."

He? Ava sat up straighter. "Okay. I'll be right out."

In the living room, she found Logan Diffenderfer sitting awkwardly on the linen sectional. He got up when she walked in and made a motion like he might hug her, but then he pulled back. "Hi," he said, sitting back down. "I sent you a bunch of texts, but you didn't respond."

"I haven't looked at my phone all day."

They could hear Ava's mom banging around in the kitchen. Given that her mom had absolutely no idea how to cook, Ava figured that this was just a cover so she could stay close by.

"My mom said you brought my homework?"

"Not really. It's all online. I just wanted an excuse to see you."

"Oh?" Ava was proud of herself for holding his gaze. "Why?"

Logan shifted uncomfortably. "Uh...well...I, uh..." Ava had never seen Logan flustered before. It was weird. It was also charming. "I was worried about you. It was such a big weekend, and then Jordan said you were out sick today. When you didn't return my texts..."

"I'm not sick. I mean, technically, yes. But I don't have a cold or anything. I have depression."

"Oh," he said. "I didn't know that."

"Not a lot of people do. I used to be embarrassed about it, but I'm not anymore. It's just this thing I have." It felt good to say it out loud.

If Logan was freaked out, he didn't show it. "I'm glad you told me."

"Logan," she said, "do you still want to know why I hate you?"

He answered without hesitation. "Yes."

Her mom came out from the kitchen holding a spatula like a prop, which it basically was. "Do you kids want dinner?"

Ava wanted to kill her mom. Then she remembered how amazing she'd been today and felt bad about it. "We're fine, Mom. Can we have a minute, please?"

Her mom disappeared back into the kitchen. Ava sat down on the couch next to Logan.

"Do you remember freshman year when the school was going to drop me out of advanced classes?"

Logan shifted in an uncomfortable way. "Um…"

"I know that you know. I know because I heard you talking about it."

Logan looked down. "Shit." She could tell he was remembering. "That day at cross-country practice."

She nodded. "I was under the bleachers."

"Why?"

"Because I was having a really bad day and I couldn't be in class anymore. I took the bathroom pass and that's where I ended up."

She remembered hearing his voice. She remembered the sound of the coach's whistle. It terrified her because it made her realize that school was over. She'd been sitting under the bleachers for more than five hours. That was the moment she knew something was really wrong with her. She tried to speak. She tried to ask for help. She was going to ask Logan Diffenderfer. He was her best friend's boyfriend. He was safe. He would pull her up and she would be okay. Only it wasn't okay. Logan was laughing. At her.

"You called me an idiot," Ava said.

Logan shook his head. "Shit. Ava. It had nothing to do with you."

Ava still remembered it clearly. Staring at the ground and realizing that she couldn't physically stand at the same time that Logan was talking about her. She remembered the exact words. *I can't even understand how she can be that much of an idiot and the school just doesn't care.* He was talking to Malik and Grayson from the team. They were laughing at her too. *She's so obviously dumb,* Logan had said. *The only reason they're letting her stay is because of her mom.*

Ava remembered lifting her head slightly when she heard that part. If Ava had had the emotional energy back then, she also probably would have questioned why the school didn't go through with their threat to kick her out of the advanced track. But she didn't. So she didn't know. Not until she heard it from Logan Diffenderfer. *She basically lawyered up. Sent her mom in there to yell at the principal. I heard her mom was like, "If you drop my daughter, I will make your lives a litigious nightmare, blah blah blah."* Logan had done a not-terrible imitation of her mother. *That's the only reason they didn't kick her out. They should, though. She's so dumb. Some days I look at her and I'm just like, "Are you even literate?"*

"You are not an idiot," Logan said from the couch next to her. "You were never an idiot. I was."

"I know." She said it with a slight smile. "But it took me almost four years to figure that out. I didn't know about my mom yelling at the principal. It made me feel so stupid and so weak at a time when I was already feeling stupid and weak."

"You are neither of those things." Logan sighed. "Everything I said, it had nothing to do with you."

"Then why'd you say it?"

Logan stood and walked to the fireplace. He put his hand to his temple like he couldn't believe this. "Because I was humiliated. They were kicking *me* out of advanced classes, and Malik was teasing me, and I was embarrassed."

Ava didn't know any of this.

"It was my fault, though. I'd been lazy about studying. But Mrs. Geller liked me, and she didn't think I should be punished so severely, so she told my parents what your mom had done."

Mrs. Geller taught advanced freshman English. Ava always felt self-conscious around her. You could tell she didn't believe that depression was a real thing. For a while, it made Ava not believe it either.

"She thought she was helping me out," Logan said. "She said that if my parents raised a fuss to the principal, they'd have to keep me too. But my parents wouldn't do it for me. They said that it was my fault and that I deserved the consequences. They were right. The school kicked me out for the rest of the semester. I worked my ass off, and I proved to them that they should let me back in."

Ava didn't remember him not being in class. That period of her life was such a blur.

"I had no idea," Ava said.

Logan came back to the couch and sat down next to her. "I wish I'd known. I wish you'd told me. I always thought you were such a—"

"Bitch?" she asked.

"Just to me. I couldn't figure out what I'd done. I'm sorry, Ava. *I* was an idiot and I'm sorry that I hurt you."

"I accept your apology."

"Friends?" he asked.

She nodded. He put his hand out and she shook it.

"Friends," she said. Their hands lingered for a moment before they both pulled away.

CHAPTER **TWENTY-ONE**

THE NEXT three weeks that led up to college application deadlines were some of the tensest that CJ could remember. Excluding, of course, the beginning days of Ava's depression, Martha's parents' divorce, and the time when Jordan's foot got stuck in the mall escalator, which doesn't sound like that big of a deal but was actually really scary. CJ tried to remind herself that getting into college wasn't life or death. So far it wasn't working very well.

On the day that her Stanford application was due, the girls ate lunch together in the cafeteria like they did every day. Jordan was casually scrolling through Instagram when she sat up suddenly. "Senior Superlative ballots are out." She held up her phone to show them the e-mail from the yearbook committee. CJ couldn't believe the timing. As if she wasn't already stressed enough thinking about her future, now she had to worry about her legacy as well. She grabbed Jordan's phone and looked down the list, trying to find something that sounded like her. *Best Hair, Best Eyes, Best Singer, Best Dressed, Best Body.* She crossed her arms in front of her stomach. She wasn't any of those things. She kept scanning. *Most Likely to End Up on Broadway, Most Likely to Be on a Reality Show, Most Likely to Work on Wall Street.* She wanted her classmates to remember her as someone special. Her eyes finally fell on the perfect category. *Most Likely to Be President.* That was the one. She wondered aloud if it would be tacky to vote for herself.

"Yes. It's tacky," Martha said.

Jordan took her phone back. "It's not tacky if it's true." She typed her own name in for Best Dressed.

"It's still tacky," Martha said.

"Why?" CJ asked. "If I was actually running for president, I'd vote for myself. I'd run a whole campaign. Why can't I do that for the Superlatives? Actually, don't answer that. Because I know the answer. It's because as women we're constantly taught not to advocate for ourselves. We're taught not to ask for what we deserve. Well, guess what. I deserve this. I deserve it and I'm asking for it."

CJ was cracking. She knew it. She was totally and completely cracking. It was the Stanford application. She still hadn't written a single word of her transformational experience essay, which was due tonight, and it was making her doubt everything about herself. Ava looked over at her. "If you don't calm down, I'm crushing up one of my Ativans and slipping it in your Diet Coke. Swear to god," she said. "I'll do it."

"Can I get one?" Martha asked. CJ was pretty sure she was only half joking. Martha had finished her applications, which was the easy part for her. If she didn't get a full ride, or close to it, it didn't matter where she got in. She wouldn't be able to go. CJ got angry just thinking about it.

When lunch ended, Ava grabbed CJ. "I need to talk to you for a second." She pulled CJ into a quiet corner.

"You don't have to drug me," CJ said. "I promise you. I'm fine."

"It's not that." Ava looked at her toes. "I decided to apply to Stanford. I was on the fence until literally last night."

CJ felt herself getting emotional.

"Are you okay with this?" Ava asked. "I feel like Stanford is your thing."

CJ shook her head. "Oh, Aves. I can picture you there."

Ava looked at her toes again. "I don't know. I think RISD is still my number one. But there was something about walking across the campus...even with everything else that was going on..."

CJ nodded. She knew exactly what Ava meant. Stanford

was like Hogwarts with sunshine. It was everything she'd ever wanted.

After school, CJ went straight home and sat in front of her computer. She had eight hours left. Eight hours to write something that would convince Stanford to take a shot on a girl with an average score.

Average. The word fit her. She realized that now. It wasn't just because of her score. It's who she was. Her dream had always been to change the world. To make it a better and kinder place. But how could an average girl possibly accomplish that? She thought about all her hours volunteering. Over the years, she'd jumped at every opportunity she could find. She'd built houses and she'd handed out meals and she'd sorted recycling and she'd stuffed envelopes. But the world was still the same. *She* was still the same.

Her phone buzzed with a text from Martha. Jordan's birthday was tomorrow, and they'd been working on a surprise for her. CJ responded to the text and then turned back to her computer. She read the prompt again.

Describe a transformational experience and how it has shaped you into the person you are today.

She thought about Wyatt. Then she opened Instagram to stop herself from thinking about him. Then she opened Snapchat, which she hadn't even looked at in months.

Then she looked back at her screen and tried to focus. She couldn't stop thinking about what he'd said to her. Because he was right. He *was* her transformational experience. Just not in the way he had assumed. All her life, she'd kept her true self hidden behind a perfect facade. A perfect girl with a shiny list of accomplishments and awards. He'd broken through that and found all her flaws, all her shortcomings, all the imperfections that she was so good at masking. He'd made her confront them, and he'd helped her laugh at them. He made her feel proud of who she was. Wyatt had uncovered the real CJ. And it turned out that it was the CJ she wanted to be. She was average. This time it made her smile.

She decided to call him. She got as far as lowering her thumb to his name before she stopped herself. She set her phone down. Picked it back up. Set it down again. She turned to her computer. Typed a few words. Deleted them. Typed a few words. Deleted them. Then she picked up her phone and dialed. The phone rang only once.

"Hi," said the voice on the other side of the call.

"Hey," she said. "Do you feel like going for a run?"

"God, yes," said Logan Diffenderfer.

Jordan was wearing a flirty skater dress in her signature shade of purple that looked just the right amount of sexy paired with her knee-high black faux-suede boots. She felt nervous as she gave her name to the hostess. "I'm Jordan. But I think the reservation is probably under Scott."

He'd originally made a reservation for the following night (the night of her actual birthday), but she'd overheard enough whispers to realize that her friends were also planning a surprise for her. Telling him now was almost more poetic anyway. If the date went well, they could watch the clock tick forward together. She would be eighteen at midnight. She was so excited to finally and officially be an adult. She already felt like one whenever she was around him. It's why she loved their conversations. He took her seriously. He treated her like an equal, not a child.

"Ah, yes," said the hostess. "Your date is already here." She leaned in with a conspiratorial smile and whispered, "He asked for our best table."

Jordan followed the hostess through the candlelit restaurant. Most of the tables were set for two. This was not a place for business dinners. This was a place for romance.

Scott stood and greeted her with a kiss on the cheek. "You look incredible."

"Thank you." She was nervous. God, was she nervous. She was sure the entire restaurant could hear her heart beating underneath the purple fabric of her dress.

Scott pulled her chair out for her, and Jordan saw that there was already a bottle of champagne on the table. "Oh, uh. This is really nice."

"I wanted to do something special. Since we're celebrating."

"What are we celebrating?"

"I have some news about the park."

She hadn't been expecting that. "What?"

"I think you're going to be very happy when I tell you."

He tried to pour her a glass of champagne, but she shook her head. "I...uh...I'm not much of a drinker." He set the bottle down. "What's going on with the park?"

"A lot, actually," he said. "The mayor's questions ended up having a pretty direct impact."

Jordan crossed her legs casually, trying not to look as eager as she felt. "Oh?"

"Yeah," he said with a smile. "In fact, you're getting your wish. The neighborhood won't be losing a park."

"Are you shitting me?" It exploded out of her mouth loud enough that a few heads in the quiet restaurant turned.

"No," he said, laughing. "I'm not shitting you. The developer was freaked out enough by the mayor's pressure that she was worried the whole deal might fall through. So she came forward with an incredible offer. It's going to get announced officially tomorrow."

Jordan was giddy with excitement. She thought about pouring herself some champagne. She wanted to clink her glass with his and toast the good news.

"Anyway," he said, "she's putting up a substantial amount of money for a new park."

Jordan blinked. "I'm sorry. What? A *new* park?"

"There's a parcel of unused land about half a mile from the old park. A big vacant lot."

Jordan knew the spot he was talking about. It was overgrown with weeds and scattered with litter and abandoned couches. They used to cut through it all the time until Ava scraped her leg on the rusty springs of an old mattress and had to get a tetanus shot. "It's a dump," Jordan said.

"It won't be after she drops money into it. The neighborhood gets a park *and* an office building. Everyone wins."

"Not everyone," Jordan said.

Scott leaned back and stared at her. "I'm confused. The neighborhood is getting a park. I thought you'd be excited."

It was getting a park. Just not *her* park. "What about the jungle gym?" she said. "What about the seniors who've been waiting to carve their names?"

He shrugged dismissively. "Who cares?"

Jordan cared.

"Scott. There's something I need to tell you."

He apparently wasn't too concerned about what it was, because he picked up his menu. "Sure. What?"

She took a deep breath. "Tomorrow is my birthday. Well, tonight, actually. At midnight."

He looked up from the menu. "Happy birthday. I guess we really are celebrating."

She exhaled. "Let me back up. I have a personal investment

in the park. That's why I wanted to interview the councilman. But you would never have even called me back if you knew who I was. So I lied. My name isn't Jordan James. It's Jordan Schafer."

He set his menu down.

"I lied so you wouldn't know my real age."

"How old are you?"

"I just wanted you to take me seriously. And then you did. And I got to know you. And you got to know me."

"Jordan." His voice was nervous. "How old are you?"

"I'll be eighteen at midnight."

Scott pushed back from the table so fast that he knocked his champagne glass over. It splashed all over him and all over the table. "Shit!" He stood. Jordan did too. She grabbed her napkin and tried to dab his shirt. "No." He turned away from her. "No. Don't touch me."

The hostess came rushing over with a clean towel and tried to mop up the spill.

"It's fine," Scott said. "I've got it. Please. It's fine."

"Scott." Jordan's voice caught.

The hostess backed away with the skill and grace of someone who had interrupted more than one awkward moment between couples in her time.

"Scott. I know you're surprised. But I'm still the same person."

"No." His voice was only a whisper, but it was filled with panic. "You're not."

Jordan tried to offer him her napkin, but he wouldn't take it.

"Do you have any idea what you could have done to me?" he said, dabbing his shirt more and more furiously. "My political career would have ended before it even started."

"We didn't do anything wrong. I'm an adult now. Or I will be in a few hours."

Scott looked at her with hurt and confusion. "An adult? Jordan, you're just a kid."

He took enough cash out of his wallet to pay for the champagne and set it on the table. Then he grabbed his jacket and started walking away.

"Scott. Scott, I'm sorry."

Her voice quavered and it made him stop. He turned back and looked at her, softening when their eyes met. "Happy birthday, Jordan."

"Thanks," she whispered softly.

Then he was gone.

CJ and Logan kept a slow pace for the first lap while their legs warmed up. The night was cold, and their breath stretched out in front of them in thick white puffs that fluttered and disappeared. Fluttered and disappeared.

"Did you finish your essay?" Logan asked.

"No." CJ didn't want to think about her essay. She just wanted to run.

"Are you close?"

"No."

CJ quickened her pace. Logan matched her speed.

"Did you finish yours?" CJ asked.

"Yeah. It's...done. That's all I can say. It's not great. It's not terrible. It's done."

She felt him pick up the tempo, and she moved her legs in time with his.

"I'm scared," CJ said as they settled into their new rhythm.

"Me too. What if I'm making all the wrong choices?"

CJ was more worried about not having any choices to make. She'd applied to eight schools. Seven of them were top tier. What if they didn't want her?

She ran faster. He matched her new pace. Then he ran faster and she matched his. This went on for several laps. Raise and match. Raise and match. It was unspoken that they were in a race. CJ wanted to win. She needed to win. She ran harder and harder. Faster and faster. Next to her, Logan stumbled. It was the advantage she needed to break out ahead. As she raced across the imaginary finish line, the relief exploded out of her. She could still win something. If she worked hard enough and ran fast enough, she could still win. She stopped running and turned around. Logan was right there.

"Oh," she said between deep breaths. "I thought you were farther back."

"No." He was breathless too. "I'm right here."

It was impossible to say who leaned in first. CJ only knew that one minute they were racing and the next minute they were kissing. Their lips moved together in a way that was desperate and searching, as if they both needed this more than they'd ever needed anything in their entire lives. CJ's mind went blissfully blank. She wasn't anywhere except on that track, in that exact moment, kissing Logan Diffenderfer. It took away all of her pain, all of her self-doubt, and all of her fear.

Which is why she pulled away.

"I'm sorry," she said. "I'm so sorry."

CJ ran all the way home, sat down at her computer, and wrote her essay.

Dear Stanford Admissions Committee,

I have not had the kind of experience you've asked me to write about.

I have never woken up in a hospital bed to a doctor telling me that my life had just changed forever.

I have never had to process the news that the future I worked so hard for was no longer available to me because of money.

I have never stood across the street from the mother who gave me up because I thought that just a small glimpse of her might help my world make sense.

I have never had my whole world feel like it was ending in the middle of a game of volleyball.

I have seen these experiences happen to people I love, but at most, I have only ever been a witness. I have never had a transformational experience.

I know it's only a matter of time. I know that someday the phone will ring, or there will be a knock on the door, or something will happen that will make my life forever different. I know how it will impact me, because I know how it has impacted the people I love. It will make me stronger in some ways. It will make me more vulnerable in others. It will leave a residue. But also a shine. It will be a thing that happened to me, but not the thing that defines me. It will change me in some ways. Perhaps it will change me in many ways. But it will not change who I am.

That's why I feel confident saying that the fact that I haven't had this type of experience yet does not make me any less worthy of attending your institution. I know that one single experience, one single score, or one single anything does not define me. I know exactly who I am. I am someone who deserves to attend Stanford in the fall. But I am also someone who will not be defined by the rejection if you don't agree.

Sincerely,
Clarke Josephine Jacobson

CHAPTER **TWENTY-TWO**

AVA STOOD over CJ and paced while CJ proofread her essay. It was close to midnight.

"Almost done," CJ said.

"No rush," Ava said calmly. Even though they were in a huge rush. "You missed a comma," she said and pointed.

CJ added the comma and hit the button that officially uploaded her application. She'd made the deadline with twenty minutes to spare. Now they had another deadline. Ava got her car keys out, CJ grabbed her coat, and they sprinted out the door into Ava's car. She floored it through a yellow light, and they both winced at the screeching sound her tires made when she took the corner way too fast.

Martha was waiting at the curb when they pulled up.

"Sorry we're late," Ava said as Martha opened the back door.

"It's my fault," said CJ.

"Just drive!" Martha slammed the door shut and Ava peeled off.

They pulled into Jordan's driveway with only a few minutes left. The front door was unlocked just as Jordan's parents had promised, and Martha opened it as quietly as possible given the hurry they were in. Ava unzipped the duffel bag she'd brought with her and distributed the contents between the three of them. Then they gathered outside Jordan's door and waited.

Jordan sat in her window seat looking up at the moon and wondering how everything had turned out so wrong. She was about to turn eighteen. A few hours ago, she'd felt so mature and so ready; now she felt like a foolish little girl. She looked like one too, with her legs tucked up to her chest and her sleeves pulled down around her wrists. She glanced at the clock on her phone. She had thirty seconds left. It was a strange feeling to watch time tick forward and know that absolutely nothing in her life would change. She would still be the same Jordan. There would be no great moment of clarity. No discernible shift. Nothing dramatic would happen. The seconds ticked forward. Three...two...one... she was eighteen now and everything was the same.

And that's when her bedroom door flew open.

"Happy birthday!" her friends shouted at once. There was a loud *pop pop pop* as confetti sprayed across her room. She watched as Ava, CJ, and Martha jumped into her bed, expecting to find her asleep. She laughed when CJ said, "I don't think she's in here."

"Over here," Jordan said, waving from the window seat.

Someone flipped on the lights. Jordan had forgotten she'd been crying until she saw the looks on their faces.

"What's wrong?" Martha asked.

Jordan shrugged. "Long story. Are those cupcakes?"

Ava held up the pastry box in her hand. "Yes, they are. From Confectionary Cupboard. I bought enough to make us sick."

"Perfect," said Jordan.

Ava put the box down on the floor, and all the girls, one of whom was now technically a woman, sat for a midnight picnic of cupcakes and Diet Coke.

"Okay," Martha said, turning to Jordan. "This is fun. But there are tears. On your face. Explain, please."

Jordan sighed. "You were right. Scott's an asshole." But that wasn't exactly fair. She sighed again. "No. He's not, actually. I'm the asshole."

She told them about the date, and to Martha's credit, she didn't judge. She nodded along and even said she was sorry when Jordan told her how much it hurt.

"I don't even think I liked him that much, to be honest,"

Jordan said. "I just liked the *idea* of him, you know? It was like I got to be an adult for a minute."

Ava spoke with a mouthful of frosting. "I have great news. You get to be an adult for a lot of minutes now."

Jordan took another cupcake. This was her third one and she had no intention of stopping. "I just feel like such a jerk."

"You're not a jerk." Martha said it with such conviction that Jordan actually believed her.

"But speaking of jerks," said CJ, "I have some news too."

Three jaws hit the floor when she told them that just two hours earlier, she'd kissed Logan Diffenderfer. "Wow," Jordan said. "Um...wow." She expected to feel jealous, but as she took mental inventory, she realized that she didn't. She wondered if she was just in shock.

Jordan noticed that Ava was staring at her cupcake pretty intently. "Do you like him?" she asked CJ. "Because if you like him..." The sentence dangled out there, begging CJ to finish it.

"I don't. Not like that. It was a moment of temporary insanity brought on by stress. And even if I did, I could never date someone who..." She turned to Ava, letting her own sentence dangle.

"I don't hate him anymore," Ava said. "So if you like him...And if he likes you..." Jordan watched Ava closely. Something seemed off.

"Whatever," said CJ. "I don't want to talk about boys anymore. I want to talk about our newest woman." She held up her Diet Coke can to make a toast.

Jordan motioned for her to lower it. "Hang on," she said. "There's one more thing I have to tell you. It's about the park."

She broke the news quickly. She told them that the fight was over. They'd lost. The city was going to build a new park. A different park. One that would never be theirs. "We're not going to get to leave our names behind."

"Maybe it's for the best," Martha said.

"Yeah," Ava added. "It's just a dumb tradition. We probably should have outgrown it by now anyway."

CJ turned to Jordan. "You're the only adult here. So I'll take your word for it, does carving our names into a jungle gym still seem like a big deal?"

Jordan thought about it. "No," she said honestly. "Ava's right. It doesn't seem like something that adults should care about. But this does." Jordan took a swipe of frosting and smooshed it into CJ's face.

CJ laughed as she grabbed for a cupcake. A frosting war broke out and didn't end until all four of them were covered and CJ was laughing so hard that Diet Coke came out of her nose. As they sat there, wiping frosting off their faces, Jordan completely forgot that just a few hours earlier she'd been in such a hurry to grow up.

"Open your present," CJ said.

Jordan tore the edges of wrapping paper carefully. Whatever was inside, it seemed delicate. When she saw what it was, a wave of bittersweet emotion swept over her.

"This is perfect," she said. "This is absolutely perfect."

It was a voter registration form.

CHAPTER **TWENTY-THREE**

Cleveland, Ohio
Three Months Later

THE SNOW melted early that year, and spring came before anyone was ready for it. It was always a season of change, but this year, CJ felt it more than any other. When the daffodils poked through the thawing soil, she wanted to push their little faces back under and hold them there. *Just give us a little more time,* she wanted to say. *Please. Just a little while longer.*

The city officially announced the new park and released a design sketch of what it would look like when it was done. It was going to be beautiful even if it would never be *their* park. CJ decided that maybe that was okay. The Americans with Disabilities Act hadn't even been written when the old park was built. The new one was subject to a whole different set of guidelines. She remembered her conversation at the mini-golf course with Wyatt, though. Only 50 percent of the holes had to be accessible. She looked up the park guidelines and saw that they weren't good enough. *Not good enough. Not good enough.* The familiar refrain echoed in CJ's mind. It *wasn't* good enough. But what could CJ do about it? She was just an average girl. The word made her think of Wyatt, and she smiled. She decided that she had to try. She might fail. She'd probably fail. But what if she didn't? She opened the city website and started writing down information.

A week later, it was CJ's last day at Sensational Recreational. The program closed in spring since the city used the rec center for an adult indoor-soccer league. She'd already talked to Dakota's mom about trying adaptive horseback riding during the interim. Dakota was excited, and a few of the boys were going to give it a shot too. She understood why Wyatt didn't want anything to do with it, but that didn't mean it wouldn't be valuable for the kids.

She found Wyatt at center court and walked up to him. She was holding an envelope in her hands.

"Is that a 'last day' present?" he asked.

"Not exactly. You know how the city is opening a new park?"

He nodded. "I heard something about it."

"It'll obviously follow the new ADA guidelines. But..."

Wyatt nodded. "It's still not going to be a hundred percent accessible."

"Not even close," CJ said. "But the thing is, it could be. There's better equipment out there. It exists."

Wyatt raised an eyebrow.

"Don't even ask me how many hours I've spent researching it. I've barely slept this week." She didn't feel tired, though. If anything, she felt more alive than she ever had before. "The problem is money," CJ said. "Adaptive equipment isn't cheap." She'd attended a city meeting where the subject was discussed. She'd listened carefully and waited patiently but was ultimately disappointed when they decided that they couldn't make it work with their budget. "But," CJ said, "if they had the money, they'd do it."

"Is this where you tell me you won the lottery and want to spend your winnings on a park instead of hard drugs and fast cars?"

"I'm too young to play the lottery. And I think you know I'd choose the fast cars over getting suitable playground equipment for children with disabilities."

He smiled. "Then what's in the envelope?"

"I found a charity organization that raises money to augment city funds. It's a long shot. They only have the funds for one park this year. We have to apply and they have to pick us. But why not try? I did all the application paperwork. They said on the website that personal letters really help. Dakota's mom is writing one, and I'm going to talk to some of the other parents too. But I was thinking, as the director of this program, your words would mean a lot." She handed him the envelope. "All the information is in here."

"Clarke."

It felt so good to hear her name on his lips.

"Of course I'll write a letter."

"And I want you to know that I'm not doing this out of guilt. I'm doing it because this is what the kids deserve. And, okay, I'm also doing it because I like to win and I really want to beat all those other parks. But mostly I'm doing it for the kids."

"Then let's kick the crap out of those other parks," he said.

She nodded. "Thanks."

She hoped he knew that she was thanking him for a hell of a lot more than just the letter.

April 3, 2020. It was a day that would live in infamy. It started off like any other day, but for every college-bound senior at William McKinley, it would not end that way. Because at exactly seven PM, Eastern Standard Time, the majority of universities across the country would release their acceptance and rejection information through an online log-in system. There were still a couple of schools who liked to do things the old-fashioned way with an e-mail that would arrive at some vague point that day. Boston University was one of those schools. Ava, CJ, and Jordan had all applied there. Ava still clung to the small hope that maybe they would stay together next year. Martha had ended up applying to only two schools, and one of them, MIT, was in Boston too.

School was tense that day. Most students were too antsy to do much learning, and the majority of teachers didn't even try to rein them in. It was the one day of the year when everyone was allowed to keep their phones in their hands. During first period art, Mrs. Simon introduced the class to the style of Jackson Pollock and encouraged everyone to get out their aggression by flinging paint wildly at their canvases. Ava didn't know if it was the new antidepressant that Dr. Clifford had prescribed for her or if it was the action of hurling paint, but she felt remarkably at peace with whatever news she would get later. Next to her, Logan heaved a giant glob of deep-blue paint at his canvas. "It's my goal to splatter this thing in the school colors of every place that might reject me. That's Duke blue." He dipped his brush into a blob of cardinal red and flung it violently.

"Stanford red?" she asked.

He nodded.

It *had* occurred to Ava that she and Logan might potentially end up on the same campus next year. It had also occurred to her that she didn't totally hate that idea. She admitted to Dr. Clifford that she had possibly the teeniest, tiniest hint of a crush. Not that it mattered. CJ still claimed that kissing Logan was a mistake, but Ava didn't want to get in the way if that wasn't true. She watched him fling another giant glob of cardinal red.

By lunchtime, there was still no news from Boston University. Things got so tense that the girls, who had never been regular truants, decided to skip fifth period. If they were going to sit around and be freaked out, they may as well do it outside in the gorgeous spring sunshine.

They sat on the lawn of the athletic field and tried to keep one another distracted between glances at their phones. CJ just kept hitting refresh over and over and over. It was hard to watch.

"Maybe we should go to Denny's," Ava said. "Blow off the rest of the day and eat our feelings."

"I'm down," said Jordan.

"In," said Martha.

"Sure," said CJ. She hit refresh again as she stood up. "Oh my God!" she screamed, when a new e-mail popped up.

Jordan and Ava were already grabbing for their phones. Jordan hit refresh on hers first and saw the same e-mail that CJ was reacting to. "Oh," Jordan said. "God, CJ. You scared me."

"What?" Ava asked. "Is it BU?" She stealthily hit refresh on her own e-mail.

"No." Jordan looked up from her phone. "The yearbook committee sent e-mails to all the winners of the Senior Superlatives."

"God," Martha said. "Those things are so stupid." But Ava saw Martha reach for her phone and check.

"I'm Best Dressed, bitches," Jordan said victoriously.

Ava smiled when she read hers. "I got Most Likely to Be the Next Picasso." She turned to CJ. "What did you get?"

CJ tossed her phone aside. "What does it even matter? These things are so stupid."

Next to her, Martha agreed. "You're right. Totally stupid."

"Why?" Jordan asked Martha. "What did you get?"

Martha put her phone away. "Nothing. I mean I got nothing."

"Don't feel bad," Jordan said. "We have a big class. Not everyone gets something."

CJ sighed. "You're lucky you didn't get anything. This is so embarrassing."

"It can't be that bad," Ava said. "What did you get?"

"I'm not telling. It's mortifying." CJ flipped her phone over.

"Okay," Jordan said. "You don't have to tell us." Then she quickly grabbed CJ's arms and pinned them to her sides. "Ava! Grab her phone!"

CJ was much stronger than Jordan and quickly freed her

hands, but Ava already had the phone. "Got it!" CJ lunged for Ava and she took off running. "Martha, go long!"

Martha put her hands out and Ava tossed her the phone. It was a terrible throw, but Martha managed to make a dive for it. Right as CJ caught up to her, she turned and tossed the phone to Jordan. A game of monkey in the middle commenced.

"Come on, guys," CJ said. "You know I'm like way more athletic than you, right?" But after running back and forth a few times, she threw up her hands. "Oh, whatever. Just read it."

Jordan was the one who had the phone in her hand when CJ gave up. She opened the e-mail at the top of CJ's in-box and read it out loud in her most dignified yearbook committee voice. " 'Dear Clarke, We regret to inform you that the admissions committee at Boston University is unable to offer you…' " Jordan immediately stopped reading. "Oh shit. Wrong e-mail. Shit, CJ. Shit, shit, shit. Here." She handed CJ her phone back. "I'm sorry."

CJ took her phone and read the rest of the e-mail from Boston University. "Oh," she said flatly. "Well, shit."

Jordan glanced at Ava and Martha helplessly. Then she looked at CJ. "I'm so sorry."

"No. It's fine. I'm okay. It wasn't my top choice anyway. Don't worry about it. I know you and Ava are dying to check yours. So go ahead."

Jordan and Ava traded a look.

"You guys," CJ said. "Please. I know you must be dying right now. Check your phones."

They each demurely reached for their phones. They kept their reactions small and contained, but it's not like CJ couldn't read the looks on their faces. "Congratulations," she said.

"Thanks," Ava said sheepishly.

"Yeah, thanks," said Jordan.

The bell rang and CJ stood.

"Screw BU," said Ava. "Come on. Let's go to Denny's. A moment like this calls for Moons Over My Hammies all around."

CJ shook her head. "I don't feel like it. I'm going home." She started to walk away but turned back. "Oh, and my yearbook thing, I got Tallest. So that's how I will be remembered by the class of 2020. As the tallest." CJ turned and walked away.

CHAPTER **TWENTY-FOUR**

THE TICKET booth seemed smaller than usual that evening. Martha was sitting on the tiny stool in the tiny box of that room when she logged into MIT's admissions portal. It didn't seem right to be in such a small space when she was getting such big news, but she had to know. She read the letter once, then put her phone away. She felt like crying.

She drummed her fingers against the counter and didn't notice when Logan Diffenderfer walked up to the window. "One, please," he said.

Martha took his money and slid him a ticket. He laughed when he saw the title that was printed on it.

"What?" Martha asked.

"I didn't even check to see what movie you were showing." He held up his ticket. "*The Graduate.* How apropos."

"I've never seen it before," Martha said.

"Is the theater busy tonight?"

"Are we ever busy?"

Logan smiled. "Then you need to join me."

Martha locked up the ticket booth and met him in the lobby. They picked two seats in the back and settled in as the opening credits rolled. Dustin Hoffman appeared on-screen, and then there was a long moment of silence.

"I love this opening sequence so much," Logan said. "Right away you get the point. This is a guy who has no idea what he's doing with his life."

"I can relate." She thought about MIT and felt like crying again. The silence on the movie screen was unsettling and Martha fidgeted. Just when it seemed like the silence was going on for too long, a song that Martha had always loved started playing. *Hello darkness, my old friend.* "You're right," she said. "This is very apropos."

"Did you hear back from the schools you applied to?" Logan asked.

"I only applied to two. Cleveland State and MIT."

He read the heavy inflection in her voice and asked her if it was bad news.

She shook her head. "I got into both."

"Congratulations."

She shrugged. "I got a full ride at Cleveland State," she said. "I should just go there. It makes the most sense. MIT didn't offer me any scholarship money."

"But…?" he asked, still looking at her.

"I don't want to stay in Cleveland, Logan." She wanted to go somewhere different and try new things. She wanted something bigger. Bigger than the tiny ticket booth and the tiny apartment and the tiny life that would be hers if she stayed. "What about you?" she asked.

"I got into Stanford."

"Congratulations."

"Thanks. I guess. I got in a couple of other places too. But my parents are expecting me to say yes to Stanford. That's what they want."

"What do *you* want, Diffenderfer?"

"Not that."

Logan's eyes went back to the screen. The sad song continued. It was the perfect soundtrack for what they were both feeling. Martha felt their hands touch on the armrest. It was an accidental brush, but neither of them moved their hands away. Martha thought that the only thing that felt strange about sitting in the dark with Logan Diffenderfer and talking about their futures and their fears was that absolutely nothing felt strange about it.

When the movie ended, Martha didn't get up. She knew that Logan would want to sit through the credits like he always did. She didn't mind. She was thinking about the movie and how you never really know where life is going to take you. She decided that this was okay. The mystery of it was half the fun.

Martha turned to Logan. "Hey," she said. "Did you get voted anything for the Senior Superlatives?"

"Yeah. But it's stupid."

"Mine too. I hate it." She'd lied when she told her friends that she didn't get anything. She was too angry and humiliated by how her classmates saw her. "I got Most Likely to Never Leave Ohio."

Logan laughed slightly. "Maybe they got ours backward."

"Why? What did you get?"

Martha felt Logan's elbow brush against hers on the armrest as he told her. "Most Likely to Be President."

Jordan wrapped her hands tightly around the steering wheel. She was worried she was going to crash if she didn't totally focus. She was still thinking about what the letter from Northwestern said. *Wait-listed.*

She turned off the main road and pulled into the parking lot of Councilman Lonner's district office. She knew there was a chance that Scott would already be gone for the night, but she didn't think so. He'd told her that he couldn't leave on Fridays until he'd logged all the constituent concerns he had heard during the week and sent them to the councilman. The list was often so long that it kept him there until midnight.

The nice woman who worked at the front desk was

already gone, and most of the offices were dark. Jordan peered around the front desk and called out softly, "Hello? Anyone here?"

When nobody answered, she walked around to the back. There was a light coming from an office. It was Scott's. She walked up and said the only thing she could think to say. "Hi."

"Jordan."

She'd startled him.

"Hi," she said again.

He glanced around as if they might get caught. "You have to go. I can't see you."

"Actually," she said, "you have to see me."

"Jordan…"

"I'm registered to vote in the district. I'm a constituent and I have a concern. I want to tell you why I think Memorial Park deserves a second chance."

———————

CJ sat in her bedroom with the door closed, staring at the obscene vase that Wyatt's mom had given her. She decided that she would take it to college with her next year. It was the perfect size to hold pens.

She logged into Skidmore's admissions portal first. She had decided to save Stanford for last. The Skidmore form letter popped up immediately. *We're sorry…* She didn't need to read anything after that. She logged into the next school. And the next. The rejections came quickly. She only saw the word "congratulations" once. She barely registered it. She still had Stanford left, and she said a silent prayer before she logged in. *Please*, she thought. *Please.*

CJ was seated at the desk her father had originally built for her oldest sister. It was the only hand-me-down that ever fit. She'd spent so many hours sitting there, studying, writing papers, and staying home from parties to prepare for the SATs. She'd logged so many hours of hard work at this desk that it almost didn't seem fair to be sitting at it when Stanford informed her that *I am very sorry to let you know that we are unable to offer you admission to Stanford University.*

CJ snapped her laptop shut.

She was lacing up her running shoes when her phone buzzed. She didn't even look at it. It would be Ava or Jordan or maybe even Martha calling to find out where she got in. She couldn't tell them. Not yet. She went into the kitchen, where her dad was watching the game and her mom was starting dinner.

"I'm going to Ohio State next year," she said. They both looked slightly stunned. "It's the only place I got in." Her dad muted the television, but CJ was already halfway out the door. "I'm going jogging."

When CJ arrived at the track, it was during that weird period of time after the sun had set but before the automatic field lights turned on. She would have twenty minutes of pitch-blackness to run through. *Perfect*, she thought. All she wanted to do was run and let the darkness swallow her up. She'd only taken a few steps when she saw the silhouette of a person approach. CJ couldn't see the person's face in the dark; she could only make out the absolutely unmistakable shape.

"I'm so glad you're here," CJ said.

Jordan sat across from Scott while he took out his yellow legal pad and grabbed a pen. She took a deep breath and told him what the park meant to her. She told him about the day she'd met her three best friends there. She told him how they used to dream about growing up and adding their names to the jungle gym. That they would go there every fall a week or two after senior night and run their fingers along the new names. That they would plot and plan and look forward to the time when it was finally their turn. She told him how she was scared that she might drift away from her friends next year when they weren't all together anymore. And how leaving their names carved into that wood was the only way she could be sure that a piece of them would always be together.

When she was done, Scott put the cap back on his pen. "I'll type this up," he said. "And I'll pass it on to the councilman. But"—Scott set his pen down—"none of this is going to make a difference. I'm sorry. The park is getting torn down."

"I know," she said, standing. "I just wanted a chance to be heard." Jordan put her hand out professionally. "Thank you for your time."

Scott took her hand and shook it.

"Bye, Scott," she said.

Just as she was stepping into the hallway, she heard him say her name.

She turned.

"Where are you going to college next year?"

Jordan paused. "George Washington University."

The moment it was out of her mouth, she knew it was the right decision. Even if she got off the Northwestern wait-list, she would still choose George Washington. It felt like a million years ago when Ms. Fischer had handed her the brochure and suggested that she apply. Now Jordan knew that it was the right place for her. She wanted to be in Washington, DC.

"You're going to make one hell of a journalist someday, Jordan."

"Maybe," she said. "Or maybe I'll be something else. I still haven't decided for sure. I'm only eighteen, after all."

———

Ava squinted at CJ in the darkness. "How could you tell it was me?"

"Nobody else is as short as you."

They were mismatched as friends in so many ways.

Height was just one of them. But they aligned in all the ways that really mattered.

"I stopped by your house when you weren't answering your phone," Ava said. "Your parents are worried."

"Then I guess they told you I got into only Ohio State?"

Ava nodded.

"It's a good school," said CJ.

"I don't think they're worried about you going to Ohio State."

"I know. They're worried I'm going to crack. But I'm not. I'm okay. It's the right place for me, I think."

"Really?"

"I'm working on being at peace with my failures. I think I'm getting better at it. What about you?"

"Oh, I'm a master at failing." But Ava knew that's not what CJ was asking. "You want to know where I got in."

CJ nodded.

"I got rejected from Georgetown and Wellesley."

"Idiots," CJ said. "I'm pretty sure you're just trying to make me feel better. But still, they're idiots. And what about Stanford?"

"I got in."

"Congratulations."

"You can be pissed at me."

"I'm pissed I didn't get in. I'm not pissed that you did. I'm really proud of you."

"Thanks."

"And RISD?"

Ava nodded. "Yeah."

"Damn, Ava."

"I know. I don't know what I'm going to do. My mom said she'll support me in whatever decision I make."

"Do you think she's telling the truth?"

"Yeah. I do, actually."

Ava thought about the moment that she'd found out. Her mom had been sitting next to her when the letter from Stanford popped up on the screen.

Congratulations! On behalf of the Office of Undergraduate Admissions, it is my pleasure to offer you admission to Stanford's class of 2024.

Ava had actually screamed. Next to her, her mom had kept her cool. She kept the same poker face when the good news came from RISD. "Looks like you have a tough choice ahead of you" was all she'd said.

"It *is* a tough decision," CJ agreed. "I guess that's the advantage of getting into only one place. Bet you're super jealous of me."

"So jealous."

Ava laughed and CJ gave her the biggest hug ever. "Hey," CJ said, pulling away. "Do you mind if I ask—just because I'm incredibly curious about what a successful

Stanford essay sounds like—what did you write about? For your transformational-experience essay?"

Ava knew everyone assumed she'd written about the moment she met her birth mother or about being diagnosed with depression. And while those things were both certainly transformational, they were far from the most significant thing that had happened to her in her life so far. "I wrote about that day at the park. The summer before kindergarten. When I met you and Jordan and Martha."

"What?" CJ said. She couldn't have been more surprised.

"Yeah. It basically changed my whole life. I wouldn't be who I am if I didn't have the three of you as best friends."

CJ laughed. "That is such a good answer."

"Then why are you laughing?"

"It's so simple. And so perfect. And something I could have written too." But then she shook her head. "No, it's not, actually. I wouldn't have written about it in the same way. I love you, Aves. I'm super proud of you."

"I'm proud of you too."

CJ smiled. "You know, I'm kinda proud of me too. Wanna go for a jog?"

"Hard no," said Ava.

CHAPTER TWENTY-FIVE

MARTHA WALKED past Old Navy and Chico's and turned into the Army Recruitment Center. The young sergeant stood as she entered, and she walked right past him too. Major Malone was at her desk doing some paperwork when Martha appeared in front of her, jumpy and tense. "Hi," Martha said. "Do you have a minute?"

"I would invite you to sit, but you seem…" The sentence did not need to be finished. Martha was in no position to be still. "How about we take a walk?"

"Sure, yeah." Martha shoved her hands in her pockets. "A walk would be good."

It was a nice spring day, and they stepped outside, where the air was fresh and everything was blooming. "So," Major Malone said. "Why don't you tell me what you're looking for?"

Martha was too nervous to be anything other than honest. "Well," she said, "I'm basically looking for someone to pay for college. But also...maybe more."

"Okay," Malone said. "We can work with that. There are a couple of options. One, you enlist. Give the army five years, then you go to college on the GI Bill. Everything is paid for."

"I don't think MIT would let me defer for five years."

Malone stopped walking and looked over at her.

"What?" Martha asked.

"You got into MIT. That's really impressive. What are you planning on studying?"

"Mechanical engineering. At least I think so."

Malone smiled in a kind way. "Good for you. And good for the army. Those are skills we need. I have no doubt that after five years doing engineering in the army, MIT would happily readmit you. But that doesn't seem like what you want."

Martha shook her head. "I want to go to college. I want that experience."

"Then let's talk about an ROTC program. We pay your tuition and you owe us four years after you graduate. A little more if you also want us to pay for graduate school or flight school."

Martha stopped walking. *Flight school.* She felt goose bumps dot her arms. "Can I ask you a question?"

"Of course."

"What's it like to fly a helicopter?"

A wistful look spread across Malone's face. "I won't be able to explain it. There are some things you can't possibly understand until you try them. Is that what you want to do?"

"I don't know. I don't know what I want to do." The uncertainty scared her almost as much as anything else. Not in a bad way, though.

As they walked more and talked more, Martha thought about all the profiles of military women she'd read in the last few days as she worked up the courage to walk through that recruitment office door. She'd wanted all her preconceived notions about the military to be proven true. Instead, she'd found women marching in Pride parades and using their high ranks to make changes. She'd found women who came from money and women who came from nothing. She thought she'd find one type of woman and instead she'd found everything. Everything except an excuse not to at least have a conversation with Major Malone.

Martha hadn't had a lot of choices in her life, and now that this one was in front of her, she was scared. This made her think about the person she was named for. When people thought of Martha Washington, they always pictured the white-haired wife of the first American president. But before she was Martha Washington, she was

Martha Custis. Before she was Martha Custis, she was Martha Dandridge. And before that, she was Patsy. Just a little girl from a large family who learned how to read and write at a time when women didn't usually do that. She was a girl who wanted more out of life than what was being offered. That's what Martha had in common with her great-great-great-great-great-great-great-grandmother.

She was brave enough to want more and she was brave enough to go after it.

CJ was so used to getting bad news that she almost didn't know how to process it when she got the mail that afternoon. She stood in her front yard reading and rereading the letter until she was finally convinced that it was real. Then she went straight to her car.

Wyatt was the first person she wanted to tell. She drove to his house, knocked on his door, and a minute later, his mom answered. "CJ. It's so good to see you."

"You too. Is Wyatt here?"

Katherine shook her head. "He's on campus with his dad."

"Campus?"

"OSU." She was smiling now. "He decided to go back in the fall. They're taking care of some paperwork today and meeting with someone from the Office of Disability Services. The school has been great so far. Fingers crossed."

CJ knew it wasn't her place to be proud of him, but she couldn't help it. She was. "Is it okay if I leave something for him?"

"Of course. I'll make sure he gets it."

"Give me one second."

CJ took the letter out of the envelope and wrote a note at the bottom of it. She felt weird writing the words that she was writing while standing so close to Wyatt's mom, but Katherine did a good job of not staring. CJ finished and stuffed the letter back in the envelope before she could second-guess herself.

"By the way," CJ said, "I love the vase you gave me. I love it so much. This is going to sound hokey, but it reminds me that life can change in an instant, and it's up to us how we deal with it when it does."

"I appreciate that. I know my pottery is far from perfect."

"That's why I love it so much. Even with its flaws, it's still one of the most beautiful things I've ever seen."

Wyatt's mom smiled. "Thank you, CJ. That's incredibly kind. Everyone else tells me they look like dicks."

CJ laughed. "Not at all."

CHAPTER **TWENTY-SIX**

THE DAYS grew longer and the humidity settled in. Summer was impossibly close and everyone knew what that meant. Their time as seniors was almost over. Jordan's stomach was in knots when it came time to be photographed for the Senior Superlatives. It's not that she was nervous about what she was going to wear. She knew that whatever she picked would be amazing now and totally out of style when she looked back on it in ten, twenty, thirty years. No, she wasn't nervous about the outfit. The reason she was on edge was because Logan Diffenderfer was going to be the one taking the picture, and she knew it was the perfect time to finally be honest with him.

She met him inside the auditorium. He was setting up a makeshift photography studio, and she watched for a moment while he hung a blue sheet for the background and set up a few light stands. He looked like a real photographer.

"Hey," he said as she walked up. "I didn't hear you come in. Perfect outfit."

"Thanks."

She was wearing a corset top that her grandmother had helped her embellish with straps and a frilly skirt in red, white, and blue that her younger brother said made her look like she was running for president.

"Take a seat whenever you're ready," he said, motioning to a black stool in front of the drape.

When she sat down, he walked over and touched her shoulders, positioning her in a way that would best catch the light. "Just like that," he said.

He lifted his camera and took a couple of test shots. After he checked the digital images, he looked up at her.

"Is something wrong?" he asked.

She knew her expression was heavy. "I need to say something and it's a little hard."

Logan lowered his camera. "What?"

"When I broke up with you freshman year, I lied about why I did it. I told you it was because I didn't have feelings for you anymore, but that was a lie. God, it was *such* a lie. I was head over heels for you."

Logan set his camera down on the table. "Why are you telling me this now?"

"Well, there was a very specific reason why I had to break up with you."

"It was because of what Ava overheard me say, wasn't it?"

Jordan nodded. "She was so hurt and she was going through such a hard time. And she was—*is*—one of my very best friends. I couldn't stay with you."

"I understand. I don't hold it against you."

"It was really hard for me to lie to you. I just want you to know that."

"Jordan—"

"Hang on. I need to finish this. I was in love with you for a very long time." She took a deep breath. "But I'm not in love with you anymore. I'm always going to care about you as a friend, but that's it."

"I care about you as a friend too." Logan smiled warmly, and she knew he meant it.

"I know you do. You're a good guy, Logan, and I know that if you thought something might hurt me, you wouldn't do it. So what I'm saying is, if you've been worried that I still had feelings for you, and if that's maybe held you back from pursuing someone else...you don't need to do that anymore."

Logan smiled. "You're a really good person, Jordan."

"I know," she said. "Now make me look fabulous."

"You got it." He lifted his camera and took the shot.

CJ was at her desk looking at the Ohio State online course catalog when her phone rang. "Hey, Logan," she said. "What's up?"

"You got a second to talk?"

This sounded serious. "Sure," she said with slight concern. "What's going on?"

"We kissed," he said rather matter-of-factly.

"I know."

"We kissed and then we never talked about it."

"I know that too."

"Can we? Talk about it?"

CJ walked over to her bed and plopped down. "Yeah."

"Good. Because I never knew if it meant something to you or if it was just one of those things that happen."

CJ stared at the ceiling and tried to figure out the best way to tell him that it *did* mean something to her. "Logan, the truth is, I was such a mess that night. I was overwhelmed and freaked out, and I needed someone. You were there for me when I needed it." She was grateful for that. "So I guess what I'm saying is, it did mean something. But not like a romantic something. What I really needed that night was a friend. I just got wrapped up in the other stuff."

Through the phone, she could hear Logan exhale. "I feel the exact same way."

"Really?" CJ sighed with relief. "I feel so stupid. I was just so caught up in college applications and all that pressure that was on me—"

"Yes. Exactly!"

Logan said some other things, but CJ didn't hear any of it. Because it was at that exact moment that she swore she saw a horse walk into her front yard. She sat up. It couldn't be a horse. She went to her window and looked out. It was definitely a horse. Right there on her lawn. And the horse was not alone.

"Uh, Logan. I have to go." She hung up before he could respond.

CJ ran to her window and threw it open. "What the hell are you doing?"

"Clarke Josephine Jacobson," said Wyatt from the saddle of a beautiful brown horse, "I've come atop this mighty steed to give you a message."

CJ smiled. "I'll be right out."

When CJ opened the front door, Wyatt was waiting for her. He'd taken up a very regal, very George Washington pose.

"You're crazy," she said as she walked up to him. "How did you even get this thing here?"

"This *thing* is named Cocoa Puff."

"Hi, Cocoa Puff," she said. Then she looked up at Wyatt, seriously craning her neck to do it.

"So this is what it's like to be taller than you," Wyatt said.

"Seriously, Wyatt. How did you get a horse into my development? I don't even think we're zoned for this."

"Can you not with the questions right now?"

CJ made a big show of closing her mouth.

"I got the letter."

CJ smiled. She was so proud. The nonprofit had picked them. Their park was going to get all the money it needed to make it wonderfully inclusive.

"I also got the message you wrote at the bottom of the letter."

This time she didn't smile. She was too nervous about how he would respond. Her hand had been shaking when she'd written it. *I should have you kissed you in the bathroom that day. But you should have kissed me too. We were both afraid. How about we be afraid together?*

CJ looked down at her feet. There were hoof divots all over her father's freshly mowed lawn. Everything about this was crazy. "Aren't you going to say something?" CJ asked.

"No, Clarke. There's absolutely nothing I want to say. I just want to kiss you."

She looked up. Wyatt draped his hand down and CJ took it. He squeezed. She squeezed back. Twice.

"What's that?" he asked.

"It's how my friends and I say 'I love you.'"

"Well, then. Here." He squeezed her hand twice.

Then he helped her up onto the horse. She put her arms around him and he turned his head. This time there was no hesitation and no fear. Their lips found each other like it was the easiest, most wonderful thing in the world.

When they finally pulled away, Wyatt spoke. "So...you wanna ride off into the sunset?"

CJ nodded. "Yes. Yes, I do."

CJ held on tightly and thought about how she never wanted to let him go.

Martha stood at the glass door of the movie theater and felt impatient. Logan was late. She wouldn't blame him if he was having second thoughts. A second later, she saw him turn the corner and half walk, half jog to the door. Martha opened it immediately. "You're late," she said.

"I know. I'm sorry. I was coming from my therapist."

"Oh. Okay, then. I just thought maybe you'd changed your mind."

"Nope," he said. "I'm all in."

Martha took a breath. "I can't believe we're really doing this."

"I know," Logan said. "Me neither. I think there are going to be a lot of shocked people when they find out."

"Screw 'em," Martha said. "They'll get over it." She

took another breath. "Okay. Let's make this official." She reached into her pocket. "This is your employee key." She slid the key off her key ring and handed it to him. "Do not lose it or Ben will take twenty-five bucks out of your paycheck."

"I won't."

"So how did your parents take it? When you told them you're taking a year off and working here?"

"They freaked. *Totally* freaked, actually. But whatever. I think they'll come around once I reapply to schools next year. If I get into a good film school, I'm hoping they'll relax a little bit. And if they don't, oh well. It's not their life."

"No, it's not."

Martha finished showing Logan around and helped him turn on the popcorn machine. Then there was nothing left for her to do. "Okay," she said. "I think that's it. So this is good-bye."

"Later," Logan said.

But Martha wasn't really saying good-bye to Logan, she was saying good-bye to the theater. It had been good to her. She walked out the door and let it close behind her. She looked back only once.

Martha pulled her phone out of her pocket and looked at the text chain with Victoria. It was long now, and it took her a second to find the question she loved to read and reread. The one that had taken all of her bravery to ask.

Were you upset because you have feelings for Logan Diffenderfer or because you have feelings for me? It's a loaded question. Because I have feelings for you.

"Martha."

Martha looked up. Victoria was standing at the corner waiting for her. "That took long enough," she said.

"What was I supposed to do? Guys always take longer to learn things."

Victoria made a scoffing sound. "Men." Then she put her hand out. Martha took it and let Victoria pull her in. Their lips met and Martha felt that same electric jolt that she'd felt when Victoria had first responded to her text.

Because I have feelings for you, dummy.

Martha and Victoria kissed on the corner. It went on and on for what felt like forever, and Martha thought that it was nothing like kissing a boy. It wasn't like kissing Hermione Granger either. It was so much better.

The only thing I have to fear is fear itself. The only thing I have to fear is fear itself. The only thing I have to fear is fear itself.

Ava had been on a Roosevelt kick ever since CJ had given her the book. Now the words cycled through her mind as she walked to the park. Dr. Clifford had suggested that it might be helpful to make a list of the things she'd done in her life that were brave. That way she could see that she was actually a lot stronger than she realized. It was definitely helping. She looked back over her accomplishments.

Turning down RISD was brave.

Saying yes to Stanford was brave.

Giving the letter to Logan Diffenderfer was brave.

She'd written the letter out on a sheet of notebook paper and then shoved it through the slats of his locker on the last day of school before she could change her mind.

Dear Logan,

This weekend I'm going to go see the new park that the city is building. I want to have memories there so when I come back on break or during the summers, it'll have meaning to me. I'm bringing my sketchbook. Because sitting on a bench and sketching will be a good memory to have. But there's one that would be even better. A first kiss with a guy I care about. I like you, Logan. Not as a friend. Although that too. If you don't feel the same way, then my memory will be of sketching. And that's okay. So no hard feelings. But if you do feel the same way, then I'll be there

*on Saturday at two pm. Meet me and
let's make a memory. —Ava*

Even though the new park was still under construction, it was easy to see its potential. Everyone was talking about the cool new jungle gym and the fact that all the equipment was going to be wheelchair accessible thanks to the organization CJ had found. The benches had already been installed, and Ava was going to sit down on one and watch the landscapers work.

She looked at the time on her phone. It was one forty-five. She would have a few minutes to sit down and catch her breath and remind herself that *the only thing I have to fear is fear itself.* But as she came around the corner, her expression shifted.

"You're early," she said.

Logan Diffenderfer stood up from the bench and walked toward her.

"I know. I couldn't wait."

CHAPTER **TWENTY-SEVEN**

"CAN WE please try to be a little quieter?"

Jordan had already asked her friends to keep it down, but nobody was listening.

"I thought I was supposed to be the uptight one," CJ said, making absolutely no effort to lower her voice.

Ava and Martha weren't any better. They were still laughing at a joke that Martha had made.

Jordan took the key out of her pocket. "Seriously. *Shhh.* Scott loaned me the key only because I promised we wouldn't get caught. So we need to be quiet."

She slid it into the lock and pulled back the chain-link gate. It was the same gate that had kept them from entering the park on their first Friday as seniors, a night that now seemed like a million years ago. The gate wasn't protecting a proposed development site anymore. The office complex was almost done.

"Okay," said CJ, as soon as they were inside. "Who brought the goods?"

Ava put up her hand. "Me." She reached into her bag and pulled out a skewer.

Martha took it from her. "A skewer?"

"Yes. A skewer. What's your problem? It's perfect."

"It's actually totally perfect," said Jordan. "So let's get on with this. We go in alphabetical order, right? Out of fairness?"

"Definitely," said Martha. She handed the skewer back to Ava.

They walked around to the side of the building. To the spot where earlier that day a layer of fresh concrete had been poured. It was still wet, just waiting for them to leave their mark. They went one by one, carefully printing the letters into the soft cement. When they were done, they admired the list.

Ava Morgan
CJ Jacobson
Jordan Schafer
Martha Custis
Class of 2020

There wasn't a lot to say after that. Nobody gave a big

speech or anything. Writing their names down was enough. After they were done, they walked out and shut the gate behind them.

They'd driven separately since they were all going different places afterward. Ava had plans to hang out with Logan at the theater, and Jordan was going to meet her grandmother to work on sewing some new clothes for college. Martha's dad had let her borrow the car to drive downtown to meet up with a group of MIT freshmen who had found one another online.

CJ was the only one who didn't have plans. As she unlocked her car, she watched her three best friends drive off in different directions. After this summer, they wouldn't see one another every day anymore. But that was okay. She knew they would always be in one another's lives.

Her phone rang and Wyatt's name flashed on her screen.

"Hey," she said, answering. "I thought you were with your family tonight."

Wyatt's father had finally gotten the courage to reach out to his younger brother, and they'd been slowly working on repairing the damage between them. They had plans to finally introduce each other to their families tonight.

"I'm still with them," Wyatt said. "But I had to call you to tell you the craziest thing."

CJ turned the car on and pulled away from the curb. "Do tell." She glanced in the rearview mirror and watched the park, or rather the place where the park had once been, disappear from view.

"My uncle has a son."

CJ smiled. "I knew it. I was right, wasn't I?"

"You were right. He's great, Clarke. Really great."

CJ knew who he was talking about. Because she knew Wyatt's last name, of course. She'd even asked him about it. It was such a unique name. Such a uniquely awful name. When he told her that his dad had a brother, she'd wondered if maybe Logan might be his cousin. They'd thought about it and speculated, but Wyatt didn't want her to talk to Logan about it. It was his dad's business, and he wanted his dad to move at his own pace.

"It's kind of like having a brother. I'm excited. He had to leave just now. I guess he's got a job at a movie theater or something. But we're going to hang out tomorrow, just the two of us."

"That's amazing."

And it *was* amazing. CJ felt goose bumps all over her arms.

"Anyway," he said, "I have to go. I just wanted to call to tell you that. Oh, and I have to tell you one more thing."

"What's that?" CJ asked.

She could hear the smile in his voice. "I love you, Clarke Jacobson."

The goose bumps spread from her arms to her entire body. "I love you too, Wyatt Diffenderfer."

EPILOGUE

Washington, DC
January 20, 2049

WYATT AND I are seated beside each other on the West Front of the Capitol Building. We're surrounded by politicians and dignitaries and a crowd of onlookers so deep that I can't see where they end. I know that every little movement of mine will be scrutinized, so I'm doing my best to keep my shoulders back and my posture presidential. Wyatt thinks that now is the perfect time to try to make me laugh. He leans over and whispers into my ear, "Hey, Clarke."

"That's Madam President-Elect to you," I whisper back. And in just another few minutes, it will be Madam President.

But then he whispers something else, and I can't stop the small laugh that escapes my lips. I play it off with a wave to the crowd and they cheer in response. Wyatt has just reminded me that all these people think that the first time we kissed was on a horse in my front yard. I told the story in an interview once, and it quickly took on a life of its own. Everyone assumed that that was our beginning, and we let them. But the truth is, I kissed him once before that, on the side of the road, and he didn't kiss me back. Our love story has never been perfect. Just like me, it's flawed and complicated. I wouldn't change a single moment.

I lean over and make it look like I'm telling him something serious. "Well, there are a few people here who know the truth."

I look two rows behind me and see Ava, Jordan, and Martha. I had to bump a couple of people out of position to get them these seats, but it was well worth pissing off a few members of Congress to have my friends this close. Dakota and her mom are here too. They were also there with me on the Senate floor the day I introduced the health care bill with a speech that made people sit up and take notice of the freshman senator from Ohio.

I was never supposed to have won that race. I was the underdog by about a mile and almost pulled out. But on the day I was thinking of quitting, my campaign manager drove me to the only office space we could afford for my campaign headquarters. It was in the building where Ava, Jordan, Martha, and I had all carved our names when we were seniors. I decided then that I would never quit no matter how hard it got. Those names reminded me that I wasn't scared of losing and that some of the greatest moments of my life had come from my failures.

Still, there were days that felt impossible and nights when I didn't think I could keep going. It was during those times that I would sneak around to the side of the building and trace my fingers around the letters of my friends' names. I always went down the list in alphabetical order. Out of fairness.

Ava Morgan. She's Dr. Morgan now. She got her PhD in psychology—also from Stanford. She liked the one-on-one work of counseling, and she kept up with her painting, taking her art to a whole new and spectacular level. Ava always thought of herself as the quiet one, but the truth is, the way she expresses herself on the canvas means that her voice is louder than any of ours. A couple of years ago she founded a nonprofit that uses art to help kids work through their trauma.

Jordan Schafer. Jordan did exactly what she always dreamed of doing. She's a journalist. She covers the political beat at the *Washington Post*, where she's destroyed more than a few political careers with her award-winning investigative work. Thankfully she's promised that she'll never write anything that will take me down. Unless I do something to deserve it.

Martha Custis. Martha traveled the farthest to be here today. She and her wife have been living overseas ever since Martha's promotion. Martha knew it was what she wanted from the moment she flew her first combat mission. So in the end, she followed in the footsteps of her great-great-great-great-great-great-great-grandmother's second husband, George, and became a general in the United States Army.

From the podium, the Senate Majority Leader announces that it's time for me to take the oath of office. I quickly glance back at my friends. They know that they are on camera, so their expressions change only imperceptibly. But it's enough for me to notice. They are proud of me. I smile back. I'm proud of them too.

Most people still say that it was that speech on the Senate floor that set me on a path to one day become president. Other people point back earlier, to the class I took during my freshman year at Ohio State University, the one that inspired me to volunteer on my first campaign. Or even earlier than that. Back when I was just a wide-eyed kid who believed she could change the world. There are so many moments that led me to this podium today. But if we're looking for the exact one that started it all, credit goes to Ava for pretty much nailing it in her Stanford essay. Because the most important moment in my life was a warm day in late summer when I met my best friends. If it wasn't for those three little girls, I would not be the woman standing here today.

The Senate Majority Leader continues her preamble. The words she says are not new. They've been said on cold January mornings many times before. I can see them on the teleprompter. *It is my great privilege and distinct honor to introduce the Chief Justice of the Supreme Court, who will now administer the oath of office.*

Now is when she's supposed to direct everyone to stand. But earlier in the morning, I asked her to make one small change, which she does.

She looks out to the crowd and says, "Will those who are able, please stand."

Beside me, Wyatt squeezes my hand twice. Then he lets go. He knows I need it back for the part that comes next.

I take a deep breath, I step forward, and I raise my right hand in the air.

ACKNOWLEDGMENTS

Writing a novel always seemed like it would be a solitary endeavor. Until I sat down to write one. This book simply would not be a book without the incredible network of people who read early drafts, helped me with research, talked me down, talked me up, and simply were there for me. In no particular order:

Bob Stevens. Okay, this one actually *is* in a particular order. You are my best friend, the love of my life, and my biggest supporter. Thank you for telling me I could do it when I didn't think I could. And for keeping the dog and me both fed during that time.

Kate Testerman at KT Literary. The most incredible literary agent and friend a girl could ask for.

Pam Gruber, Farrin Jacobs, Hannah Milton, and the entire team at Little, Brown. Your thoughtful notes made this book into what it is. Thank you for pushing me. You didn't just make this a better book. You made me a better writer.

To the people and organizations who helped me with research: Hollywood, Health & Society; the Bay Area Outreach & Recreation Program; Camp Cheerful; and Lieutenant Commander David Daitch.

Kristen and Jonathan Lonner. For letting me ask a million political questions, for making me dinner while you answered them, and for teaching me "rose and thorn." My "rose" is that I have you in my life. My "thorn" is that we couldn't figure out a way to save the park. I think it was the right choice. Thank you for helping me see that.

To my early readers and note givers: Lynn Sternberger, Diana Ramirez, and Monica Mitchell. Special thanks to Monica for being my guide to all things Cleveland and for giving me the address to her childhood home so I could drive by like a creeper when I was in town doing research.

Mark Sarvas. An incredible writing instructor and friend. I always knew I wanted to write a novel, but I never knew where to begin. Thank you for showing me the way.

To The Shamers and to my Cluster. You know who you are, and you know that I couldn't have done this without you.

Javier Grillo-Marxuach. A former boss, a current friend, and a consummate mentor.

Jason Katims. You taught me how to write from the heart. I will always love my *Parenthood* family.

Josh Hornstock. I owe you my entire career.

Joanna Coles and Holly Whidden. My life and career changed forever when you let me tell your story.

Every strong woman I know has a group email chain with a handful of other strong women who are always at the ready for advice, pep talks, and reality checks. I'm so lucky to have such a group in my life. (Listed in alphabetical order out of fairness.) Amber Benson, Cecil Castellucci, Kate Rorick, Liza Palmer, Margaret Dunlap, and Sarah Kuhn.

To my high school friends. (Also in alphabetical order. And only with maiden names. Because high school.) Anna Soellner, Carey Coffey, Carla Naumburg, Kirsten Handelman, Mara Ashby, Nikki Bramante, and Valerie Kinsey. There are pieces of each of you in these characters.

To The Ripped Bodice. For selling me so many incredible books and for letting me sit in your store for hours while I wrote my own. On that note, thank you to every bookstore, coffee shop, diner, hotel lobby, and Ikea (no, seriously) that provided me with a space to write.

To Stephen Cross. For posting that terrible picture of me from our eighth-grade yearbook on the night of the 2016 election. I'd completely forgotten that I was the girl considered most likely to be president. It meant a lot to me to remember.

And finally, to Jennifer Hansen for forcing me to run one final marathon, and to Allison Alley for agreeing to get dragged along too. (Honorable mention to Jeff Cohen, who logged almost all the miles with us despite the fact that he wasn't even doing the damn race.) As we ran those miles and talked and talked, an idea popped into my head about a group of friends who push one another to go farther, to dream bigger, and to be their best selves. That idea turned into this book. Thank you.

ABOUT THE AUTHOR

Sarah Watson is the creator of the hit TV series *The Bold Type*, which the *New York Times* described as "*Sex and the Single Girl* for millennials." Previously she was a writer and executive producer of the critically acclaimed NBC drama *Parenthood*. She lives in Santa Monica, California. *Most Likely* is her debut novel.